A Simple Stitch, A Common Thread

Third Edition

By

Deb Obermeier

Words Matter Publishing

P.O. Box 531

Salem, Il 62881

www.wordsmatterpublishing.com

ISBN 13: 978-1-947072-02-2
ISBN 10: 1-947072-02-1

Library of Congress Catalog Card Number: 2017940175

ACKNOWLEDGEMENTS

சில

The re-release of A Simple Stitch, A Common Thread is very important to me. It allowed me to make a few revisions based on feedback from my readers. It also afforded me the opportunity to include some of the family recipes that is talked about throughout the chapters. I want to thank my husband for being so patient while I sat with my laptop "writing a book" as I would say every time he asked me just what I was in such deep thought about.

I would like to thank my family for encouraging me to keep writing. Including them in the process, sharing my progress and getting a nudge when I needed help to keep me focused.

I want to remember my brother, Davey. He had a journalism degree and was an excellent writer. Throughout this process, he casually asked me how the book was coming along. When it was first released, I was so proud, I sent him a signed copy. A couple of months later, he called me from his home in Florida. He said to me, "When you said you were writing a book, I thought good for you. But as I read it, I was impressed. It was very well written. I needed to tell you that. Please continue to write." That call meant more to me than I can say. I lost my brother to a sudden illness in December 2015, just 6 months after that release. He sent me a Christmas gift every year, one with a special meaning. A few months later, my nephew, Dan, sent me a large, handcrafted sheep. My brother bought it while traveling. For those who don't know, the cover of the first release had a sheep sign with the name of Eliza's shop, A SIMPLE STITCH on it. He bought this sheep so it would encourage me to keep writing. I miss him, but my sheep still sits on a shelf in my den doing double duty. Reminding me of Davey, and encouraging me to keep writing. How could I not?

Dedication

❦

I am dedicating this to my granddaughter, Emmilee, who inspired me and kept up with the year and a half process while writing this novel. It was on a trip to Arizona in October 2010 when I went to meet my new grandson, Bennett. He is the 7ᵗʰ of now 9 grandchildren in my daughter's family. Each trip always inspired creativity. There was usually a baking day or crafting of sorts. This trip, there was the "Granny, we need to write a book" suggestion. So with that, we found pencil and paper, a somewhat quiet place to sit and came up with our story line. They have always been fans of the prairie stories of olden days, their ways, and wisdom. Emmilee thought we needed a storyteller to reflect on things past. We created the town, named our characters using family names. Eliza was short for Elizabeth, my Great-grandma's name, Memaw, and Pop became Mimzie and Papa and down the line, using names from grandkids and everyone through the generations. We were specific to their trade, their position in the era of the story line, even planning a family tree of sorts.

When I returned home from that trip, I pulled out the paper full of penciled notes and just could not let this go. I began to write.

With the continued encouragement from Emmilee, and eventually getting my daughter and daughter-in-law involved, I continued the year and a half long process, e-mailing chapters or calling and reading something I was excited to tell. Getting input when I got stumped or stale added interest and characters.

As I came to the ending, it was bittersweet. I was closing the page on this wonderful group of friends that I had created and shared their lives with for so long. I would miss them very much and still, do. Emmilee and I continue to reflect on things that were said or done, and simple thoughts that make their way into our many conversations.

At many family functions when we start to have too much fun, they still give me that look and tell me, "You are starting to act like Aunt Mildred!"

I take that as a compliment. She is my hero!

So thank you again, Emmilee, for the inspiration, encouragement, and involvement while creating this very special story we told together. Just look what we did!

I am hopeful to involve yet another granddaughter, Amanda, with her illustrating. She has been drawing since the age of 4. She is now 12, and she continues to amaze us with her works. It will be my pleasure to include her visions throughout my stories. With that being said, I cannot wait to see what we do next!

Love, Granny

Chapter One

**An amazing sunrise and a fresh pot of coffee
to start the day at A Simple Stitch....**

৵৽৵

It was an amazing sunrise. The slice of orange on the horizon looked as if God was opening the shade to a gorgeous day. Eliza paused to admire it from the window on the way downstairs to her shop. This is her favorite way to begin the day.

Living above her small yarn shop, A Simple Stitch was a bonus. Her daily routine began with a prayer for guidance, thanksgiving for her blessings, forgiveness for her shortfalls and a good morning to her Grandma Mimzie. A locket hangs from a thin gold chain around her neck that carries the picture of Mimzie when she was but a young girl. She starts the coffee, turns on the music and faces a new day.

Eliza lives what she considers a simple life in the small town of Spring Forrest where she was born, went to school and returned to live after college. Her roots are strong and her heritage her focus. Whenever she starts to feel insignificant, she drifts back to memories of Mimzie and finds herself engaged in the most interesting conversations with whoever happens to be around at the time. One of the things her customers look forward to is her gift of storytelling. Many of her stories are of Mimzie, her life, the values she instilled in those around her, and her many accomplishments.

The coffee was ready. Pouring a cup, she stands in the front door gazing out at the quaint Main Street that her shop shares with so many merchants. Over the years they have become like her family.

It is fall, and there is a chill in the air. Only a few weeks until Thanksgiving. Across the street, at CJ's Café, she checks out the daily specials on the blackboard. In the fall a rather stocky scarecrow holds the menu surrounded by an arrangement of pumpkins, squash, and mums at his feet, only to be relieved of his duty the day after Thanksgiving by one of Santa's elves. On the menu today is a favorite of hers, Harvest Squash Soup garnished with roasted pumpkin seeds and warm rolls. She knew what she would be enjoying this afternoon. Mimzie's family recipe that she passed on.

She and CJ became close after he returned to Spring Forrest. It wasn't a difficult choice to make. After six months at college, he knew that home was where he wanted to be. His love to cook and create new recipes paired with his personality was a perfect combination for opening a Café. The timing for such an opportunity was a blessing, and just what this corner needed.

Perhaps this morning would call for a couple of logs in the open hearth of the oversized fireplace that graces her sitting area. Many groups have gathered here through the years to share patterns, conversations, and helping each other with life in general. Hours go by quickly while crocheting or knitting as they chat. The coffee is endless as these evenings often times run well past closing time when the group gathers. Everyone looked forward to their times together. Eliza didn't mind the late hours. It felt more like a house full of company than a late evening at work.

She loves this time of year. Just before she closed last night, the UPS driver dropped off several boxes of new yarns that will be great for holiday patterns. Most of her customers make choices now for projects they will complete for next year. Knitting and crocheting projects are somewhat time-consuming and not often worked on as a priority but as a means of relaxation and reflection. To some, it also provides a social outlet.

The new colors for winter are wonderful. Sage greens and rusty reds, with a tweedy black and cream fleck throughout. I would love to make a scarf from this, Eliza thought as she unpacked the skeins of yarn. They were high quality and had a comforting feel. These won't be on the shelves long, she thought. A new display and a quick clean up and it was time to flip the sign and let the outside in to share in her day.

She heard a far too familiar sound coming from behind her counter. It was Cody, her companion. He found the packing papers from the shipment and as any four-year-old cat with pent up energy would, he decided to browse through it to see what he could stir up. His golden fur with a subtle stripe blended with the paper. That should keep him busy for a while. He was good company for her on long nights, and there were many long nights.

The bell on the door clanged, and a familiar voice broke the morning silence. It was Olivia, such a kind person, often stopping in to drop off a basket of muffins from a new recipe she was trying out.

Looking at the sale table on her way by she finds a few skeins of brightly colored yarns left from summer and scoops up the bargains. "These will make wonderful scarves for the children, we are trying to provide for more than fifty children in need this winter," she said taking her finds to the counter.

Always curious and willing to help, Eliza asked, "Is it just our county, or have you expanded your group to try and serve other counties?"

"Oh no, that is just in our county," Olivia quickly explained. "The need is great. Many families have come on hard times they hadn't felt the strain before."

"In that case, I'm going to give you an extra 30% off this purchase," Eliza smiled. "You are having a profound impact on our community. Your generosity is certainly contagious. Keep up the good work," Eliza encouraged as she placed the skeins in a new holiday bag. "And thanks again for the muffins. You know I'm always willing to test a new recipe."

As Olivia said her goodbye's and closed the

door, Eliza drifted away for a moment. She had a deep admiration for Olivia, a stay at home mother. Olivia is busier than ever, constantly looking for a need. The baking she does generates income to help offset the expenses of the charity she founded, 'A Snug Around the Neck,' a non-profit organization for their county that has been a huge undertaking. In the past two years the number of volunteers has doubled but unfortunately so had the need. Eliza is always on the lookout for a potential customer to send Olivia's way.

Suddenly, the bell on the door brought Eliza back to reality as three ladies entered. Laughing and non-stop chatting, the first thing they noticed was the display of fall woolens. It didn't take long to realize only one of these ladies enjoyed needlework. Two of the three quickly set their sights on the fireplace and oversized leather chairs. "Oh, we have been on the go since early this morning," one said as she sat down. "Now, this is where I belong," she exclaimed as she snuggled in with her friend quickly joining her in the other chair. "All that's missing is a fresh, hot cup of coffee!"

"Where are you ladies from?" Eliza asked as she joined them.

"Texas," Jayne said as she introduced herself, "one of the adventures the three of us often throw together." Her heavy southern draw was quick to validate that statement. "And this is Allie and Sara," pointing as she introduced the others.

"What on earth brings you this far from home, on

some special adventure?" Eliza asked. "Surely it must be more than yarn!"

"Oh no, not yarn," Allie laughed. "Never touch the stuff! Jayne's niece Annie moved to this area recently, and we have come up to surprise her and see how she has settled in."

Not knowing an Annie, Eliza questioned a bit more. "Annie who, if I might ask? This is a small town, but not that small. I can't say I've had the pleasure of meeting her."

From the shelves near the door, Jayne spoke up, "Simpkins, her name is Annie Simpkins, and she teaches at the grade school, fifth grade. She just moved to the area late this summer in time for the new school year."

"Okay," Eliza replied. "She teaches with my friend Abigail. She hasn't been in or joined us on a group night yet, but we hope she does. She is young, and we don't want to be too pushy and scare her off," she said with a smile.

"Oh, you won't scare her," Jayne said. "Annie always has been very inquisitive. That's one reason she chose the fifth grade. They have the same curiosity she still exhibits. When she was about eleven, her dad talked her mom into letting her get her first horse. She had always wanted to be a rodeo star. Annie tagged along to horse and cattle auctions whenever she had the chance. They had neighbors at the ranch down the lane, and she would slip off after school and watch them train horses. When she got a bit older, she helped. There was always a market for well-trained horses, so it was a never ending challenge. Learning from them helped her train and care for her own horse at such a young age. She was a natural and never tired of helping at the other ranch. Mr. Carson, the ranch owner, taught Annie how to ride as well as any of them. She never entered any serious competition. Instead, she got involved in helping at a neighboring ranch that offered workshops for handicapped children. That allowed her to share her love for horses, and she quickly found working with the kids with disabilities was far more rewarding than her own riding career. From the summers she spent with the kids came her decision to be a teacher. She landed her first teaching position here, packed up and moved. This is her first time so far away from home. Annie lost her mom several years ago and has tried to be there for her dad. She knows he is lost without her mom, and so is she. The holidays are going to make it a tough time for both of them, her being so far away for the first time. We thought if we came and checked on her we could see how she was really doing and perhaps put her dad's mind at ease. And that is how our adventure began!"

"Well, this is quite a story," Eliza said, as she brought over three mugs and a fresh pot of coffee. The coffee quickly made this stop their favorite by far! "Would anyone care for a muffin?" Eliza offered bringing the basket of Olivia's muffins.

They couldn't decide what was more enjoyable, the fireplace, coffee, muffins or the company. The recipe was a keeper. Eliza poured herself a cup and poked the logs on the fire as she enjoyed her company.

As they finished, Jayne brought a basket of yarn to the counter. "This one is on me, add the coffee and muffins to my ticket," she said. "I found some wonderful yarns that will work up nicely."

Eliza was quick to correct her, "The coffee and muffins are on the house in this shop. I see you have made some very nice choices in the yarn though. What are you going to make? I like to get ideas from my customers."

Jayne replied with enthusiasm, "I plan to knit Annie an afghan for Christmas now that she is in an area that gets colder than Texas. I hope it will keep home close at heart when she curls up with it at the end of the day to relax and think about things back home."

"I think that is a wonderful idea," Eliza replied. "After you send it to her, maybe that will inspire her to join us. We'll teach her how to knit, or crochet and she could return the favor and send you something she created. You may need a hat and scarf for visits. Hopefully, they will be often and when you're in the area, stop in. I always try and have new stock with the seasons. The fall and winter bring in the rich colors like you chose, the thicker yarns just waiting to be worked into heirlooms. In the spring, the colors are new and fresh, like the season when the warm edges out the cold, the soft pastels and lighter weights are reminiscent of Easter bunnies and chicks. Summer soon brings in bright colors, the sun and sea, brightly colored flowers and beach balls. Tote bags seem to be the patterns of choice. Before we know it, here comes fall again. Every season sparks curiosity and new patterns to be shared here in the shop."

"I Promise we won't come to town without stopping

in. The girls don't mind the time I spend on my interests, heaven knows I spend more time in the kitchen utensil stores than I'd like, and they don't even give away a cup of coffee!" Jayne declared.

"Now, as you continue your adventures around town be sure to plan lunch at CJ's Café. The lunch special today is a favorite of mine. The soup is an old family recipe for Harvest Squash Soup. My Grandma, Mimzie, made it every weekend in the fall and winter, so it warms my soul. Ladies, it has been a pleasure meeting you. I hope to see you again before you leave for Texas. Perhaps you could bring Annie with you. I'd like to meet her, even if she is brought into a local shop by way of three Texans!"

Jayne assured her their plan was to have lunch at CJ's Café. "After lunch, we will stop in with Annie. I'll have her pick out yarn for a hat and scarf. That'll give us a chance to introduce her to you and show her this lovely shop." With that, she turned to her friends and said, "This way we can tell her dad she has a friend to take her under wing and give her the guidance she may need." The three agreed as they bid Eliza goodbye and continued their journey.

The rest of the morning was fairly uneventful. Eliza was able to work on a knitting project she had started. Her work was hit and miss between customers. She often sat and crocheted or knitted for an hour or so in the evenings just to wind down and relax. She expected it to be an interesting afternoon when her three new Texan friends came back with Annie. Several more customers were in and out before lunch. She put away her knitting and enjoyed chatting with each, helping with decision making and guiding them on their way to new projects.

It was lunch time before she knew it. She made a quick call to CJ's Café for a carry out before the special ran out. Eliza was so proud of her nephew, returning to his roots and opening a successful business just across the street from her. This brought them even closer than they were before he left for college. "I'll have it ready in 10 minutes," replied CJ, knowing she would request her favorite.

"I'll be there to pick it up and if you have a minute I've got something to tell you," she said, trying to spark his curiosity.

"Always time for you Eliza," knowing her, she would make it interesting.

Flipping her sign to 'CLOSED' with a note saying back in 10 minutes, Eliza locked up and ran across the street to the Café. As she walked in, the aroma of the soup and fresh bread made her stomach rumble. CJ was behind the counter as usual, with her lunch ready, patiently waiting for her colorful conversation.

"How are you doing today Eliza?" he greeted her. "How's business? I saw you had a big delivery this week, getting ready for the holidays?"

"You know it. Time is flying by. It will be Christmas before we know it," she replied. Then she went on to tell him about the three from Texas. "Have you met Annie Simpkins yet?"

"If I have in passing, I didn't know her," he replied. "What does she look like?" his curiosity kicking in. Not sure of that herself, Eliza told him they were coming in for lunch today, and bringing Annie with them. She had suggested they try the special. After that, they planned to bring Annie over to the shop with them.

"I'm anxious to meet her," she said, "I'll keep you posted," and she grabbed her lunch and started out the door.

"Talk to you later," CJ shouted.

Snuggling down in one of the leather chairs in front of the fireplace, she opened the bowl of Harvest Squash Soup and savored the moment, letting the aroma of fall take her back to the Homestead. It was one of the first things Mimzie taught her to make. Well, that and Blueberry Muffins with fresh picked blueberries. It was so easy for her mind to wander. They named the old Homestead 'Slipknot Farm.' She loved the nickname because it spurred so many cherished stories from their past. She enjoyed her soup while thinking about the upcoming weekend. She tries to spend part of every weekend out there but especially looked forward to it in the fall.

CJ didn't let her down. The soup was wonderful, as usual. By the time she finished the homemade rolls and a fresh pumpkin cookie, she was ready for a nap. CJ didn't forget Cody either, adding in his usual treat.

Any thoughts of naptime quickly fled as the bell on the door, once again, reminded her she was open for business. Friday afternoon browsers. Sometimes she enjoyed these low maintenance customers, not really wanting to learn anything, just shuffling through and trying to be polite. Eliza was happy to oblige them, asking if there was anything, in particular, they were looking for.

"No thanks, just browsing," one elderly lady replied.

"Take your time and ask if you have any questions," Eliza smiled and went behind the counter to sort through her unopened mail. Soon they wandered out the door to make their way to the next shop.

Before she knew it the clock chimed one. The morning had raced by, she thought to herself. The bell on the door brought her attention to three familiar faces from this morning with Annie in tow, just as they promised. Of course, Eliza knew from their personalities Annie would not be able to change their say in the afternoon plans.

Jayne quickly took Annie by the arm, "This is Eliza. We've been telling you about her."

"It's a pleasure to meet you, Miss..." and then she looked at Eliza with a blank stare, "I'm sorry, I don't know your last name."

"Eliza, my name is Eliza," she repeated as she took Annie's extended hand in hers. "I am so happy to meet you. I have heard about you from these three amigos of yours. What a pleasure. I'm surprised I haven't met you before now. They tell me you are teaching here and settled in our town."

"Well, that is true," Annie replied. "I have been busy trying to get my home in order. It's the first time I've actually set up housekeeping on my own, except in a small dorm at college. I'm enjoying it, although things are a bit bare. And then there is my classroom. I have so many ideas rushing around in my head, and my class, they are such a joy. I just love this age. I'm so sorry, I tend to ramble on about myself when I'm a bit nervous. Your shop is lovely, just as my Aunt Jayne described it."

"Why thank you, dear," Eliza replied. "It's home to me. I want everyone to feel as comfortable here as Cody, and I do."

"Is Cody your husband?" Annie questioned with a warm smile.

"Oh no, dear, Cody is my overgrown lump of a cat that goes everywhere with me, and at times, places without me that he really shouldn't. It's just him and me wandering around the shop and my home upstairs. We long for the drive out to Slipknot Farm after church every Sunday to renew our energy and get ready for the new week. My Grandma, Mimzie, moved there when she first married my Grandpa, Caleb Jaxon. They built the Homestead from ground up, and it has remained in our family. I found Cody there one Sunday afternoon. I was sitting on the porch enjoying the sunshine, and I heard a faint cry. It kept coming closer and finally, there appeared a little-wet mud ball, so small and so weak it was all he could do to let out a squeak. I brought him in, cleaned him up and got some warm milk down him, and he has been by my side since. At times, I'm not sure who rescued who. He is a very good company on long nights."

"I understand that completely," Annie said with a sparkle in her eye. "I feel the same way about my horse, Pete. He is still in Texas. I miss him terribly. I don't know when I'll be getting back there to see him. Dad keeps him groomed and fed, and the kids nearby keep him exercised. Sometimes I wonder if Pete misses me at all."

"Well, of course, he misses you, honey," Aunt Jayne stepped into the conversation. "And your dad misses you even more than that old horse does. That's why I got my gals together and headed your direction. We are taking back a full report of how well you have settled in. Now that we know you have made a new friend in Eliza that will put his mind at ease. Why the next time we see you, I'll just bet you will be a regular at her shop. Now," Jayne ordered, "let's get busy and pick out the yarn you want me to use for a hat and scarf. I'd like to start on it during the ride back home."

Annie looked around for the other two ladies, and they had already settled in the comfy leather chairs enjoying the fire. Cody didn't take long to get acquainted either. He was curled up on Allie's lap, as cozy there as she seemed to be. Sara had picked up a magazine from the nearby basket and enjoyed it while soaking in the warmth from the fireplace.

Witnessing this, Annie said to Eliza, "I think I'm really going to enjoy this shop of yours, even though I can't knit or crochet a stitch!"

Eliza, with a smile on her face, replied, "That is only a matter of time, dear. You will be working up yarn like a pro before you know it. Tonight is our regular group, all local ladies that gather and work on projects and discuss everything from kids to husbands, recipes, upcoming events or even new movies coming out. So many times the discussions lead to thoughts of the past, sparking memories and getting the story telling started. Before we know it, the clock is chiming to remind us how late it is then we scurry to pack up and have one last snack and cup of coffee before we call it a night. It started on Tuesday evenings, but it ran so late for a school, and work night we moved it to Fridays and have been gathering for about three years now. They call the group "Girls Knit Out" and are just like family. You are more than welcome to join us whenever you are ready."

"I will, I promise," Annie said and started toward her Aunt Jayne as she was taking her purchase to the counter. "Wow!" she exclaimed before she realized how that must have sounded, "You are certainly going to be busy with that armload of yarn!" She could only imagine the wonderful projects her Aunt had in mind. Just thinking about it made her even more anxious to learn to knit or crochet. She was looking forward to this, even though she didn't know the difference, it didn't matter, it involved making friends, not just projects. She had high hopes that Spring Forrest would seem like home before the first school year ended.

"Well, come on girls, let's keep moving," Aunt Jayne declared, "we're burning daylight!"

"Oh, do we have to?" whined Allie, like a little girl, "I don't want to wake up Cody. He's so cozy on my lap." Knowing they would leave without her, she managed to rustle him off onto the floor and gather her things. "I didn't think I could have such a nice time in a yarn shop," she said

15

as she gave Eliza a quick hug goodbye. "Someday, I may learn to do something with this stuff and actually make a purchase. It has been a pleasure though."

"Same here, I can't tell you when I have had such a nice afternoon," Sara said as she waved good-bye.

Eliza waived back and reminded Annie of her promise. Just as the door started to close, Annie poked her head back in and asked, "Is there any way I can get your recipe for the Harvest Squash Soup served at the Café? The guy that waited on us told me it was your recipe."

"That guy is CJ, and yes, it is," Eliza replied. She continued to tell Annie about the recipe, how it was handed down from Mimzie and how she made it every Sunday at Slipknot Farm. If you have a minute, I'd be glad to tell you all about it," Eliza encouraged, never giving up a chance to tell about her heritage.

Annie said, "Well, we have nothing but time." She smiled, picked up Cody, and sat down in a big leather chair by the fireplace. Just as she expected, the others joined her.

Eliza pulled up a couple more chairs and began to talk. She placed a couple more logs on the fire and sat down on the edge of the hearth. "My Grandma, who I have always called Mimzie," Eliza began, "was born and raised about eight miles out of town. Her parents settled and homesteaded the acreage as everyone did in those days. Life wasn't easy. They had to be self-sufficient for everything. They raised livestock for food, crops to feed the livestock, chickens for eggs and a couple of work horses to pull the wagon and the plow. They also had sheep for wool and food and a milk cow. Any surplus was taken to town to sell. With the cash, they purchased things like sugar, coffee, flour, and yard goods. Everyone helped each other in times of hardship.

Growing up, Mimzie was the tomboy, always making pets of the animals on the farm. She was always right out there with the men and boys working the fields, planting, and tending to the garden that provided food for the family. All extra food they grew went to help the neighbors. Mimzie liked to plant something different each year. One summer she had an abundant crop of squash, so she had to come up with recipes. That's where the Harvest Squash Soup recipe originated. They canned the fresh vegetables like the tomatoes and green beans, made pickles from the cucumbers. The vegetables like onions, potatoes, yams, and squash were stored in baskets in the fruit cellar for the winter. The soup quickly became a favorite on Sundays after church. Left on the stove to simmer while they went by horse and wagon, regardless of the weather, it was a welcoming treat to come home to, warming them through. Of course, there was always fresh bread to go with it, and butter, not margarine, creamy fresh churned butter. The old butter churn is still at the Homestead.

A few years after Mimzie and Caleb married they made the Homestead their first home, naming it Slipknot Farm. They later created their brand using their initials, C&C, for Caroline and Caleb, and the J for Jaxon, tying the C's together resembling a slipknot. So," Eliza continued, "to carry on the tradition, I still go to Slipknot Farm every Sunday after church, spend the afternoon, and I try to make

Harvest Squash Soup at least every other Sunday. If you would like to learn how just plan to tag along Sunday after next. I'd love to show you the Homestead. I still have some animals there, and it is a perfect way to start a new week."

Jayne spoke up, "Oh, I wish we weren't leaving so soon, I would love to join you."

Annie just smiled, promising her Aunt that she would be sure and send pictures.

Another twenty minutes had passed. The familiar clang of the bell reminded Eliza she was still open for business.

The four gathered their belongings and started for the door, all talking at once about the Homestead. This, she thought to herself, is exactly why she loves her shop. There's always room for new acquaintances that quickly turn into friends.

"How may I help you?" she said, turning to the ladies that just entered the shop, looking for an adventure of their own.

Chapter Two

**An abundance of laughter when friends gather,
and muffins...**

ᔥ∞ᔤ

The Friday night group, 'Girls Knit Out' was pouring in, early as usual. This is one obligation no one is late for. All talking at once, they started pulling chairs around the hearth and unloading their projects. Olivia brought a container of muffins like the batch she shared with Eliza earlier. That quickly got everyone's attention.

"You know why we love you, Olivia, don't you?" Rosie shouted out across the group.

Olivia blushed a bit, and then smiled, "Yep, and that's why Eliza always has the coffee ready, too."

They began the session with a pot of coffee and a snack, then put it all aside so they could work on their projects. Once the hooks and needles come out the creativity starts to flow. This sparks conversations, compliments and a new idea or two. Sooner or later, a memory comes to mind, and the story telling begins. Eliza usually ends the evening with another pot of coffee while they reach a stopping point on the projects and another story reaches a happy ending.

Tonight Eliza couldn't wait until everyone was situated. "Has anyone met Annie Simpkins yet?" she asked as she brought over the coffee pot to make a round. "She teaches the fifth grade and moved to the area this summer from Texas."

Abigail spoke up, "I know her, a darling girl. She teaches with me, and my daughter Sydney is in her class. Why? Did you hear something about her? She isn't unhappy, is she? She can't leave, the kids just love her!" Abigail had Zoey, her Great Dane, by the collar, and was leading her to the hearth, getting her situated with Cody for the evening. They routinely curl up together while the group's in session. Looking at them, they almost seem as happy to be here as the ladies.

"Hold on," Eliza said, trying to stop Abigail from getting so worked up. "It just so happened that she was in the shop this afternoon. Her Aunt Jayne and two friends, Allie and Sara, stopped in this morning to look at yarn goods. We got to talking, and I learned they came from Texas to see how Annie had settled in. Her dad's missing her and worrying so much, they drove up to help put his mind at ease. Theirs too, I suspect, although they would never admit it. They spent the better part of the morning here, then after lunch at the Café, they brought Annie in with them to introduce her and pick out some yarn."

"Was it Harvest Squash Soup day today? I just thought of that," Lilly said as she joined in the conversation.

"And I missed it! Eliza, is this Sunday Harvest Squash Soup day at Slipknot? It's on my mind now, and I won't be satisfied until I have a mug."

"It's next Sunday. I've invited Annie to drive out with me after church, and I'm going to share my recipe with her. Give me a call if you plan to drive out. It may be a perfect way to get acquainted with her. She doesn't know how to knit or crochet but says she has a desire to learn. She thinks it may help her pass the time this winter.

She would be a good candidate for 'A Snug Around the Neck' too, Olivia. Have you met her yet?"

Olivia was in deep thought and then replied, "I don't think we've been introduced. Has she been at church?"

Kate, the newest member of the group, still fairly new to Spring Forrest, spoke up, "I haven't met her, but I did see her at the library one evening. I didn't realize she was the newbie or I would have welcomed her. She was talking about her fifth-grade class project."

"What kind of muffins are these, Olivia?" Rosie asked. "I may need four dozen or so for an Open House set for two weeks from Saturday at the Real Estate Office."

Olivia quickly took notes, as she replied, "they're called The Best Chocolate Chip Banana Muffins Ever, and the general consensus so far is everyone that has tried them seems to agree."

It wasn't unusual for Rosie to order six dozen or so for an open house. The potential buyers were not so many in numbers, but everyone at the Realty has their share with morning coffee long before any Open House signs are displayed.

"Got you down for six dozen, Rosie, you know four dozen will never be enough." Olivia gave her a wink and a smile, knowing her best friend wouldn't give her any problems. "After all, lots of cold kids out there this time of year. It's for a good cause." That sealed the deal.

"Six dozen is fine," Rosie winked back, "but when I can't wear my jeans because of your muffins, I'll expect you to help me do something about it."

Eliza chimed in, "Rosie, are you sporting a muffin top!" The room roared with laughter. Rosie looked totally lost.

Olivia spoke up, "You'll have to enlighten us on that one."

"Well," Eliza started, grinning from ear to ear, "you know when you try to button your favorite jeans, then you lay on the bed to zip them up, has happened to all of us from time to time. Well, you finally stand up, take a breath if you can, and relax, that roll hanging over your waistband... MUFFIN TOP!"

Rosie started to laugh, they all joined in, some were out of control, and even Eliza had tears streaming down her cheeks.

Finally, Rosie caught her breath and said to Olivia,

"Make it eight dozen. I don't mind sporting the roll now that we have a name for it!"

It took the group a good ten minutes to gain their composure. They love to start the evening off with a good laugh. It added life to their years. After all, wasn't that why they gathered?

"Could someone help me start this new row on the hat I'm trying to crochet?" asked Lilly. She had started a new pattern with granny squares worked around the brim and a row midway through the hat and the most darling scarf that matches it. Still new to the group, this was only her third project. Although she hadn't yet married or had children of her own, she has three nieces and a nephew back home in Minnesota. She sends them letters weekly and tries to include something interesting from her new hometown. Since working in the Emergency Room at the local hospital, she had met many of the townspeople, unfortunately not under the most pleasant circumstances. If it weren't for social outlets, her high-stress job as a trauma nurse in the ER would take its toll on her. When she decided to become an RN, she knew she would love helping people. Many situations arise that could have been prevented. Lilly believes in teaching when she can to prevent problems, rather than be there to pick up the pieces. She was very lonely when she first relocated, but Eliza quickly took her under her wing and got her started crocheting. Now this group is like her second family. Lilly enjoys the fellowship at the church on Sundays more than anything and has quickly become a part of their congregation.

Rosie pulled her chair next to Lilly reaching over

and taking her hook and yarn from her. She could see the frustration on Lilly's face. "Just relax, sweetie. There isn't anything going on with this project that can't be fixed," reminding Lilly this was her outlet to relieve stress, not create it. In a few minutes Rosie had her back on track, explaining the pattern, and on her way to finishing up another hat to send to a niece. After all, Minnesota will be much colder this season than anything they would see here in Virginia. "So, are you going to do the scarf to match in the same threads?" Rosie asked.

Lilly just smiled and replied, "If you are there to keep me straightened out when I make a mess of it, too." Then, she leaned over and gave her a quick hug and went right back to her crocheting.

Rosie found her way to the coffee pot and freshened her cup. Then she took a little time to look at the new stock. She was in between projects right now. With the holidays around the corner, she was thinking of crocheting a bag for her husband's secretary. That would be a project that could easily be completed on a Friday evening or two.

She was one that could whip out a project in record time. She not only taught half the group to read patterns but recruited most of those in the group. Working in the Real Estate office part time gives her the edge on changes in the community, those coming in and going out, and all the gossip that goes with it.

Eliza joined her to look at the new yarns that just arrived suggesting the reds and greens with the black tweed. That would make up into a bag that could be used throughout the season.

"Are you planning on a purse or larger, like a tote?" Eliza asked.

"Seems totes are more functional this time of year, with running errands and going to the post office. Nothing huge, but substantial, that's for sure," Rosie answered, picking up several skeins of the red and the green. "Perfect," she smiled as took them to the counter. "I just love the thought of the holidays coming, with most of my family close by and Chloe coming home for Christmas break. I have so much to look forward to."

Keeping busy suited Rosie. After Chloe had gone away to college last fall, she struggled with adjusting to an empty nest. The Real Estate office occupied some of her time, but with her husband gone on business so much, not many realized the lonely times Rosie was going through. Her focus was always on keeping Chloe involved in dance, tumbling, and cheerleading later on. There was always somewhere they had to be.

Eliza picked up on the trials she was going through and tried to help Rosie with reassurance when she could, keeping it between the two of them. Rosie liked knowing what was going on around her and enjoyed conversations around town, but when it came to her life and feelings, she was a very private person. She probably got that from her mother. Her family grew up in the country and kept to themselves. It wasn't until she married Mark, an executive in his company, that she became involved socially. Nurturing his need to entertain at home and in the community, she quickly learned how to make any event a success.

Kate and Abigail were busy on their knitting projects. Kate was a very well read woman. She, being the Librarian, had such a love for the written word and was able to read patterns like they were simple recipes. She hadn't been knitting that long but picked it up as if second nature.

Abigail started talking about Annie. She worked with her at school and had a good academic relationship with her. They had attended a couple of teacher's conferences together and had lunch now and then, but hadn't really gotten to know her personally. This, she realized after Eliza told them so much about her.

"Kate," Abigail questioned, "have you been introduced to Annie, the fifth-grade teacher yet or did you say you had just met in passing? It seems the two of you may have a lot in common, both being new to the area."

"I would really like to meet her. Perhaps when you come to the library next week you could bring her by," Kate suggested. "Seems that would be good for both of us, not knowing everyone around town yet. It could give us a chance to see what we may have in common."

As Eliza passed by to see if they needed their coffee warmed up, she invited Kate to come out to Slipknot Farm on Sunday after next with her and Annie to learn to make the infamous Harvest Squash Soup. If Lilly made it out, it would be a great afternoon.

"I'll stop by El & Em's Farmers Market and pick up

some extra squash in the morning," Eliza said. "This is the perfect time of year for soup and homemade rolls."

"What will we do about dessert?" Kate questioned. "Should I bring something?"

"Oh, no, we never bring things to eat to Slipknot. I'll pick up a few apples, and we can make an apple crisp. That should just about make for a perfect meal. Anyone else in?" Eliza asked as she looked around the group. She loved the idea of a gathering at Slipknot in the fall. "Just let me know next Friday if you can make it. The more, the merrier."

"Oh, look at the time," Lilly said. "I have an early shift tomorrow, and it is going to be a very long day. I need to start packing up."

Lilly was off next weekend and was making plans to join the girls at Slipknot Farm. This would be her first time there. She has heard a lot about the Homestead from her Friday's with the group. Eliza had shared many stories over this past year. Although she missed her family in Minnesota, she knew she was blessed with the company she kept in her new hometown.

"Would you like to take the extra muffins to the ER tomorrow, Lilly?" Olivia offered. She never passed up the chance for free advertisement. Everyone around the hospital was familiar with Olivia. It wouldn't be the first time Lilly brought in Saturday morning treats.

"Sure will, I never pass up a chance to point business in your direction," said Lilly, grinning so that they all knew the thought of a 'Muffin Top' was running through her mind. "So, Olivia, how many members do you have active in your charity now?" Lilly asked.

"Well, A Snug Around the Neck has fourteen members now, which I feel in the two short years we have been working together, we have helped a lot of families with children," she said with pride.

A Snug Around the Neck meet on Wednesdays, each member taking turns to host the meetings at their homes. That saves the cost of renting a hall or going out somewhere. The hostess provides lunch. A lot of ground is covered during their Wednesday meetings. Families with needs are referred and discussed. Then they spend time deciding where the handiwork finished since the last meeting will be distributed, and where the money they raised will be spent. After all, they are there to help, not see how big they can grow a savings account or stockpile their goods.

"Who came up with the name, 'A Snug Around the Neck'?" Kate asked.

Olivia quickly spoke up, "Mimzie, of course."

One of Mimzie's favorite sayings, when Eliza was growing up, was "Quick, come give me a Snug Around the Neck!" It has always stuck with me. One evening while we were all together and discussing the cause, Olivia expressed the growing need for a name for her charity. Something special that would relay the full meaning of the organization. Eliza spoke up, and they had a name. She was so excited when Olivia announced she would like to call the charity 'A Snug Around the Neck.' Eliza silently felt a warm feeling, like this was a tribute to Mimzie, the most important woman in her life. After all, Eliza's strength came from the values Mimzie instilled in her.

"I'm ready to tie this color off, a good place to stop for me," Abigail said. "Zoey, start waking yourself up over there. You aren't spending the night." Zoey just rolled her eyes, then followed with a yawn, and stretch, and she was on her feet. Cody looked up at her, got up, yawned, and stretched, and they both walked over and sat by the door with their backs to the crowd, as if saying, "we're up, let's go!"

Everyone was stirring, packing up and making another pass by the muffins. It wasn't long, and they were all on their way home.

Lilly waved as she left, shouting back, and "I hope I don't see any of you tomorrow!" They all laughed, knowing exactly what she meant.

"That girl is full of compassion," Rosie said. "I've heard when she is in the ER, she can calm a family and patient down in seconds. She uses that voice of hers, and it seems to calm the situation almost immediately. That is a true gift. Not many of us could handle situations like that. Not all have a positive outcome. How difficult that must be to deal with, then go home alone. Here, I feel sorry for myself because my daughter has gone off to college to pursue her career. How lame am I!" scowled Rosie.

Eliza stepped in quickly. "Now Rosie, you have been

doing so good, don't get down on yourself, we all have our strengths."

Listening to Eliza, Rosie just smiled and started to gather her goods. "I cannot believe how fast time goes by when we all gather," she said as she put her chair back and reached for her coat. "We should plan a Friday night sleep-over! That would be a hoot." She just laughed at herself all the way to the door, knowing deep down that wasn't going to happen.

Rosie has a way of always leaving them laughing.

Soon, all had gathered their belongings, not forgetting the dog, and were on their way home. Eliza looked around the shop, amazed at how considerate her friends were, almost leaving things in better condition than they were when they arrived. She called to Cody and turned out the lights. As she started up the stairs to her apartment, she stopped to look out the window. She relaxed and gazed at the stars and the moon, shining down so brightly, she could feel God's grace enveloping her, ending her day the same way she started it, by counting her blessings.

Eliza loved her apartment. Not only was it convenient living right above her shop, but it was the perfect place to rest and renew. As she entered the door at the top of the stairs, she felt as if she were stepping back in time. She had owned this building more than twenty-five years and restored the integrity of the apartment back to the original era. It was the perfect home for her antiques, heirlooms, and the things she had collected at auctions and estate sales through the years.

There was a portrait of Mimzie hanging in the entrance hall at the top of the stairs made from the old photo kept in the locket Eliza wore. This was one of the few she had, as taking pictures wasn't priority in those days. An album was kept on her bedside table with the rest of the photos from her childhood and family. When she gets restless, she pages through them and lets the memories comfort her. Perhaps that is why she is so quick to remember the stories of the Homestead and the things Mimzie shared with her as she was growing up.

Kicking off her shoes, she went into the kitchen to put on the tea kettle. It was late. Often times, she fixes a cup of tea to relax, wind down and go over the events of the day. She turned on the water to draw a nice bath in her claw foot tub, threw in some bath salts and lit a few candles. She loved the scents this time of year. She recently picked up a few new candles at Flora's Unique Floral Boutique. These are Autumn Spice. It's a warming scent of pumpkin and cinnamon sticks. With a pair of favorite flannel pajamas laid out, her cup of tea in hand, and the tub ready, she flipped the switch that lit the antique chandelier she had installed above her tub some years ago. It came from an estate sale of a family friend, so it was a sentimental find. It was perfect for relaxing in the tub and reading or flipping through a magazine. Not tonight. She just wanted to lay back, rest her head on the rim of the cold iron tub and go over the events of the day. She had, after all, made friends, near and far. Eliza wondered why Annie had been brought into her life at this particular point in time, holding tight to her beliefs that things happen for a reason, not just by chance. Eliza couldn't wait to see what the big picture held.

Finishing her tea and the water cooling down, it was time to get out and cozy up.

Turning on the light by her overstuffed chair, she propped up her feet and leaned her head back, letting out a long relaxing sigh. Fridays are always long, busy days. Having another cup of tea, this time Sleepy-thyme to help her relax, she let her mind start to wander. Thinking about the early days when she was looking for her niche in life, wanting to do what she loved, she never imagined that she would have a shop that offered all the things she dreamed of. Her customers and friends were as important to her as the income the shop provided, allowing her to live in her own hometown.

Picking up her pen and notebook that lay by her chair, she made a few notes. This is her thinking spot. Many of her ideas come to life right here. Sunday she would take a few extra supplies to Slipknot and maybe do a bit of extra cleaning. Sounded to her as the following Sunday may become quite an event. She just loved the time she was able to spend at the Homestead. When friends gathered, it was even better. So relaxed, she didn't even think of turning on the TV. Many times she tries to find an old movie to get lost in. But not tonight. Tonight she was content with her tea, Cody curled up on her feet and the thoughts of a week from Sunday. She was anxious to get to know this new friend, Annie Simpkins. Very anxious, indeed.

Chapter Three

A drive out to Slipknot Farm, lunch on the porch and an interesting request...

Awake before her alarm went off, Eliza's feet hit the cold floor. "My, it is a brisk morning," she exclaimed as she closed the bedroom window.

Even at a young age, she slept with her window open a couple inches, about the height of an old wooden thread spool. By doing so, her favorite quilt and flannel pajamas don't get too warm. Being snuggled in the warm covers felt good, bare feet on a cold wood floor, not so much. She turned on the coffee and hopped in the shower to warm up, wake up, and get the day off to a good start. Saturdays this time of year can be hectic in the shop. She was anxious to get moving.

The sun was shining through the window. She pulled back the curtain, thinking how much better business is on a sunny day. Early fall, you take it day by day. Even though the winters are fairly mild, the weather sometimes changes without warning. Mimzie always said if you want to know what the weather is doing, put your hand on the window to see if it's cold, or step outside and see if you get wet or your hat blows away. She wasn't much for listening to a forecast. Depending on the Farmer's Almanac was a way of life as soon as she was old enough to read one. Eliza followed her interest in the little catalog, making notes in them, comparing the years the same as Mimzie did. There is a bookshelf at Slipknot with back issues kept in date order. It was fun picking a year and flipping through the notes to see how close the little book was with predictions and advice.

Dressed in her favorite orange sweater and jeans, she was ready to start her day. Pouring another cup of coffee, she called Cody and started down to the shop. Making her usual stop on the steps by the window, she took in the day. It felt good.

Continuing her routine, prayers, good morning to Mimzie, and another pot of coffee for the shop, she went to the front door to check out the daily menu. CJ was busy making changes to the chalkboard.

"Good morning!" she shouted across the street, knowing full well she would startle him, and she did.

After he had fixed his mistake, he bid her good morning the same.

"So, what's on the menu for today, anything I can't live without?" she said with a chuckle.

"Never!" he replied. "After all, most of my recipes

came from that family treasure box of yours, and what didn't was inspired by something you mentioned in one of your long-winded stories."

Today felt like the start of a brisk fall day. CJ was hoping it was a busy one bringing in a nice crowd for breakfast and lunch. The specials were French toast with fried apples and fresh ham for the breakfast crowd, and Potato Soup with his infamous Grilled Cheese for the latecomers looking for lunch. That, along with his usual menu, there was plenty to choose from on a Saturday around town. Everyone loved his French toast. CJ baked a special cinnamon-raisin bread the day before, to get the perfect texture to absorb the egg mixture without getting soggy. He added a few secret ingredients to the egg batter for flavor. When the aroma fills the air, it almost pulls the passersby in by their noses. He created his signature grilled cheese sandwiches, not just buttered and grilled, but dipped in a special batter and dredged in finely ground pretzel crumbs. The perfect combination. Once you have had one of these, grilled cheese as you know it will never be the same.

"Did you get apples at El & Em's?" she asked, knowing he buys local any time he can.

"Where else?" he replied. "I also picked up some fresh scallions and some new potatoes for today's soup."

It's very busy at El & Em's this time of year. Just on the edge of town, the girls have produce all summer and open their pumpkin patch in the early fall. If you are energetic, or particular, you can go out to their gardens and pick your own vegetables. There are a few apple trees, some blackberries, and a grape arbor. They have a very good business generated by visitors, but the townspeople are still their best customers.

"While you were out, did you notice how their pumpkins looked this year?" Eliza asked. "I'm planning to drive out this morning before I open. I need a few more butternut squash and apples for next Sunday at Slipknot."

"Have special plans?" CJ asked, knowing she goes out there every weekend.

"Our conversation about Annie Simpkins at Girls Knit Out led to Lilly missing Harvest Squash Soup at the Café and before we knew it, she and Kate planned to join Annie and me at Slipknot to make a batch a week from Sunday."

"Annie Simpkins, is she the school teacher that was in the Café yesterday with the ladies from Texas?" CJ asked, trying not to be too conspicuous. "They all had the Harvest Squash Soup, said they never had anything like it. They said you suggested it. They sure weren't in any hurry and left a really nice tip," he finished.

"They came back to the shop after the Café so I could meet Annie," Eliza explained. "CJ, I felt so close to her almost immediately, like she was someone I've known for years. Perhaps because her Aunt told me so much about her when they were in the shop earlier, I can't quite explain the feeling."

With that, Eliza said good-bye and turned to wander

back to her shop. CJ watched her cross the street, thinking he had never seen her react like that to new friends or a new acquaintance. He detected some kind of bond between them. This got him thinking how he wouldn't mind seeing Annie come in for lunch from time to time. Her Texas draw was a fun change of pace. Shaking it off, he went back to work on his menu.

"Finally," he said as he finished. "I've spent way more time out here than I had planned," he mumbled, turned, and went in to start prep for the breakfast crowd.

CJ's Uncle Ben was in the store room getting out the cinnamon raisin bread to start slicing. Next, he would wipe off the tables, open the curtains and get the dining room ready for the day. They open within the hour, and he had a lot to do. At times, CJ didn't know what he would do without his uncle there to give him a hand, but more than that, keep him company. Where Uncle Ben was concerned, the feeling was mutual. He admired the young man CJ had become, as if right before his eyes. He watched him go through the awkward teen years, his voice changing and his face breaking out, competing in sports and trying his hand at dating. It nearly broke his Uncle's heart when he left for college. He was homesick for CJ when it should have been the other way around. Uncle Ben has been by CJ's side and helping him ever since the day he heard CJ was coming home after six months away at school and had bought the Café. They worked like a well-oiled machine, the two together, one picking up where the other left off. It warmed Eliza's heart to see her brother and nephew across the street from her shop, sharing opposite corners of the main street in the town they were all raised in and enjoying successful family businesses.

I'm going to sweep off the walk," Uncle Ben said, as he put away his cleaning supplies.

"That's great," CJ agreed. "Everything is under control behind the counter, and we're almost ready for breakfast."

While he had a few minutes, CJ started washing the potatoes and chopping the scallions for the soup. He would start it, so it had time to simmer and let the flavors blend before lunch.

As Ben went out the door, he saw Eliza heading out of town in Bittersweet. That's what she named the old 62 Chevy truck. She had it overhauled and painted a burnt orange after she inherited it from Mimzie. This old truck had logged many a mile hauling sheep, goats, feed sacks, hay bales, and anything Mimzie came upon that was for sale or free by the side of the road that she could make use of. That was a trait she handed down to Eliza. When Mimzie passed away, Eliza inherited the old truck and the truckload of memories that go with it. Bittersweet just seemed to sum it up in one word.

"Guess Eliza is heading out to El & Em's this morning before she opens up shop!" Uncle Ben shouted back to CJ at the counter as he swept the sidewalk. "That old gal is as full of energy as Mimzie was, two of a kind, those girls... two of a kind," almost mumbling to himself as he finished the walk.

Pulling up at El & Em's Market, Eliza honked at the girls. Early Saturday mornings seemed to be the busiest time for the farmer's market shoppers. The earlier there, the better selection. Eliza went around the counter and gave Ellie and Emmilee a hug. "Perfect day isn't it!" she said as she walked back around to the customer side of the stand. She had watched the cousins grow up together living just down the road from the field that is now their marketplace. Even at an early age, they were out in their small gardens planting and tending to their "crops" as they called them. Their favorites were sunflowers and pumpkins. Early on they shared the fruits of their labor with all the neighbors.

"Next Sunday is Harvest Soup at Slipknot, and it looks like I may be having company. I'm going to need several nice squashes."

They displayed their fresh produce in bushel baskets lined along the front of the stand. There was an abundance of butternut and acorn squash, new potatoes, sweet potatoes, and apples so shiny and perfect they could have been in a magazine. The girls also had a nice selection of pumpkins, of course, in all shapes and sizes picked and ready. A great time saver for a day when time matters. Eliza picked up some carrots and potatoes and a few fresh leeks as well, thinking ahead about a pot of vegetable soup for this Sunday and then plenty of leftovers for the week. The fall can bring on some busy days.

Quickly loading her produce in the back of the truck, she bid the girls goodbye, offering an invitation to Slipknot next weekend if time permitted. They were busy on Sundays this time of year taking advantage of giving families with kids a place to come and enjoy a great fall day.

Back with plenty of time before she opened, Eliza carried the produce up to her kitchen. She arranged the vegetables and fruit in the extra-large wooden bowl she kept on her counter. Enough with the playing house, she scolded herself, then ran down the steps like a kid in a hurry. She flipped on the coffee pot, flipped the sign to open, unlocked the door, and was ready for business. Cody sat in one spot as she circled around him with her antics. Something about a Saturday morning always got her off to a child-like start.

Glancing out the window, she could see CJ had a great breakfast crowd. Not surprising though. The crisp air has lots of people out and about.

There were customers from near and far in and out of the shop today. Many customers were new, while others make it an annual trip this time of year. The day went by in a blur. It was time to flip the sign and close the shop for the day. Just as she reached to lock the door, she caught a glimpse of CJ reaching for the handle.

"What brings you here?" she said as she opened the door to let him in. "This is rare, you coming to my yarn shop! Want me to teach you how to knit some new pot holders?"

"No, nothing like that," CJ stammered, obvious he didn't know how to start off the conversation. "Just thought I'd see what you were up to this evening," he said as if he were fishing. "I know you are going to Slipknot tomorrow and I just wondering if anyone was going out with you."

"Oh," Eliza replied, knowing now what he was trying not to come right out and ask her. "If you are wondering if Annie Simpkins is driving out with me tomorrow, that's not in the plans. She will be the following Sunday, not that she said anything about being busy tomorrow. You could ask her to go to church with you. It would probably be good for the both of you."

"I've only met her once and not even been introduced at that, and that is not why I'm here or what I'm asking, or why..." he stammered as he could see he was quickly digging himself in a hole. "I was just thinking about driving out to the Homestead tomorrow. Won't be but a few more weekends and I will be opening on Sunday's before Christmas. Just wanted to have a day in the country before we got bogged down with the holiday customers," he said, feeling a bit like he justified his need for the trip.

"Oh, now I understand," Eliza said, winking at him, only to set him off again.

Turning beet red, he stood there shaking his head. "Well, I just thought I'd offer some help if you had anything you need to do before winter since I had the time, but if you are going to be like this, I may as well just stay home!" he shouted back at her.

They had such a good relationship. Eliza being the youngest of the four children growing up, and Rachel, CJ's mom helping her so much after the loss of their parents at such an early age they have always been inseparable. Eliza was so excited when CJ was born, she took a shining to him, and he has been her shadow since he was old enough to crawl. They enjoy picking at each other, one dishes it out, the other dishes it right back. They both started laughing, and Eliza grabbed him by the shoulders, shook him while telling him how much she would appreciate both the help and the company if he would be so kind.

"I'm glad you came to your senses! About time you see what you almost missed out on. Free help is hard to come by. Especially good help. So, I'll see you there around noon," he said as he turned to leave. As he opened the door, he reached up and flipped her sign to CLOSED. "I know you've got a lot to do this evening to get this old shop in shape before Monday, so I'll get out of your hair. Glad I could give you a good laugh!"

Eliza quickly finished the shop and headed upstairs to put her soup on and make plans for tomorrow. Since CJ was coming out to help, she may try and plant the mums she had sitting on the porch and get the daffodil bulbs in the ground. The weather is just right for planting bulbs, and the mums would have plenty of time to take good root before the cold sets in. As she gathered things to load up, she piled them just inside the garage. Many times she thinks how nice it would be to live at the Homestead and have the lifestyle Mimzie cherished, but she loved her shop, apartment, and the convenience. This was not the time in her life to make a major change. After all, at the Homestead, Mimzie had her husband to keep her company. Eliza would miss her customers and friends if she isolated herself out there. So for now, she will enjoy her Sundays and an evening now and then while considering herself fortunate to have a busy life. She was looking forward to spending the day with CJ. He was so much fun to be around.

The church was a short six block walk, and Eliza had a perfect morning for it. She loaded the truck and didn't want to park it piled full in the Church parking lot. This also gave her a little extra time to let her mind wander and do a little window shopping as she passed by the local storefronts. The town stays closed on Sundays, except for a few before Christmas. They have strong family values and feel Sundays are for sharing time with families and friends. CJ has carried this belief with his Café hours, serving only breakfast and lunch. He feels supper time is family time, closing at 2:30, giving any late customers time to finish without being rushed.

Eliza hadn't seen the display in Deb's Mugs & Muffins window. Deb changes her menu with the seasons. Fall is also one of her favorite times. She, like Eliza, followed her heart when she opened this quaint coffee shop. It is a great place to sit in the afternoon to recharge. She has special roasts for all of her coffee beans and has a wonderful recipe for hot cocoa that brings people back every winter. Often times, she paints themes for the season on her store windows. As Eliza passed by, she realized just how long it has been since she stopped in to have a cup of coffee and chat with Deb. They enjoy brainstorming, usually coming up with some ideas to give the upcoming season a new approach. She'll have to stop by this week if time allows.

The arrangements in Flora's Unique Floral Boutique windows are just gorgeous, Eliza thought to herself as she walked by. She has a tremendous talent. Many times Eliza brings her natural dried flowers, nuts, berries, pine cones, and seed pods from the Homestead. There is a beautiful arrangement hanging above Eliza's mantle that Flora made one Christmas using an old kitchen grater as thanks for the treasures. Time getting away, Eliza steps it up a bit to get to Church on time.

As she entered the church, she could see the benches were full. A wonderful turnout. Their congregation was strong and continuing to grow. The sounds of children learning to sit through the service were present and cherished by those knowing it was this blessing that kept the church alive and well. After a few songs, a powerful message and some fellowship on the front steps, everyone was on their way, refreshed and spirits renewed. As Eliza drove out to Slipknot, she found herself with the windows down, singing and taking in the day. Her faith is what kept her strong. She learned at a young age that it isn't up to someone to make you happy. If you live your life for God and put other's needs first, even the smallest random act of kindness can bring happiness to you. Eliza lives this belief to the fullest. She keeps her acts of kindnesses to herself, knowing that she is following her heart, letting God show her the way. For this, she is grateful and knows this is why she lives such a blessed life. A perfect day, with the sun in her face, she notices some of the foliage starting to turn. Thanksgiving is just two weeks away. This year has gone by quickly.

Slipknot brings back so many memories of growing up in the country. There was always a garden to be tended to and plenty of fresh fruits and vegetables of the summer.

She remembers making jam with Mimzie, the old kitchen, all of the canning jars and listening to hear each one 'ping' as they sealed.

As she turned into the lane to the Homestead, she sighted a few deer in the nearby field. "Hope they keep clear of the tree I planted this summer," she mumbled to herself, honking her horn to see if they would scatter. The deer in this area are so accustomed to people, they don't scare easily. They did stop grazing and look at her as she passed by, almost as if they were greeting her with a hello! Not happy, she honked again as she continued down the long lane. The porch that ran the length of the cabin was always a welcome sight. She loves to sit out in the summer while cleaning berries or breaking beans from the small garden she still tries to tend to. The distance from town and the business of the shop in the summer often keep her from taking care of it as well as she'd like to, but it still produces fresh vegetables for her and her family. She counts on the girls at El & Em's for variety.

As she got out to start unloading, Cody jumped from the truck, out in the sun to stretch, and then headed for his favorite spot on the porch.

She could see her old mare, JoJo, and the three sheep, Sadie, Sophie, and Sugarplum, coming across the pasture. First things first, she thought, as she headed for the front door with her arms loaded. Pushing the heavy wooden door with a welcome creak, she unloaded her cleaning supplies on the farmhouse table. One more trip to get the groceries for next weekend and the soup she made for lunch. The sun was warm, and there was a slight breeze. It was going to be a gorgeous and productive day.

She went outside and opened the wooden shutters that were kept latched during the week. This wasn't for security, but to carry on the tradition. The shutters saved many a night sleep when the wind and lightning went on for hours in the spring. She was afraid of storms growing up, now she watches them safely from inside, finding it a relaxing way to pass an evening.

With carrots and apples in hand, she walked toward the fence that surrounds the barn. There were the girls, all lined up to greet her. Giving each a treat and a scratch behind the ears, she looked around for Uncle Oliver. He moved out to the Homestead after he lost his wife and now lives in the summer kitchen he remodeled into a cabin. He certainly is a lifesaver, keeping the animals fed and watching over the place. His old truck is gone, but he'll be home by evening. Sunday is his errand day as he stocks up and visits with friends on his way home.

Back to the kitchen, she fills a large jar with ice cold water and drops in a few tea bags to set out on the porch step to brew. The soup pot on the stove goes on low, and she begins to dust the kitchen and living room. This great room combination houses so many of the original pieces of furniture Mimzie used daily. There isn't much dust to take care of, she just enjoys going through the motions and stirring her memories. With the floors being old planks, it is easy to sweep and rarely needs a damp mop. Since she has company coming out next week, she will do a little extra just to freshen it up. As she started out to shake the old braided rug, she saw CJ driving in. She waved, excited to see him. She loved having a companion around while working.

He stopped, hopped out of his truck and pulled out a life-size scarecrow he made from some old overalls and flannel shirt that belonged to Uncle Ben. Then he unloaded three huge mums in full bloom.

"What on earth are you doing?" Eliza shouted at him with excitement in her voice! "Where did you get such beautiful mums? And why does that scarecrow remind me of Uncle Ben?"

CJ just smiled. "I knew you wanted next weekend to be special like Mimzie would have had it in the fall."

Knowing how important the Homestead was to Eliza, CJ was always thoughtful in that respect. He went to the barn for a shovel and gloves, then took a few minutes to brush JoJo.

Back out to the porch, he scratched out a half circle for the mums and brought a hay bale to sit the scarecrow on, leaning him back on the porch railing.

When Eliza finished inside, she walked out to see how his progress was coming. She took a step back in awe of his welcoming display. She couldn't believe her eyes. "I have always loved the arrangements at the door of your Café, but this time, you have outdone yourself!" she exclaimed as she walked toward him.

He could see in her eyes she was coming to give him a hug. He waited. Smiling, he hugged her back. They have a special connection. She's always been there for him when his family wasn't around to pick him up. That he will never forget.

"I'm glad you like it," he said. "Keep them watered, and these should bloom till you come out to decorate for Christmas. They seem healthy enough that they should have time to root and come back next summer. We'll put the scarecrow in the barn after Thanksgiving. You may be able to use him in the garden next summer. That is if Uncle Ben doesn't figure out where his overalls went!"

"Great!" she replied. "I thought that scarecrow reminded me of someone."

They laughed as they walked in arm in arm, looking forward to a bowl of soup and a long talk.

The table out back was set and ready for lunch. Taking their soup, bread, and iced tea out on vintage trays and sitting in the old willow chairs overlooking the pond always made lunch taste better.

"It's a nice afternoon. I'm sure glad there's a breeze today," Eliza said as she passed CJ another piece of bread. "Got warmer than I thought it would, but this time of year, you never quite know what to expect."

He agreed, finishing his soup, pouring them both another glass of tea. "Couldn't have asked for a better way to spend my Sunday."

"I saw you out at the barn chatting with JoJo earlier," Eliza said. "You know that old mare looks forward to your visits. I think it would do you both good to take a ride now and then. Probably add some life to her years. She is getting some age on her you know."

CJ just smiled. He remembered when Eliza got JoJo. Thought she was just the best thing ever. She was less than a year old. They sort of grew up together, the two of them.

"Wouldn't be the Homestead without her," he replied. "She's like a fixture out here, just hope she isn't too lonely. Doubt those dumb old sheep are much company to her!"

As they sat and pondered their thoughts, soaking up the sun, Eliza spoke up, "I just want to thank you again for coming out and planting the mums and bringing that adorable scarecrow. That means a lot to me. Your company means even more."

"You don't have to thank me. I can see it in your eyes. I just wanted your outing next Sunday to be special. After all, you have first time guests coming out. We want the old Homestead to welcome everyone, just like Mimzie would have, don't we?" Smiling, CJ picked up the tea pitcher to refill his glass.

Eliza was surprised to see their conversation open up. CJ was usually very quiet about his thoughts and spent most of his time just kidding around with her. Today, he began to talk about his own life. Deep down he knew this is where he belonged. He would never trade Uncle Ben's company for anything, and most days doesn't know what he would do without him. Although at times, he felt very lonely. He admitted thinking about having a nice home and starting a family someday. The Café provides a good income, and the thought of expanding has crossed his mind. For now, he doesn't want it to lose the small Café charm.

Suddenly, Annie Simpkins became part of their conversation. CJ was curious about her background, comparing his decision to leave school and return home to her choice to finish school and leave home. They discussed Eliza's conversation with Annie's Aunt, her love for horses from an early age, and how she helped the kids with disabilities at the stable down the road from her. They talked about the loss of her mom and her father's concerns. It took a lot of courage for her to pick up and relocate so far from home with no family or friends, especially starting her first teaching position.

"So, did she have a horse of her own growing up?" CJ asked. He remembered how the sight of JoJo made him feel when he returned to the Homestead.

"She has a horse. Her parents got him for her when she was twelve. Named him Pete, and he is still with her dad. They have a small stable for him, but I'm not sure he gets regular attention since Annie isn't there," Eliza filled him in. Knowing that was probably one of the hardest things to leave behind, she felt for Annie. "When she comes out next Sunday, I'll be sure to introduce her to JoJo and let her know she is welcome to give her all the attention she wants to. That'll be good for both of them. Now, I need to get moving. You sit and enjoy the afternoon as long as you like," said Eliza as she picked up the tray from the table and started to the back door.

50

CJ followed and helped her with the dishes. "I noticed a few pots of mums on the porch. Anywhere, in particular, you would like them while I have the shovel and water out?" he asked.

"I thought I would put them around the corner posts of the fences on each side of the lane road. What do you think about that?"

"Sounds good to me. Want me to put the daffodil bulbs in around them while I'm at it, or did you want them planted somewhere else?" CJ questioned as he was picking up the pots.

"Sounds even better! That's a couple of things I can cross off my list. You certainly have made my day better. Thank you for that," smiling at him, she picked up the bulbs and walked along with him.

The job was done in no time, the tools put away and after another visit with JoJo, he was about to call it a day.

"I guess I'll head back to town if you don't have anything else for me to do around here," he said as he came in the front door. "I watered the mums again so they should be in good shape until mid-week. You may want to leave a note for Uncle Oliver."

He walked over, gave Eliza a hug, and then started out the door. Half way out, he turned and came back in.

"What would you think about having a family gathering at the Homestead this Christmas? I know everyone has plans around the holidays and travel is a bit more difficult, but I thought if we let them know early enough it could work out. I just feel the need for the family this year more than ever," he explained. "I'll set aside time to help you with the decorations and the cooking. The baking could wait until everyone gets here and we could do it together like we did when I was a kid," he finished with a child-like excitement in his voice.

"You remember about the family baking?" she questioned him, "But you were so young. That really stuck with you. Seeing how creative you are in your own kitchen makes a lot of sense."

"So will you call Mom and see what she has planned this year?" looking at her as if waiting for a promise. "After all, you being the little sister, you always get your way!" he winked, "and you know you are my favorite Auntie!" Smiling ear to ear, he gave her a peck on the cheek, turned, out the door he went and jumped off the porch, missing all the steps like he did when he was a boy.

How could she say no to that?

Chapter Four

Introducing Annie to Slipknot Farm, baking with yeast, stories of the past and new friends for a lifetime...

The drive home from Slipknot was nice. Eliza had the evening to relax and regroup for the upcoming week. As much as she loved her shop, she made it a rule to stay out of it on Sundays. This gave her a sense of having the day off.

She couldn't get her mind off of CJ. They spend time in passing most days, but not often a visit like this. A family gathering at the Homestead for Christmas would be wonderful. They have their family reunion in mid-July. It started as a tradition many years ago, and no one has ever suggested anything different. The more she pondered the idea, the more she loved the thought of a new Christmas tradition.

Losing their parents at a very young age, Mimzie and Papa were there to fill the painful void. Oliver was the oldest, already 17 and Ben was 15. They were in high school.

Rachel, CJ's mom, was 11 at the time. Eliza had just turned 4. She didn't remember much about her mom and dad, but Oliver often told her stories of them and continued doing so even after he returned to Slipknot, helping her take care of things after the loss of his wife, Mary.

Finally home, with her hands full and Cody at her feet, Eliza flipped on the light at the top of the stairs and greeted Mimzie as she passed by. A quick shower and retiring in her favorite chair, she put her feet up on the ottoman and picked up her address book from the side table. Time to call Rachel. Eliza knew she would be the one to get the word out. She would e-mail everyone. Eliza never had the desire to learn to use the computer. She loved the simple lifestyle she had chosen. Besides, she had her big sister for times like this. As the phone rang the third time, she heard the familiar voice on the other end of the line. They hadn't chatted in quite some time. Maybe longer than either realized. After a quick 15 minutes of catching up, Eliza told Rachel about the day she spent at Slipknot with CJ and how surprised she was when he asked her to help plan a family Christmas at the Homestead this year.

"So, you want me to see what kind of response I get? I suppose that would be a start." Rachel said.

"Unless you have a better idea. CJ has his heart set on sharing this Christmas with the family, just the immediate family. Save the big reunion for July." Eliza answered.

"I'll send out an e-mail then get back with you on Wednesday evening, and we can talk about the response if that's all right with you. In the meantime, you talk to

Oliver and Ben. You know they don't have e-mail, and you see them often anyway. How are they doing by the way?" Rachel asked.

"Oh, they are fine, doing just fine. Oliver is content at Slipknot. It has been extremely hard on him losing Mary so suddenly. It doesn't seem like three years have gone by. He's sure a lifesaver for me, keeping an eye on things and helping with the upkeep. As for Ben, he's still CJ's right hand, helping at the Café daily. That's a double blessing. I'll make sure Molly knows about the Christmas plans. It's not like it would be a priority for Ben to pass it on to her," Eliza said. "Well, it's getting quite late, and we both have busy days ahead. I'll say goodbye for now and talk with you on Wednesday. I miss you, Sis. Can't wait for the feedback. I think I'm getting as excited about the gathering as CJ."

"Me, too," Rachel agreed. "Good night."

Finishing up a few notes, Eliza realized the time. She turned off the lights and readied herself for bed. Opening the window just right, she pulled down her quilt and crawled in. Now to clear her mind so she could get some rest. This idea of a gathering was rather exciting. What a great way to spend a holiday. And, oh, to decorate the Homestead for a family Christmas, what a blessing that would be. Tired from the day, she drifted off to sleep.

The first of the week seemed to go by in a blink. It was already Wednesday evening. Rachel called just as she promised. She was full of news about family plans.

Oliver's oldest daughter, Sophie, and her husband

would make the trip. They had planned Christmas at their house this year, so it wasn't difficult to convince their daughter Celeste to spend the holidays at Slipknot. Their son Carson and his wife Julie were excited to make the journey to Slipknot as well. Carson had been there when he was younger, but Julia had only seen pictures and heard stories. What a great way to spend their Christmas, especially since it was the first one they would share with their son, Jaxon, now 3 months old and so far he had only met his Auntie Celeste and his over-ambitious Grandparents. My how Great-Grandpa Oliver would be thrilled. As for Rachel's daughter, Beth, short for Elizabeth, named after Eliza, she had already talked to CJ and planned to be there.

"So, it seems we'll have several generations together!" Rachel laughed. "Now that you know what you're in for, is there anything I can do to help?"

Eliza, with her mind going in circles, trying to grasp the news, took a moment, then asked, "When will everyone be arriving? Did they give you any idea how long they can stay? Are they going to be sleeping at Slipknot, because my apartment is available if anyone is uncomfortable with the crowd?"

About that time she realized how ridiculous she must sound, rambling on, as though the questions racing around in her head were pouring out of her mouth. She hated it when that happened!

Rachel stopped her. "Eliza, it will be fine. They have your number, and I'm certain they will call you soon. Everyone seems as excited as we are. You can discuss their needs with each of them. Oh, how exciting is the thought of an old-fashioned Christmas. I know you will make it all the more special, you and CJ that is."

Eliza was overwhelmed. Her sister was always the older, more mother-like figure. She wasn't much on complimenting or encouraging Eliza with choices she made.

"Thank you for that, Rachel," she quickly replied, "and I mean that. It means so much to me that they are willing to travel during the holidays, and with CJ's help, we will make it as special as they hope it will be."

"I know what you're both capable of, and I have no doubt that it will be amazing. Just don't over-do it so that you and CJ are worn out and can't enjoy the celebration. It's going to be quite an undertaking. Could I send you some money for food or any extras that you'll need for the crowd? I'd be more than happy to do that since I can't be there to help you get ready. Please," Rachel asked with a strong concern.

"I'll be ok, don't worry about that part," Eliza assured her.

"We'll see," she replied, "but for now, I really must go. I'll call you next week Monday, or sooner if anything else comes up. Enjoy your planning. Tell CJ to call me one evening when he has time." Rachel said her good-byes.

Eliza sat there for a few minutes, just to get her emotions settled down. Never did she think she would have such a Christmas to look forward to at Slipknot.

Much too excited to start getting ready for bed, Eliza picked up the phone. She knew Oliver would be ecstatic. After a few rings, she heard the familiar voice on the other end.

"Hello, Ollie here," the deep voice came across.

"Hope you weren't dozing on the couch," she said cheerfully, "I have some news for you." "Oh, please tell," he replied.

Always the curious one for news, she had his full attention. "Well, I just got off the phone with Rachel, and it seems there is going to be a family Christmas this year at Slipknot. Are you up for a little extra work and a lot of excitement?" she questioned.

"What do you mean by a 'little' extra work and whose idea was this anyway?" he grumbled. "Sounds like something you would instigate, but you always save the reunion for summertime. Is someone sick, gonna die, need to see everyone for a very last time?"

"Stop, Oliver! Whatever has gotten into you? Are you still half-asleep? This isn't the conversation I thought we'd be having. It's going to be a good thing, CJ's idea as a matter-a-fact. He asked me when we were out last Sunday if a gathering at Christmas would be possible. Rachel sent out some e-mails, and it seems quite a few can make it out, including Carson and Julia with their son, your Great-Grandson whom you've only seen pictures of. Now, is that better?" She waited patiently for a reply.

"Carson and Julia are going to make the trip with

the little one!" his voice now filled with the excitement she had first expected to hear. "And what about Celeste, is she coming with them, and Sophie and Jack, they would be devastated if they were looking at Christmas alone? You know how they love the holidays."

Eliza assured him they were all planning to make the trip, along with Rachel and her family, and of course Ben and Molly would join them, even though, they most likely would go home later in the evening. "So, are you up for it?" she waited for his reply.

"Couldn't be more ready if you told me they would be here tomorrow," he said, then let out his familiar chuckle. "Just make a list, I'll do whatever I can to help. You knew they named the little guy Jaxon, didn't you? Mimzie & Papa's sir name. Great idea, and so thoughtful. I told them how much that was appreciated."

She did know that assuring him, they would have been very proud. She knew she could count on him. "I may try and come out for a while tomorrow evening so we can sit and chat a bit about the plans. I wanted to drop off a few things for Sunday anyway. You know I'm having friends out, don't you?"

"So that's why I thought Ben was sitting on a hay bale among the mums the other evening until I got close enough to tell someone had made off with a pair of his bib overalls and shirt. Was CJ out to help you with that?"

"Sure was, that's when he broke the news to me that he wanted to do Christmas at Slipknot. I could tell he was up to something, the way he lingered after the work was done, but he sure caught me off guard with his idea. After the initial surprise, I've been just as thrilled about the plans. He certainly has the family excited. Guess you want to get to bed soon," she paused. "I'm not going to be up much longer either." She bid him good-night. "I'll call if I can't make it out tomorrow."

"That'll be just fine. Sleep tight," he said as he hung up the phone.

Sleep, Eliza thought to herself. How am I going to be able to lay my head down and go to sleep? With all this excitement of the holidays, she suddenly remembered that she had a big weekend to get ready for. Business was picking up, autumn guests were back, and she was entertaining on Sunday. Lots of good things to get ready for. This is the lifestyle she loves. The busier, the better. Especially when it is a 'good busy' as she likes to call it.

Knowing she was going to have to burn off some energy to get a good night sleep, Eliza got out her recipe box, pulled out a stack of cookie recipes and sorted through them. What can I whip up tonight that will be good for Sunday, she thought to herself. Then she had it. GGG's Chewy Chocolate Cookies, one of the recipes her momma had made when she was a young girl. Mimzie taught them all to cook and bake as soon as they were tall enough to reach the counter from a stool. In fact, the very stool still sits in the kitchen at Slipknot. Eliza had her turn on it just the same. Quickly gathering the ingredients she had her mixer beating the butter and sugar while she was whisking together the flour, cocoa, and other dry ingredients. She added them to the bowl with the butter mixture and her dough was almost perfect. The last, but very best ingredient, the dark chocolate chips, the really good quality ones that made these cookies even better than the original recipe, and a handful to snack on while baking, of course. The oven was pre-heating, and he had three cookie sheets ready by the time it beeped. The first tray in, these take exactly 9 minutes per sheet. They puff up nicely, but as they cool on the rack, they flatten out and stay chewy. As she put the last tray of cooled cookies in the crock bowl, she set two aside and poured a glass of milk. Cody, sitting at her feet, was waiting for a splash in his bowl. He always knew when the milk jug came out. She covered the bowl, put her glass in the sink and turned off the lights. Now she was ready for bed.

She didn't have the time or energy to drive out to Slipknot on Thursday evening, so she called Oliver and post-phoned their plans until Sunday evening.

The Girls Knit Out was held in passing, everyone having commitments. Rosie stopped to visit but had another open house at the Real Estate office set for Saturday morning. Olivia was by to drop off some muffins and pick up a few things from the sale table but didn't stay to work. There were several other events going on around the school and in the community that involved friends, families, and a lot of volunteering. It was an early evening, but for once, that was okay with Eliza.

Plans were set for Sunday. Saturday was busy with a lot of lookers. This was common at this time of year. There were also familiar faces coming in to see what she had in for winter. With a nice fire going, she took the time to sit and chat a bit with some of her out of town customers that she only saw this time of year.

Closed and the shop ready for Monday morning, a light supper and a warm bath were in her plans. She needed to catch up on her rest. After all, Sunday was the day she had been waiting for since Annie stopped in the shop with her Aunt.

Bittersweet was loaded and ready to pull out right after church. Annie planned to meet her for the service and ride out with her. Eliza knew she would be welcome and welcomed she was. Annie couldn't remember a time she had been made to feel such a part of the community. She was starting to feel like this was a place she would call home.

After church, Annie reached into the back of the truck and pulled out her satchel. "I brought clothes to change into when we get to the Homestead. I love my comfy clothes on the weekends. Being dressed for school every day, it's a nice change," she smiled at Eliza. "I hope you didn't go to a lot of trouble for this. I know you must be very busy at the shop this time of the year. I've noticed the increased traffic around town. It's very exciting to feel like a part of things, especially with the holidays coming up so quickly. I'm so afraid this will be a hard time for my dad and me this year. But I don't want to bring this day down with my whining and feeling sorry for myself. I'm blessed by my new friends and wouldn't do anything to put a damper on today!" Annie said, perking right up. "It has to be a great day. I brought my red cowboy boots!"

Bittersweet was heading out of town with the windows down and Eliza telling Annie about everything and everyone they passed along the way.

"Lilly and Kate will be out in an hour or so. Lilly took an early shift this morning at the E.R. Kate is the Librarian. Have you met her?" Eliza asked.

"In passing, at the library, but we haven't had a chance to talk," Annie replied. "Are any of your other friends coming out?"

"Abigail and Rosie had other obligations.

You might know Abigail from school."

"I teach with Abigail. I have her daughter in my class."

"I want to make a quick stop at El & Em's. I'm sure they have a few fresh picked apples. We're going to make an apple crisp for dessert. It'll only take a few minutes. Have you met the girls yet?"

"Actually, I have," Annie replied.

As they walked up to the counter, El & Em greeted Annie and Eliza with excitement in their voices. "I suppose Annie told you she came out last weekend and made plans to bring her class," Em told Eliza. "What are you doing out this way today?"

"We are having a gathering at Slipknot and need a few apples for a crisp. Perfect day for it, don't you think?"

"Oh, you couldn't have requested a more perfect afternoon," El replied. "We're hoping for a nice crowd today. Pumpkins are at their peak."

"These should do quite nicely," Eliza smiled, picking up a half dozen bright red apples. She handed Em the money, and they were back to Bittersweet continuing their journey in no time at all.

"Won't be long now," Eliza said, as she made the turn. "Slipknot is just at the end of this lane. Anxious?" she teased.

"Are you kidding, I've been so excited about this since we first made plans. I have so many things going through my mind about how it's going to look, and the cooking, that's going to be such a treat!" Annie rambled. "Oh, there are three deer, look they are staring at us. Aren't they afraid?"

"Afraid? I wish they were afraid," Eliza said as she blew the horn. "They look as if they were expecting us. I hope they didn't eat the mums CJ planted last Sunday."

"Oh, was CJ out last Sunday? Is he planning to be out today?" Annie perked right up. "I haven't had a chance to go back to the Café since that first trip with my Aunt. It was amazing. I was really hoping to go there one morning for breakfast. I heard it is really good. We were talking about it at school. Lots of interesting conversations take place in the teacher's lounge!" she rambled.

"No, he isn't planning on this afternoon unless his plans changed. He stays clear when we have a girl's day. But he did know I made plans and came out to help with a few things last Sunday. Wait till you see the arrangement he put out to greet us. We're here!"

"Wow! What a welcome. Did he make the scarecrow? And the porch, it is just what I was hoping it would be, all the way across the front of the house. I can't wait until next summer when I can sit on the swing and spend an afternoon reading a favorite book! OH, my, if you invite me out next summer that is. I am assuming too much too fast. It is just that I'm so excited," Annie said, holding her hands to the sides of her face. "I'm embarrassing myself."

Eliza reached across the seat of the truck, took her hand, and said, "I'm thrilled to see the excitement in your eyes. Please don't hold anything back. I love to share the Homestead, and it pleases me to make my guests happy. We're going to have a wonderful time, and please know you are welcome to come out anytime, whether I'm here with you, or you just drive out to spend an afternoon relaxing alone. Now, grab your bag, and I'll show you around."

As they got out of the truck and started up the stairs, Annie pulled out her camera, told Eliza to turn around and smile so she could snap a picture. She wanted to remember her first trip out to Slipknot. She got the scarecrow and flowers in the foreground. "Perfect!" she said as she scurried up the steps.

As Eliza opened the big wooden door with its familiar creak, Annie was taken by the entrance. It felt as if she had stepped back a century in time. They meandered through the living room and dining room, stopping and admiring each piece of furniture, questioning Eliza of their history. There was a hutch and buffet, several old wardrobes throughout the house, and an old daybed positioned under the large window in the living room, perfect for a nap. Many of the pieces were either handed down or hand-made by family. The kitchen was a sight to behold. It housed the old stove with a warming shelf, the massive cast iron sink with double bowls and drain boards on either end, all in one piece with the backsplash attached and an old ice box used before there was electricity.

Amazing." That is the word Annie used over and over as they explored the Homestead. The house was much bigger than Annie had expected, but as Eliza explained Mimzie and Papa had five children, and she started to get the picture. With four bedrooms across the back of the house, it allowed family and guests to have a comfortable place to stay. Before they knew it nearly an hour had passed.

"I suppose we could start the soup. Lilly and Kate should be out soon," Eliza suggested.

"I hope they like me," Annie said, hesitating. "I don't know a lot of people here yet, other than at school. I'm anxious to make friends, but I'm trying not to put too many expectations on the day. I'm already overwhelmed by the Homestead itself."

Eliza just stood there for a moment, smiled at Annie and said, "How on earth could anyone who gets to know you not love you? You are an amazing young woman, and I can't wait to learn everything about you. You're going to have more friends than you ever imagined."

They both smiled as Eliza reached for the old wooden recipe box in the jelly cupboard. "This is full of family recipes, starting with Mimzie's mom, who would have been my Great-Grandma, through my generation, and this year I have added a few of CJ's favorites. I guess there is no end to the collection."

"Why would you want to include CJ's recipes in a family collection that dates back so many generations? Don't you think that takes away from the history?" Annie questioned. "Isn't it something that you would want to keep in the family? I realize the Café is an important part of the town, and you and he seem close, but it seems the recipes he shares with you should be kept separate."

"Annie, didn't you know CJ is my nephew?" Eliza asked as she studied the look of complete surprise on her face, watching it turn a bright shade of red. "Guess not!"

Annie began to stammer all over herself, then they began to laugh and laugh and laugh. More so about the surprise, not the situation. "So he is your nephew, you are his Aunt Eliza. Why didn't I know that? How did I miss it? How could I miss it?" Annie rambled in that familiar way she did when she got nervous.

That is one of the things Eliza had learned of Annie's personality, just one of the features that made her so endearing.

"CJ is my sister Rachel's son, and she has a daughter, Beth, short for Elizabeth, named after me actually. I shortened mine by leaving off the second half, she shortened hers by leaving off the first, so it works out perfectly. Momma and Daddy were gone when I was only 4, so we moved in with Mimzie and Papa to live, Rachel, being older, took me under her wing and liked to play Momma to me any chance she had. We have a special bond." Eliza quickly stopped herself. "Now who is rambling?"

Eliza found the recipe for the Harvest Squash Soup. "We will work here on the old work table."

She got out the squash and cut it in half long ways, removed the seeds and placed the squash cut side down on a large baking sheet. "Now, this goes in a 300-degree oven for about 20 minutes to soften the squash enough to peel it. While they are roasting, let's get the dough punched down and make the Butterhorns. I started it this morning to let it get the first raise in before we got here. I love to cook with friends, but I like to visit more!"

"Are we really going to bake in that old stove? Is it hooked up to anything, or does it burn wood?" Annie quizzed.

"Oh, no, today we will do our baking in the new oven over by the window. The old stove belonged to Mimzie and it still works, but I found through the years it's nice to have a larger more efficient model at hand when we are getting down to some serious cooking," Eliza explained as she shoved the two sheets of squash in the hot oven. "Have you worked much with yeast dough?"

"Not at all. That is one thing that really intimidates

me," Annie confessed. "But, I have always wanted to learn. Looks like my lucky day."

"Can't learn any younger, at least that's what Mimzie always said," Eliza smiled as she brought down the large glass jar of flour. "Dust the board and your hands, and then punch your fist right in the center of this dough, taking out any frustrations you may have. Being so young, you probably don't have much troubling you."

Annie laughed. Then, as she started around the table, she gasped! "Oh, what is that?" Annie pointed to the large red stain on the floor by Mimzie's old cook stove. "Was there a massacre here in the days of the Cowboys and Indians?" she giggled.

"Not exactly a massacre," Eliza winked. "More like a raspberry juice dilemma. Oh, I feel the need to tell you a story, but don't stop kneading that dough."

"My momma loved to make and attend to a garden as soon as she was old enough," Eliza went on, "and was always full of ideas for canning and growing different things. One afternoon she was out on the edge of the woods and came upon a raspberry patch. Roger, her brother, was with her, and before they knew it, they had two buckets of berries. So, she had the idea to make jam. Well, Mimzie helped her outside at the wash stove to cook down the berries and strain the juice. She instructed her when it had cooled, bring it on the kitchen stove and they would cook it into jelly. So anxious, when the juice had cooled, Momma brought in the pot, almost more than she could handle, and as she reached the cook stove, called to Mimzie that it was ready. Well, you see the little stool that we all stood on to learn to cook? Momma didn't, and there she went, head over heels over a pot of raspberry juice and was sitting in the puddle when Mimzie came in the room. Momma was in tears of horror and Mimzie was in tears of laughter, not at Momma, but at the situation. 'Well, look at your white apron,' Mimzie said to her. 'I think we may have found a new way to make our plain old white wool red!' Wiping her tears, it was only a few minutes until the Homestead was roaring with laughter and a new idea had been born. The stain on the floor never came up, and now, it is just another story in the history of Slipknot."

Enjoying every minute kneading the dough, the story added to the memory. Annie worked with Eliza's direction, and before she knew it, she had twenty-four of the oddest looking Butterhorns either of them had ever seen. Not only were they misshaped, but no two were the same size.

"All I can say is, they may not be perfect to look at, but that never hurt the taste yet! Get out that camera of yours, you need a picture, your first try at yeast bread. Bet there won't be any left when lunch is finished."

Eliza tilted the pan for the picture as she complimented her for a job well done. They placed them on a shelf built under the windows made especially for cooling pies and raising bread. Today the sun warmed it nicely.

"These will rise for about 30 minutes while we finish the soup and then we'll be ready to start the apple crisp."

The squash had roasted and cooled enough to handle while they chopped the rest of the vegetables for the stock, using an old cast iron pot that had been one of Mimzie's favorites.

"Now we can add the diced squash to this old crock bowl, pour a couple of dippers of broth over it, and take the potato masher and work it just as if you were making mashed potatoes. You have made mashed potatoes haven't you?" Eliza teased.

"Yes, at holidays my momma let me be the one to mash the potatoes when I got old enough, but we did use an electric mixer. I know that's a shock to you, but it worked quite nicely. This potato masher though, it gives me a greater feeling of the pioneer days. That's what I want to be a part of now. I want to learn it the old way, not that I'm saying you are old...because I just know you aren't, old that is!"

And with that said, Annie was as red as the wooden handle on the potato masher, and Eliza was laughing at her tripping over her words.

The rolls had doubled, and the soup was simmering nicely on the stove. Eliza had the apple peeler clamped to the work table and gave Annie another lesson on how to do it the old way! Once again, in amazement, she couldn't understand how such a tool could peel, slice and core the apples in a simple cranking of a handle. They were ready in no time. The square baking pan that was hanging on the wall was just the right size, and the apples filled it nicely.

Eliza made the crumble, covered the apples and slid it into the hot oven just as the rolls came out.

Annie was bouncing around the kitchen with joy when she saw her Butterhorns. Her first attempt, and oh, they looked wonderful and smelled even better.

Just then, the door opened with a familiar creak and there stood Kate and Lilly.

"What on earth is going on in here?" Kate said as they stood in the massive doorway.

"I'm starving, and I hope we are hearing the cries of success, couldn't handle a failure right now. I've had my heart set on this day out for two weeks," Lilly said as she walked in and gave Eliza a hug She held out her hand and said, "You must be Annie. I've heard about you, all good I assure you, and couldn't wait to meet you. I'm Lilly."

With an introduction like this, how could they not become close friends?

Kate stepped in, took Annie's hand, and with a simple introduction, the room sounded as if they had known each other all their lives.

"It smells even more wonderful in here than I imagined it would," Lilly said, as she held tight across her stomach, trying to muffle the grumble. "What can I do to help?"

Eliza helped Lilly get out the dishes and linens to set the table. She had the back porch ready. It was so pleasant out there last Sunday afternoon, and the weather was just as nice, it should be perfect.

"I need to get something from the car," Kate excused herself. As she went out the door, she quickly turned back and complimented Eliza on the scarecrow and mums. "What a great setting this would be for a group picture if Mr. Oliver would be around this afternoon to take one, that is. After all, this could be the start of a great tradition." She hurried back up on the porch carrying a pumpkin that had the top cut out and an arrangement of sunflowers filling it.

"What a gorgeous arrangement!" Eliza exclaimed. She loved surprises like this. "What a wonderful idea, using the pumpkin as the vase. Did you come up with this on your own?"

"I wish," Kate answered. "I suppose I could have taken the credit, but I stopped by Flora's while in town. I told her I would like something unique for the outing today. She did a nice job, didn't she? But then, she always does. I'll take it out back. Come on, Lilly, I'll help you set the table."

The porch was ready Annie was just blending the cream into the soup, and Eliza was toasting pumpkin seeds in an old iron skillet on the stove. Just as they carried everything out for lunch, the apple crisp was coming out of the oven. "Perfect timing," Eliza exclaimed.

As they sat around the table, Eliza asked they join hands as she gave the blessing, for what a blessing this day was.

"Well, Annie, how do you feel having your first

cooking lesson from the master?" asked Kate. "If you want to learn it right, ask Eliza."

Annie was overwhelmed. As she tried to tell everyone how much this day meant to her, she became blurry-eyed and had to stop mid-sentence. "I'm sorry, I didn't mean to sound so foolish. I'm just so thrilled about being here, together with all of you. I have been so lonely lately. I don't want this day to end."

Lilly quickly picked up her glass of iced tea, raised it at the table and said, "This calls for a toast, to us, new friends, and old places. To the first of many gatherings." As they all clinked glasses, Lilly then finished with, "Now, could we please eat! I'm starving!"

The next hour and a half passed quickly sharing wonderful food and conversation.

"What is over there?" Annie questioned. "Am I seeing water?"

"Yes, there is a pond over there, and behind the small shed is where Momma started her first garden," Eliza explained. "Over by the barn is the old summer kitchen, which is where Oliver, my oldest brother lives. He converted it into a cabin when he moved back after his wife passed away. I don't know what I would do without his help. He takes care of the animals and the few chickens we still keep, and in the summer helps with the garden. More important than that, he helps maintain the integrity of the Homestead. There is a lot to take care of out here, but we think it's worth the effort."

"I need a walk. Do you want to go over and see Eliza's horse, JoJo and her three best friends, the sheep Sophie, Sadie and Sugarplum??" asked Kate. "We could take some apple peels for them. They love attention."

After spending the better part of the next hour walking around, greeting the animals and doing a bit of exploring, it was time to clean up and start winding down the visit. Eliza put some coffee on and got out the crock of cookies. They enjoyed them as they packed up the truck.

Annie couldn't stop talking about JoJo. It made her feel lonely for Pete, her horse that she had since she was twelve. It had been one of the hardest things about leaving home. Not seeing Pete, but more so, not being with her dad. She suddenly realized she hadn't talked to him all week. Now in the midst of this great day, Annie began to feel homesick.

Eliza quickly noticed Annie's mood sadden. "What are you thinking about, dear?" she asked. "You seem a bit blue. Are you all right?"

Annie explained that seeing the horse and spending the day together made her think about her dad and Pete. It seems like an eternity since they were together. Now the holidays were coming, and she realized how difficult it was going to be.

"Why don't you saddle up JoJo and take her for a ride?" Eliza suggested. "She would love it, and it might be just what you need to end this perfect day."

Annie's eyes lit up, and her smile came back instantly.

"Really! I could take her for a ride!" Annie exclaimed. "How exciting!"

In a blink she was off to the barn, Eliza barely able to keep up with her, and in no time, Annie was trotting down the field road as if she and JoJo had been friends forever.

Oliver caught a glimpse of her as he drove in. He stopped at the barn with Eliza. "That wasn't CJ. Who just rode off on JoJo? That looked like a girl?" he commented.

"That was Annie, she's the fifth-grade teacher, here for her first school year. She's from Texas. It is going to be difficult for her to spend the holidays alone, and I'm not sure if she will be up for the long trip to home. Her horse is there with her dad, so I thought JoJo might just be the perfect way to end the day here at the Homestead, and it was."

Eliza and Oliver chatted about the plans for Christmas. There were a few things for Oliver to get started on. Because he had constantly maintained the grounds and outbuildings, it wasn't going to be difficult to get the things ready for the crowd. She could now see the excitement in his eyes that she had only heard in his voice until now.

With JoJo brushed and back in the corral, Annie with her belongings in the front seat of Bittersweet, and Oliver waving good-bye from his front porch, Eliza started slowly down the lane leaving Slipknot until the next time. She smiled, driving back with the windows down, watching the sunset knowing it was the people that made it more special than the place itself. She couldn't have asked for a more perfect day.

Chapter 5

Annie drops by 'Girls Knit Out' with chocolate cake and coffee! She's one of us now…

The alarm sounded. Monday morning came quickly. Eliza made it through her morning routine in the shop, her mind on Sunday every time she had a moment to daydream. Business continued to pick up. It seemed more people were out and about in town enjoying what autumn had to offer.

Abigail stopped by to check out the bargain table for deals that could be used for A Snug Around the Neck and ask about Sunday. They chatted a bit, then the doorbell clanged, more customers were coming in.

"Will you be here for Girls Knit Out?" Eliza asked as she looked toward the customers coming in. "We'll talk about the weekend then. Hope you can make it."

"Yea, see you then. Hope you have a busy week." Abigail smiled as she walked toward the door.

"Well, ladies, what can I show you today?"

Eliza greeted the group, and the next two hours went by in a blink. This was a group that plans a trip every fall. They take turns choosing the destination and outings. The leader this year happened to be a regular customer of A Simple Stitch and comes to town every fall. Two pots of coffee later, and a steady stream in and out of the comfy chairs, many new ideas had been discussed, and a great deal of winter work was planned.

"Are you ladies staying in town tonight?" Eliza asked as she packaged their purchases.

"We are staying overnight, but not here in Spring Forrest. We have reservations at an Inn closer to home. We'll head that direction later this afternoon. But before that, we still have to shop Main Street, can't miss Flora's Unique Floral Boutique, and several other stores. We have reservations for a late lunch at CJ's. I thought that would be a good rest stop before we finish. It is only a forty-five-minute drive to the Inn."

"Well, I thank you for making A Simple Stitch a stop on your trip. I won't have to tell you to have a good time, I can see that's on your agenda. I applaud you for that. Most women never get the chance to get out and truly enjoy themselves," smiling, Eliza walked them to the door. "Enjoy town, and have a good lunch."

Lunch was also on Eliza's mind, but too soon the day was at an end. As she finished up in the shop and as she flipped her sign to CLOSED, she noticed CJ's message on the blackboard. Not his usual menu, but words of wisdom.

Very unlike him, she thought. What is going on in that young man's mind?

By the time Friday evening rolled around, Eliza was ready to settle in with the Girls Knit Out, ready to relax and catch up. Seemed they hadn't all been together for several weeks. Autumn tends to be busy for everyone.

"Come on in, pull your chairs around. I have the fire just right and a pot of coffee brewing. I even made pumpkin cookies. I'm really getting into fall," Eliza said as she greeted them at the door.

Last ones in were Abigail and Zoey, both excited to gather with friends. Zoey headed straight for the hearth where Cody was already curled up waiting. He knew the drill. They assumed their usual position and were settled.

"What a great evening," Eliza said as she stood by the fire and looked around. "We're all here. We haven't all been together for quite some time. What has it been, three weeks?"

"It has been about that," Rosie spoke up. "So, what's new? Anything exciting to share? Please, I'm anxious for gossip! Someone start, and I'll pass the jar of cookies!"

"I'll follow with the coffee pot. Rosie's right, we have some catching up to do. Does everyone have a mug?" Eliza followed.

Lilly, usually anxious to just sit and listen to everyone's stories was the first to speak up. "I had the most marvelous time at Slipknot on Sunday, the best time

I've had in a very, very long time. I just want to say you all missed a great day."

Kate followed, "A great day is an understatement. We had such a marvelous time, and the food, and Annie, you have to get to know this girl, she is a gem. She was so appreciative to find new friendships. She has been here for months now and hasn't really made any good friends, just acquaintances. This is a very interesting girl, and we all need to put some effort in making her feel welcome, I'm just saying."

"See the arrangement Kate and Lilly brought to Slipknot, isn't this darling, arranged in a pumpkin. Of course, it came from Flora's," Eliza explained. "I just had to put it here on the counter, so I could enjoy it." Eliza continued to share some of the high points of the day. Annie's first try at yeast rolls and her help with the soup and apple crisp. "She is a quick learner, and I look forward to spending as much time with her as I get the chance to. She's someone that we are all going to find very special. Don't know why yet, but there is something about her."

"She is planning to take the fifth-grade class to El & Em's next Tuesday. I had a permission slip for Sydney, and she needs help if anyone would be interested. I could pass it on, or you could call and talk to her about the trip," Abigail added to the discussion, "She is all about the kids, and they love her."

"Come to think of it, I'm off Tuesday," Kate spoke up. "I think I'll give her a call and see if I could help out. That would give us a chance to spend a little more time together. Does she knit or crochet, anyone know?"

"When she and her Aunt were in with her friends from Texas, she said she had never learned. She seemed anxious to, thought it would be a nice pass-time for the winter months, especially during the Christmas vacation. She already anticipates time on her hands during the break," Eliza explained. "I think if we could get her involved, we could teach her some type of handiwork. She may even be a good candidate to join A Snug Around the Neck. Olivia, have you mentioned that to her, or have you not met her yet?" Eliza asked.

"No, I haven't. I wish she could join us on Friday evenings. We need to make it a point to invite her, perhaps that's all it would take," Olivia said. "I suppose I could take a tray of cookies to her class. I have some great fall cookie cutters. They would enjoy them, or cupcakes. I'll figure something out. Then I can introduce myself to her. I'll plan on that."

"Well, I'm sure she would welcome you. That's a great idea," Eliza said encouraging her. "Just remember, no nuts, schools don't like treats with nuts, they have a concern now for allergic reactions. No one focused on that when I was in school. If you liked it, you ate it. It's all different now."

Everyone was busy pulling out projects or magazines with new ideas and getting down to business. Lilly pulled her chair up by Rosie. "How does this look to you, are my stitches even enough? I haven't had a lot of time to work on this since you helped me at our last gathering, but I didn't want to forget what you taught me, so I stayed up late a couple nights. What do you think?" Lilly waited for Rosie's opinion.

"You are going to be a pro in no time!" Rosie took the scarf from Lilly's hands to examine it. "Your stitches are good, and as you go they will become so uniform you won't even have to think about what your hands are up to." As she handed the scarf back to Lilly, she flashed her a smile. "Now, let me see what is in my bag of tricks. What's this?" she questioned herself as she pulled out the new bag of yarn she purchased from Eliza the last time they met. "Oh, that's right. I need to make a tote for a Christmas gift. Wonder what else lurks in the black hole I call my project bag!" Without another word, she pulled out a crochet hook and started chaining.

Lilly studied her for a moment and had to ask, "What pattern are you using?"

"A pattern? What's a pattern?" Rosie looked at Lilly without as much as a grin. "Is a pattern for crocheting like a recipe is for cooking?"

"Well, I don't do much of either, but I think yes would be the answer to that comparison," Lilly replied. They both started laughing, and soon all eyes were on them.

Kate finally asked, "Okay, what did we miss? Let us in on it."

"Nothing, really, just aggravating Rosie," Lilly replied.

"It was quite unexpected, I have to say. I'm proud of her. She is really starting to shine," added Rosie. "And she is getting her stitches down to an art as well."

They pulled their chairs back into the circle. The chatter continued as the evening passed quickly. Everyone's hooks and needles working along with the banter.

"I can't believe it is already 9:45! Where did the evening go?" asked Abigail. "I think we need to start at noon It seems like while I'm enjoying myself chatting, I get so much more accomplished with my hook."

About that time, the doorbell clanged. It caught everyone off guard. The sign was flipped, the shop was closed, and the downtown area was dark.

"I hope I'm not interrupting, but just thought I'd drop by to see what this group is really like," said Annie, standing in the door holding a tray and a bag. "Is it too late for a snack in exchange for some insight from this talented group?"

Lilly stood up and quickly asked, "Did you bring some of your famous Butterhorns? They were a bit odd looking, but oh, they were so good."

Annie blushed and then stepping into the circle and explained, "I made my favorite recipe. It's my 'Mama Simpkin's Prize Winning Chocolate Raspberry Cake.' Momma tweaked the recipe for Grandma's recipe for Texas Sheet Cake and entered it in the fair. It was so exciting when she won a blue ribbon. She shared her secrets with me, and I have been making it for special occasions since.

And it's chocolate! You can't go wrong with that. I stopped by Deb's Mugs & Muffins and picked up a special coffee she suggested to go with it."

Eliza quickly came to help her carry things to the counter. As they freed their hands, Eliza gave Annie a quick hug and thanked her for stopping in. Eliza then introduced her to the ladies she had not yet met.

"I've heard a lot about the gatherings on Friday nights. You are so blessed to have such a circle of friends," she said. "It is so nice to see you and put a face to the names I hear about."

"We've been telling them about Sunday at Slipknot," Lilly stood up and started toward Annie. Taking her by the arm, she continued. "We had such a grand time. Kate and I talked about it on the phone Monday evening, going over all the particulars, and the food, that was amazing. We are so glad we got to know you and would love it if you would join our group and let everyone else get to know you, too. Please, consider it, would you?"

"I'm flattered," Annie said, her hands noticeably shaking. "I haven't felt like this in a very long time, if ever. I would love to be a part of your group. But you see I don't know how to knit or crochet, or do much of any handy-work to speak of. I can sew, and I have my mom's old sewing machine with me, but mostly use it for a little mending at times. Mom was a wonderful seamstress, but me, I would rather spend time with the horses."

"Honey, we will teach you what we know about

knitting and crocheting, and after a while, you will be teaching us something every time we gather," Rosie assured her. "My daughter Chloe will be home for Christmas break. She is in her first year at college. I would love for her to meet you. Will you be here for Christmas?"

Annie looked at Eliza as if to find strength in her eyes and began to talk from her heart.

"After Sunday at Slipknot, riding JoJo stirred so many memories in me. By the time I got home, I was in tears. Not to worry, not sadness, but feelings coming to surface that I have kept buried far too long. I picked up the phone and called Dad. I told him about the day, and Eliza, how she has become a strength to me so quickly. I told him of Lilly and Kate, and all about Slipknot. I'm certain I didn't do it justice. We talked about the recipe box, what we cooked, and how we took the time to enjoy the day. This led us to a real conversation, unlike any we have had since Mom passed away. It was long over-due. We openly discussed the holidays. It'll be difficult for both of us, especially the distance between us now. I will be here for Thanksgiving, but I found comfort in learning he will spend it with my Aunt Jayne and family. I assured him I'll be fine. With that plan in place, he said he would come here to be with me on Christmas. Hopefully, he can stay and spend some time seeing the area. I'm so happy and relieved. I was trying so hard to find a way to get home. Oh, my, I'm rambling!" she exclaimed, turning red with embarrassment. "But I feel a calm I haven't felt in a very long time. And now to be here, and a part of things, it's just a wonderful feeling."

Eliza stepped toward her, "I think we all feel the

same way. There have been times in each of our lives that we needed a friend to give us the encouragement to make it through the stumbling blocks in life. This is where our strength comes from. Our special bond. You are a part of that now," Eliza explained. "That being said, may we please cut into Mama Simpkin's Prize Winning Chocolate Raspberry Cake? I have the special coffee brewing, and the aroma is wonderful. I'm so very proud of you, Annie, to share this evening, and to bring your relationship with your dad to a new level. You are amazing. And I bet your cake is, too."

Annie helped serve the group, getting several requests for the recipe from some, and just to have her bake it from others. The evening quickly turned back to the fun, and it seemed no one wanted it to end.

Kate talked to Annie about the field trip, and they made plans for lunch at CJ's Café on Saturday afternoon. Lilly was on an evening shift Saturday and planned to join them before going to work. Olivia talked to Annie about bringing in treats to her class one afternoon, and sending information home with her students about A Snug Around the Neck. Annie agreed that was a great idea and knew it would be well received by the parents. It was 11:30 before they knew it. Midnight by the time they packed up and helped Eliza tidy up shop.

"It's been a very long time since we had an evening as eventful as this one," Eliza said with a smile, followed by a yawn. "It reminds me of when our group started some years ago. I like it!"

Annie was the last one out the door. She turned to Eliza and said, "I was so nervous to open the door to the shop this evening. I wasn't sure how I'd be received, but on the contrary, I have never been made to feel more welcome. The same goes true for Sunday. How am I ever going to repay you for your kindness?" she questioned.

"Come back next Friday evening," Eliza replied, "and be yourself. That's how. Oh, and wear your red cowboy boots. That seems to be your trademark. Now, you need to get home safely and get some rest. Emotional evenings like this have a way of draining a person. Thank you for sharing with us."

One last hug and Annie was out the door. Eliza turned off the lights to the shop and started up the stairs, Cody right behind her. Eliza paused at the top of the landing to look out the window at the stars shining bright and continued on with a content feeling and slight smile on her face. It was the end of another very special day.

Sleep came easy for Eliza that night. She was relaxed as she lay there under her favorite quilt. With the holidays around the corner, she felt a deeper appreciation of family this year than usual.

Saturday morning started out busy, and the traffic in and out didn't let up until well into the afternoon. Walking a customer to the door, Eliza spotted Lilly, Annie, and Kate going into CJ's Café. At that point, she remembered the girls talking about having lunch there before Lilly went to work. She smiled, even though the girls didn't notice her in the doorway, she was pleased to see them together. The

Café appeared to be as busy as the shop. With that, she turned and went back in to greet her next customer.

"So, what may I help you with today," Eliza approached the two ladies discussing a new wool yarn just stocked for the holidays. "What sort of project do you have in mind? Are you thinking of a Christmas gift?"

They both started talking about their ideas, families and asking Eliza for her suggestions. Quick to offer patterns and ideas, Eliza helped them finish with their purchases and walked them to the door. Just then, she noticed it was time to turn her sign to closed and lock up for the day.

"Wow!" she exclaimed out loud. What a great day. She hadn't seen a business like this in the last few years. She was thankful to see the town bringing in the visitors. It had been a concern for the past few seasons. Busy cleaning up she noticed her stomach was grumbling, so she headed upstairs to get a sandwich and sit down for a few minutes. The cleaning could wait. The late night was catching up with her.

Suddenly, the phone rang and caused her to jump. There she sat in her favorite chair, wondering for a moment where she was. Then she remembered her lunch and realized she had dozed off. Nearly two hours had passed. As she picked up the phone, her sister Rachel was on the line.

"Were you busy?" she asked. "I was ready to hang up. Are you all right? You don't sound like you feel well."

"I'm fine, actually," Eliza replied. "I had a late night with the group and came up for a snack before finishing in the shop. That was two hours ago! You woke me up. Thank you for that. I don't know how long I would have napped. What's going on?"

"Nothing special really. I had a nice talk with CJ last night and just wanted to see how you were doing. Have you been able to settle down yet, get your thoughts together, or is the excitement of Christmas more than you can handle?" Rachel probed. "CJ said he has been very busy, the Café is really bringing in a nice crowd. He has been seeing a lot of return guests."

"I have been busier in the shop than usual, too. I'm thankful we're seeing a good season. Some of it may be the fall colors. This year they are very vivid, and our temps have been pleasing. Makes me wonder what the winter will be like. I'm secretly hoping that we will see a little snow on Christmas Eve. I know it's foolish and not likely, but wouldn't it be great? Guess I'm not calmed down about it, am I?" Eliza asked. "I just want it to be special."

Rachel quickly replied, "You sound just like I was hoping you would. Anyway, I wondered if you were planning on going out to Slipknot tomorrow afternoon.

"I'm going out after church. Nothing special going on, just thought I'd try and do a little yard work. Have something on your mind?"

"Actually, I was going to ask you to look in the attic and see if you could find the Christmas stockings Mimzie knitted? Do you think they could still be there? It would be wonderful to have them hanging on the mantle when we arrive at Christmas."

"That would be amazing. There is an old trunk in the attic. I'll see if I can make it up there Sunday and go through it. There may be some old decorations up there as well. I haven't been in the attic for quite some time. I'll see if Oliver wants to come over and help. I wish you could be here to join us. Who knows what we may uncover," Eliza said with a new enthusiasm. "Do you have Thanksgiving plans in place?"

"Same as last year. We try and spend it with Robert's family, and I'm sure Beth will be here. CJ plans to open the Café like he did last year. Why do you ask?" Rachel questioned.

"Nothing really. My focus seems to have turned to Christmas, almost like I've forgotten about Thanksgiving. I plan on helping CJ with dinner at the Café. His heart is so big when it comes to this town. I admire him for being so caring at his age. Offering a Thanksgiving dinner for the elderly and alone. What a gift. Did you know he collected nearly six hundred dollars in donations to give to A Snug Around the Neck, volunteering his time and supplies? He has seen the blessings come back to him for his efforts, but you never hear him mention what he did. What an amazing son you have. If I see him out this evening, I may try and catch him. Perhaps he would want to come out and help me at Slipknot. I'll get back with you the first of the week and let you know what I find."

Realizing the time, with a quick good-bye on both ends, Eliza started back down to the shop.

This turned her thoughts to last Thanksgiving. CJ mentioned that he had started to notice even more changes in the church congregation. Many of the elderly members had lost a spouse, families moved farther away and couldn't make the trip home. There were already calls coming in to see if the Café was going to be open on Thanksgiving Day again. With an obvious growing need, he felt he was giving back to his own community in a small way. Oliver, Ben, and Molly had already committed to spending the day at the Café helping him cook and clean up again this year. They vowed to make this their holiday tradition for years to come. Celebrating their hometown in this way offered a sense of satisfaction and a fresh outlook of Thanksgiving.

Pleasant thoughts make the sweeping and dusting go quicker. Eliza rearranged some of her displays, changed out the window arrangement and cleaned out the fireplace. As she stepped outside to sweep off the sidewalk, she saw CJ leaving the Café. "How's business going?" she yelled to him.

"Can't complain," he replied, stopping to visit. "Seems busier than last year. I'm seeing a lot of return guests as well. That's a good sign. For one thing, my cooking didn't kill them, and they were brave enough to come back for more!"

"Do you have an estimate on the numbers for Thanksgiving dinner yet? You know you can count on me again. With all my family helping you, I'll feel homeless anyway!"

"Poor Eliza, I'm sorry I took your holiday away from you. But didn't helping out at the Café give you a warm feeling?"

"Warm feeling!" she replied, "I was soaked through from sweat and dishwater! But it was the best day I had in a long time, partially because I could help, but mostly because I was so proud of you. I'll be by your side for as long as you carry on the tradition."

"I knew I could count on you. Uncle Ben and Molly and Uncle Oliver asked me about this year. So it is a good thing you are planning on it, or you would be alone, very alone!" He then gave her a nudge and a smile. "What are you up to tomorrow?"

"Going out to Slipknot to see if I can find the old Christmas stockings Mimzie knitted. I can vaguely remember them, so I think I must have seen them sometime. I'm hoping they're in a trunk in the attic. Not sure what all is up there anymore. It has been years since I looked through any of it. Would you want to come out and join me? I promise not to work you too hard."

"I think I could do that, it may be around two or so before I get there. This might even be a bit exciting. Could find some real treasures," CJ said, giving his eyebrows a quick raise up and down. "But I need to get going for now. I have a few errands to run. I'll call you if anything changes. Don't work too hard this evening."

"I won't, and I hope you make it, I love the company," she winked as she waved goodbye.

Eliza finished in the shop and took an evening walk. Energized from the fresh air and exercise, she started a pot of split pea soup, putting it in her crock pot to simmer overnight. That will be lunch at the Homestead. She'd have time in the morning to make corn muffins and planned to take some fresh apples and caramel for an afternoon snack. With that in place, a nice warm bath was in her plans. Then she would settle in for a relaxing evening, looking forward to an enjoyable afternoon at Slipknot before the start of another busy week.

Chapter 6

Spending a sunny day in a dark attic full of more memories than dust…

After braving the rickety ladder, the attic door overhead pushed open with an eerie squeak. It is a good thing she played up here as a child. That comforted her, knowing there were no ghosts or goblins waiting for her. The only light was seeping through the attic vent. Turning on her lantern, she was quickly taken back by the childhood memories. She and Ben had played up here for hours. At one time there was an old box of toys including an old barn and animals, complete with the fence they set up as a corral. They planned to have a farm together when they grew up. Little did she know, someday, she would proudly own Slipknot, and her brother Oliver would be a significant part of her life.

Oliver had already left on his Sunday routine by the time she arrived. Anxious to find the stockings, she started with the attic. The yard work can wait. Besides that, she knew after stirring up the dust from the last three decades she would need the fresh air.

In the corner, she spotted a trunk. She thought it may be where the stockings were stored. She was a bit concerned about being overwhelmed by the memories. The attic held her childhood intact. She was blessed to be in a position to purchase Slipknot from her Grandparents estate, preventing an auction or estate sale. With that in mind, she knew the only things that had been taken out was the belongings Rachel, Oliver, and Ben requested. Everyone had their memory of something they cherished growing up. She felt as if she was stirring up as many emotions as she was dust. Making her way to the corner, careful not to stumble along the way, she pulled the trunk away from the wall so she could open the large lid. It had three buckles across the front that were all secured. As she opened the lid, she found a vintage yo-yo quilt. She remembered this from many years ago. Mimzie taught her momma how to make yo-yos from small scraps of fabric one winter. Not much on sewing, Mimzie spent her winters spinning the wool she had dyed and dried, knitting socks and sweaters the family could use. They didn't have the luxury of running to the local discount store when they had a need. Her momma loved to do needlework when she couldn't be out in the garden or working with her animals. She worked for hours on end to make so many of these little circles, then to put them together in such a colorful pattern.

Opening the fragile quilt to admire it, she felt a bit overwhelmed again. She had forgotten about the treasures. The memories of her momma caused a warm well of tears to fill her eyes. Mimzie took her up there to find quilts one winter evening when she a child. Now that seemed like such a long time ago. She felt so alone. Choking back tears, and dust, she gently laid the quilt back in the lid of the trunk. As she lifted the tray, she could see the Christmas stockings. The feel of the wool was still gentle on her hands. Mimzie sheered the sheep, dyed, and spun the wool and then knitted these treasures. What patience and determination this took, not to mention talent. In her day, this was a way of life. Eliza was so thankful to have this rich history at her fingertips. They were all there, including the ones that said Mimzie and Papa. How amazing. Carefully she laid them aside and continued going through the treasures.

Excited about the pieces of the past in the trunk, she was in deep thought. Just then, she thought she heard a creek behind her. She turned, shining her lantern, but saw nothing. Must be all the memories stirring up her imagination. As she reached for the stuffed animals she uncovered, she heard another noise. It gave her a chill. Still, she could see nothing. As she looked at the toys, she remembered her momma made these. One was a dog with a tag around the neck that said Ben, a bear that said Oliver, a bunny rabbit that said Rachel, and her cat that said Eliza on its collar. They were tattered from playing with them, sleeping with them, and dragging them around everywhere they went until Momma took them and put them away. Thankfully she did, or they'd be gone. Suddenly, a strange feeling came over her. Being alone in the darkness quickly overwhelmed her. She decided to put things back in the trunk for safe keeping until she had someone to help her carry them down, and go out and spend some time on the yard work. As she reached to close the lid, she felt a hand on her shoulder and heard a voice behind her. She screamed at the top of her lungs! Frozen in place, she could hardly move.

Then she heard all too familiar laughter. Whirling around, there stood CJ! He began to laugh hysterically. He didn't even try and hold it back.

Eliza was trembling. She remembered how CJ enjoyed scaring anyone he could when he was growing up.

"Guess you enjoyed that, didn't you? I hope you're happy!" Eliza scolded him. "I'll have you know you could have given me a heart attack, or I could have hurt you."

He just laughed all the more.

"Well, I was just going along with you. You really didn't scare me at all. I knew you were here all the while," she said not having much luck convincing him.

"Sorry Auntie, sometimes coming back here just makes me feel like a kid again. Hope you aren't too upset," he tried to smooth things over. "I'll help you with whatever you want today, will that make it up to you? After all, no harm was done."

"Deal," she replied, "and you think no harm was done. You did cause me to pee a little!"

Again, the laughter erupted.

"Well, that added some years to my life," Eliza said. "And trust me, I will get a lot of work out of you today. Now, if we can get back to business, I found the stockings in the trunk your mom was asking about. Would you like to see some of your heritage?" she asked starting back to the trunk. "Hold my lantern, and I'll get them out. We can take them down. They are still in pristine condition. There is so much history up here, CJ. This stirs memories I haven't thought of in years. I'm so happy to have Slipknot intact, just as it was left to us, waiting to be passed on to the next generation with the memories that go with it."

"What's that, in the bottom of the trunk?" CJ asked as he shined his flashlight on a wooden box. "It looks really old. Have you seen this before?"

"I don't remember it. Let me see if I can get it open." The lid was tight, but she managed to wiggle it back and forth, finally slipping it off. "It's a box of old pictures. They are taken in Sepia and look to be in very good condition."

"Where's sepia? I have never heard of that. Is it a nearby town, or a place they visited?" CJ asked.

"No! Tell me you are kidding!" Eliza started to laugh but quickly saw he was getting embarrassed. "I'm sorry. Sepia is the brown finish in very old pictures. That was before black and white. These have to be from very early days with Mimzie and Papa, maybe even some of their family. We really need to take these down to the table and look at what we have here. This could be another good Christmas surprise. Wonder if we can identify them and have some copies made. I would love to put together albums for the families." Eliza was so excited. "I hope they are noted on the back who and when."

She set them by the stockings and toys. Then she took CJ over to the box that held the old farm set. As they looked at it, she explained how she and Ben played for hours.

Even then she dreamed of having a farm. It was one of the reasons she was so determined to keep Slipknot intact.

"Do you want to bring it down with the other stuff?" CJ asked. "I'd like to clean it up and have it ready for the holidays. Wouldn't it be perfect on the mantle? We could arrange it with some fresh greenery and little white lights."

"Great idea. I love it. I know Ben will remember it. We won't say anything to him and see if he is surprised. I thought we could pop some corn and bring cranberries to string for the tree and mantle while we sit around and talk. There are so many traditions to pass on." Eliza's voice cracked. "CJ, you have no idea what this gathering means. I can't thank you enough for the idea."

"I don't know what it is about this year. I have so many unfamiliar feelings rushing around inside me. I want Christmas to be special, not that it isn't always. It's the Homestead. I want to share it with everyone, to let them experience the feelings we do every time we are out here together. Does that make any sense?"

"Perfectly," Eliza answered him with a warm smile. "I'm so grateful you came back to Spring Forrest. I love having you on Main Street, sharing the roots that started here. That is a characteristic that isn't instilled in everyone. I think we are a lot alike, and I enjoy passing the memories down and sharing our family history with you. I don't know what I would do if it weren't for you. I don't have anyone of my own to share these things with."

"You realize I'm the lucky one, don't you? Now, do

you want to sit up here and play, or do we want to take things down stairs? It's nearly four o'clock," he said as he started toward the ladder.

"I had no idea I've been up here that long. I wanted to get some yard work done yet today. That may have to wait," she said, following him with her arms loaded. "You start down, and I'll hand things to you. Be careful. It isn't the best ladder."

He backed partially down the ladder and reached for the stack of stockings, laid them ever so gently in a pile on the rug in the hall, and went back up for the box of photos and the toys. Just as he started back down, Eliza heard a loud noise from the hall, CJ lost his footing and screamed like a girl, hanging on with one hand trying not to drop the box. Then Eliza heard a man laughing from below.

"Come on, suck it up and get your feet back on the ladder before you break your neck. I thought I was going to be holding you and the junk you are dragging down. If I scared you that bad, how is it you braved the dark attic?" Uncle Oliver razzed him.

"I'm up here, that's how," Eliza yelled down, "and thank you, he got just what he deserved. He snuck up on me earlier. What goes around, comes around, Mimzie always said. Help us get this stuff down to the table, could you please?"

They carried the finds to the long farm table in the kitchen. Eliza told Oliver about the search for the stockings and what they came across. They decided to leave the inside work for bad weather and go out and start cleaning up. There was some furniture that was unsheltered as well as clay pots of annuals that could be stored for the winter. The mums and scarecrow were holding quite nicely, so they watered them and decided to leave the display intact for a few more weeks. Eliza didn't want it to look abandoned. The chairs on the front porch along with the swing would be left out until after the Christmas gathering. Quite often, she would sit out on the swing in the late afternoon with an old quilt, a good book, and a cup of coffee to spend much needed quiet time. Those are the days she doesn't want to see end.

"Is there anything left in the garden?" CJ asked. "I haven't been back there. Did you grow any squash or pumpkins this year?"

"I had some squash, but I don't know if there are any left that are worth picking. I know it is far too late in the season for any zucchini or yellow squash. What are you wanting?" she asked.

"Nothing, in particular, just looking for a bit of inspiration for a good fall recipe I could try at the Café. Oh, did I tell you that friend of yours, Annie was in the Café Saturday afternoon with a couple of the girls from your group. They said they had been at the shop until midnight the night before. Is that an exaggeration? Seems awful late for a bunch of old women," he snickered.

"Just when you're almost out of the doghouse, you let your mouth get the best of you. Are you ever going to learn?" she started toward CJ. "Tell me about the lunch.

Did they seem to be having a good time? I think this is an important time for Annie. She has been here for months now and still not cultivated a good circle of friends, just some acquaintances from school, in passing, but not what she really needs. I think we're going to see her personality shine very soon. Did you know she took JoJo for a ride when she was out last Sunday?"

CJ's face dropped. "She rode JoJo? No, I didn't know that. And JoJo was ok with that?"

"Are you jealous? I never thought about it, but I suppose you are the only one who has ridden her over the years. She really didn't seem to mind. In fact, they both seemed to enjoy it," Eliza continued. "Did I tell you Annie grew up with horses? She still has her horse, Pete, at her dad's ranch in Texas. Well, it's a small ranch from what I understand, not a real Texas ranch like you see in the movies. She helped out at the neighbor's ranch growing up, caring for horses and helping out with kids that came out during the summer. I think they had disabilities and the horses were therapy for them. Being able to ride the horses gave them a sense of independence they didn't otherwise have. She misses her horse almost as much as she misses her dad."

"So, the red cowboy boots she wears aren't just a fashion statement? They're real?" he questioned.

"As authentic as Annie is," Eliza smiled. "Her dad is coming to have Christmas with her. They just made plans. I know that made her feel much better. She'll be here for Thanksgiving without family. Perhaps you should mention the dinner at the Café. She would probably love to take part in that, and would be great with the people."

"I'll see. Or better yet, maybe you could just ask her. I don't see much of her anyway." CJ replied. "It would be okay with me either way."

Eliza could read CJ like a book. She knew there was more to it than just brushing off the chance to have help at the Café. CJ has always been shy when it came to girls. Guess he hasn't outgrown it yet. Eliza knew she was going to have to handle this situation with care. She was dealing with a couple that wears their heart on their sleeve, as Mimzie would have put it. Right out there with their feelings exposed and easily hurt.

The rest of the afternoon was spent cleaning out the garden. CJ was able to salvage a few squash to take to the Café to use in soup. They picked what was left of the pumpkins and set some by the scarecrow and hay bales and a few by the mums along the lane. Later in the season, they could throw them in the field. Eliza knew the deer would love a treat. Although they irritate her rubbing on trees and eating flowers and bushes, she really did admire the beautiful creatures.

Oliver came over to help put the garden tools away and see if anything needed attention through the week.

"I can't think of anything, in particular, Oliver," Eliza assured him. "You do such a wonderful job of caretaking. I'll be out next Sunday and try and clean up the old toys we brought down from the attic. CJ wants to surprise Ben and put them on the mantel for Christmas. It's still too early to start deep cleaning and freshening up for the gathering. CJ plans to help with picking out recipes and stocking the pantry."

"Time for the gathering will be here before we know it," Uncle Oliver spoke up. "Seems like I just helped you till up that garden and now it is time to till it under. Where'd the summer go?"

CJ and Eliza said their good-byes and started down the lane. She stopped by the fence where JoJo and the sheep were waiting patiently. They knew she wouldn't drive away without giving them a little attention and a snack. She pulled out some apples and a few sugar cubes. As she fed the girls, she told them about the gathering at Slipknot this Christmas. She even promised them a red bow. After all, this would be a special time. They loved company, too.

Starting back to town to get ready for another busy week, the feel of the holidays were heavy in the air. It wouldn't be long until Christmas, Eliza thought to herself as she drove away in Bittersweet. Today she felt the name she had given the old truck was appropriate for many avenues in her own life.

Chapter 7

Perfect ending to the day, and a stroll down Main…

୬ぺふ

Typically Mondays in the shop even this time of year were light on customer traffic. Thankfully, this held true for today allowing plenty of time to re-stock the yarn bins with the new products that arrived late Friday afternoon. There were beautiful yarns of cinnamon, sage, and a honey mustard that when held together made an inspiring combination. The wool was bulky, perhaps better used for knitting than crocheting, although it would be gorgeous in either. Some new patterns that would work up nicely in this yarn were placed on a small rack by the display. She unpacked several new samples for Christmas projects as well. She had learned in her years in the shop that it wasn't easy to know exactly what the customers would want. Experience gives her insight, but she also scours magazines and advertisements to see what trends were popular. There was more to running the shop than greeting customers and making coffee. Eliza enjoyed every minute and counted her blessings with each passing day.

The bell on the door clanged, and looking up, she recognized the trio of ladies that came to town every fall. They would spend a good hour or longer looking through the yarns and patterns, discussing among themselves possibilities for projects. Purchasing enough goods to get them through the year, Eliza was always pleased to see they were once again able to make the journey. They were a jovial group, enjoying their annual trip.

From here, as many do, they would head across the street for lunch at CJ's Café, another favorite attraction. They were anxious to see him again and have a home cooked meal before they ventured on. Of course, he would recognize them right away and enjoy their company as they looked over the wonderful menu and new ideas he had for fall. He knew they would claim to be too full for dessert, but as always take something with them. Then they'd stop for coffee on their trip home and savor the sweet treats.

It was nearly closing time when Olivia stopped by. She had a basket of cookies for Eliza to sample and check out the sale table.

"I thought I'd have you try these. I baked a couple of batches for Annie's class. Do you think the kids will like them?" she asked, as she and Eliza enjoyed the samples.

"Like them? These are wonderful," Eliza said, reaching for another cookie, "First of all, they are chocolate, and what is this filling? I have never had anything quite like these, not home-made anyway, and certainly not this good."

"The dough is wrapped around a caramel. Nice

surprise, isn't it? It was supposed to be rolled in chopped nuts before I baked them, but I heeded your warning, knowing not everyone could eat nuts, so I just dipped the top in cinnamon sugar instead. This may become one of my favorite recipes. Not hard to make at all," Olivia chattered as she dug around on the sale table. "Not much left in bargains today," she grumbled.

"Well, actually, I had an annual trio in today that stocks up for the year. They usually wipe me out. Let's see what I can come up with for next week. I know how important the charity is this time of year. How are things going in the community as far as A Snug Around the Neck goes, anyway?"

"There are a lot of needs out here. Each year seems the need grows faster than the charity. I suppose that is typical of most situations, it is just so obvious to me, being as involved as I am. I feel as if it consumes me, and just when I think I can't do anymore, someone comes up and tells me of the difference we've made in a troubled situation, and I find the strength I need to go on, stronger than before. It's those small rewards that drive the charity. Do you think I'm crazy?" Olivia asked Eliza, with a very sincere look on her face.

"I think you are amazing. So does everyone else that knows you and your work. Each of us envies you in our own way, wishing we could give back as much as you do. You are a very special lady, Olivia, and I mean that from the heart. Now, here, take these three skeins of yarn, make a scarf, on me."

"You don't need to do that," Olivia scolded.

"I want to. Now, no back talk. Tell me what you've been up to lately. Talked to any of the group?"

"No, not since our record-breaking session last Friday night. But I do plan to go to the school on Wednesday to Annie's class with cookies. I've got a simple version of my presentation ready about my charity. Don't want to upset that age group, but I do feel they need to realize there is a growing need in the community."

"You are absolutely right, Olivia. They are old enough to see other's needs. I imagine some in their own class could use a bit of help if the truth is known," Eliza replied. "Things aren't like they were when we were coming up, but they are difficult in a different way. Everyone has high standards in materialistic things, rather than the basics; food, faith, and helping others. We always had enough to get by and a little to share with the neighbors. That's the way Mimzie was raised, and those values were instilled in us growing up. I hold those dear to this day. Hope you don't think I'm on my soapbox, but no one looks out for each other, they are too busy looking at each other."

"You're very wise, Eliza. I need to start spending more time with you. You can bring me up when I need a little encouragement. Thank you for that." Olivia finished with a hug. "I'll put this yarn to good use, and donate this scarf in your name. See you Friday, if not before. I can share the day in the class with the group."

The bell clanged on her way out. Eliza took a moment

to check the fire and have another cookie. She was about to flip the sign to closed and didn't want to kick it up too much. The embers had died down quite nicely. She found herself sitting in one of the leather chairs staring at the embers. So many memories had been stirred up in her over the past couple of weeks. She was feeling emotional. This time of year she always found herself feeling somewhat alone. Not feeling sorry for herself, but missing her family. The holidays always rescue her, bringing her through another winter. With only two weeks until Thanksgiving, it seems as if the fall has gone by very quickly. Hmm, she thought to herself, no wonder so many people sit in these chairs and never want to leave. She felt wonderful. About that time, the bell on the door clanged. She forgot to turn the sign, and it was well after five. She turned to see who came in, relieved to see it was CJ.

"This is an unusual surprise," she said to him from her comfy chair, "won't you join me by what is left of the fire. There is a leather chair right beside me with your name on it. If you are nice to me today, I may even give you a cookie."

"A cookie, really," CJ said with a grin, as he walked toward the chair. "I think I've already found what I was looking for. Ah. I had a busy day for a Monday. How were things here?"

"Busy, for a Monday, same as you. I'm so thankful for the visitors this season. Our town needs this boost."

"Yep, I'm planning on a big crowd this Thanksgiving according to the sign-up sheet. I can use the extra income to help with the food for that. I hope we can handle the crowd," he said, as he reached for another cookie. "Hey, these are pretty good, is this a new recipe? What's inside?" he stretched the caramel as he pulled the cookie apart. "I like the cinnamon, but I bet they would be really good dipped in chopped nuts."

"Olivia brought them by for a taste test. She is making them for Annie's class. She is going to the school Wednesday and taking the cookies to the class, therefore, no nuts. She's talking to them about A Snug Around the Neck. That's just about the right age group, don't you think? And she is hoping to make Annie feel more comfortable, too. She wants to join our group on Fridays, but doesn't do any needlework." she explained. "Do you think you are going to need more volunteers to help out on Thanksgiving Day?"

"That is a concern," CJ replied. "Last year, I thought we handled things pretty well, kept a good flow. I don't know if things are worse this year, or if the word has spread, but I could be looking at double the crowd I had last year. We were hopping all day long. The clean-up alone is tiresome. We need young people that would be willing to come and spend a day for a good cause?" he smiled, knowing she would have a comeback about the age remark.

After a bit more banter, Eliza told CJ she would put it out there during her Friday night group. They may have some ideas or even some free time. As she walked him to the door, she flipped the sign and headed out for a walk around town.

Stopping in at Deb's Mugs and Muffins, she stood idle for a moment to take in the wonderful aromas of the fresh ground coffees and baked goods. The windows were adorable. Deb changes her themes with the seasons. This year, she painted a fall scene with pumpkins and cornstalks intermingled with the real pumpkins and stalks she used on the sidewalk against the wall, just under her large display window. Very clever.

"How are you doing, Eliza," Deb asked as she hurried from behind the counter to give her a quick hug, "I haven't seen you out and about in quite some time. What brings you in? Do you have time to sit and chat a bit?"

"Wow, you should try switching to decaf half way through the day. You are a bit wound!" Eliza said as she laughed at her. "I do have time for a cup of coffee, and perhaps a piece of your carrot cake if you have any left. I'll take it to go, but have the coffee here.'

Deb hurried back with two cups. As she set them on the table, she pulled out a chair to join Eliza.

"Do I smell cinnamon and vanilla? Is this one of your special roasts? It's wonderful." Eliza complimented her as she took her first sip. "I may have to take a pound of this along for Girls Knit Out on Friday. You really should consider joining us. We have a good mix of personalities."

"I've considered it and would love to, just have so many things going on Friday evenings. It's my late night. I try to get ready for Saturday mornings, which is my busiest time. It's the crowd that usually works through the week and is ready to have a leisurely cup of coffee, read a little, and get their day off to a slow start. Conversations are great here on Saturdays. You should pop in some time, bet you would see lots of people you haven't visited with in a while. I open at five-thirty a.m." she explained.

"That's long before I get up on Saturdays! Friday's get a bit late. I love your windows. Where did you get the idea to paint the stacks of pumpkins like snowmen and use the muffins for their hats? That's just adorable. And the way you leaned bags of coffee beans among the corn stalks edging the windows, mixing the real pumpkins among the painted ones. You have a way with your displays. Just amazing." Eliza couldn't say enough.

Deb went on to describe her ideas for the Christmas windows she was working on now. It gets so busy as soon as Thanksgiving is over, she has to be ready for a total re-do, usually working very late on Thanksgiving night. Friday after, it's completely transformed. She helps a few of the other shop owners as they try from year to year to carry a theme throughout Main Street. Flora is helping her with the designs. The conversation turned back to Thanksgiving and the dinner at CJ's for those with a need. Deb planned to donate the coffee for the day, not being able to help out with the meal.

"Have you met Annie, the fifth-grade teacher yet?" Eliza asked.

"Why, yes I did. She came in for a special coffee one afternoon. Wait, she was taking some sort of prize-winning Chocolate Raspberry Cake to your shop for your group. I met her then. Loved her accent, and she had on a pair of red cowboy boots if I remember correctly. She is adorable. Did you like the cake?"

"Oh, I remember now, she said you helped her pick out a blend. It was the perfect complement to the chocolate, and she did a wonderful job on the cake, too. She certainly is special. A few of us spent Sunday at Slipknot and had a ball. Do you know CJ wants to have a Christmas gathering there for the family this year?"

"He does? What on earth brought that on? Is it a special year? Has he got a steady girlfriend yet?" Deb asked.

"No, just keeps himself busy at the Café, not seeing anyone special. I think that settling down is on his mind, although he doesn't come right out and say anything. He seems sentimental this year. I know he is glad that his path brought him home. College away from Spring Forrest did not suit him. I, for one, am very thankful to have him across the street from me."

Deb brought the pot, gave them each a warm up, and returned with Eliza's carrot cake. They sat and chatted a bit more then said their goodbyes. As Eliza ventured on, she noticed Flora working in the window, changing out a display. Eliza stuck her head in the door, wanted to see what new ideas she had this fall, and offer thanks for the pumpkin arrangement. She was rearranging a display after selling her focal point.

"I hear you and Deb are working on ideas for the Christmas windows already. Let me know if I can help out with any cedar, branches, or pinecones. I'm sure I can bring in what you need," she offered.

"I'll keep that in mind," Flora said. "Everything you bring me is so wonderful to work with. The naturals are far more popular than the silks. I owe you," she smiled. "What do you think of my background in the window? Does it remind you a bit of the Homestead?"

"It's remarkable. And what a wonderful surprise. Did you have a picture for Deb to go by, assuming she did the painting that is? The fall colors and foliage look almost real."

"Yes, she painted it. It was my idea. But then many of my arrangements and ideas are inspired by the Homestead, and I wanted to share that with my customers. The pumpkin arrangements have been a hot item this fall. Most of us are seeing more customers this year."

Eliza was pleased. Business is crucial to help the town maintain its integrity and survive the slow times.

"I'll keep my eye out for treasures you might be able to use. Stop in some time if you have a few minutes to spare. Love chatting with you. Now I need to keep moving." Eliza finished and headed down the sidewalk.

She continued on, stopping in and out of several shops along the way. She hadn't taken the time to visit with the other merchants in quite some time. It was almost dusk. Enjoying her walk, she started thinking about supper. A bowl of leftover soup sounded good to her, and her carrot cake for dessert, a good finish to a productive day.

As she passed through the shop, she checked the fire one last time. It was out, the shop was tidy, she called to Cody, and they both started up the stairs. A pause on the landing, a gaze out the window, and her day was nearly complete.

"Come on Cody, time to relax, it is going to be a busy week. We need to rest up so we can go out to Slipknot on Sunday and get the yard in shape before winter." She smiled, knowing how silly she must sound, talking to her big yellow cat!

After supper, her thoughts turned to Olivia and A Snug Around the Neck. She was wondering how her visit to the classroom would be this week and trying to think of ways Annie's class could become involved in the community. Nothing too serious, but a fundraiser or event of some sort. They would become involved in helping at the soup kitchen Olivia helps to fund, or come up with ideas of their own to make money to donate. She was anxious to see how receptive they would be to her.

Being busy certainly, makes the days go by fast. She had a very productive week.

Chapter 8

Spring Forrest puts the "giving" in Thanksgiving...

ॐ∽ऽ

Hard to believe it was a week before Thanksgiving. Olivia was a bit nervous going in to talk to Annie's fifth-grade class. She was apprehensive as to exactly how this age group would react. She didn't want to upset them, but she wanted them to learn about the needs of their own community. It was not likely many of the students had first-hand involvement with charities before. She was really hoping for some positive reaction and feedback.

"Good morning Miss Simpkins," Olivia greeted Annie as she knocked on the door to her classroom. They had made plans for her to arrive around ten a.m., just before the morning recess. That would give the kids an opportunity to discuss things on the playground in a more candid setting, not to be intimidated by thinking they have to say what the adults want to hear. With that plan in place, Annie assured Olivia she would have a class discussion at the end of the day to see what their thoughts were and how they would like to try and help.

"Well, good morning Miss Olivia, and welcome to our fifth-grade class. We've been expecting you. So glad you could come and share your time with us this morning."

"My pleasure, and thank you for having me. Good morning class. I'm sure I know some of you, but you'll have to forgive me if I don't know all of your names. I hope you like cookies. I brought some of my favorites. We'll share a snack after our discussion if that suits Miss Simpkins."

"That sounds fine," Annie replied. "Now, let's give Miss Olivia our undivided attention while she tells us about her charity and how she would like you as a class to become involved. Miss Olivia, they are all yours."

"Thanks. I wanted to share with you a charity I created some years ago when I found a need in our community. I have always enjoyed baking and crocheting and anything creative, but I was looking for a hobby that could really make a difference in the lives of people in need. That's how I came up with 'A Snug Around the Neck.' There are many families that need a little help at times. A lot of ladies have joined me, and we work to make things a bit better. That's where you come in. Would any of you like to know how we could use your help?"

Hands went up throughout the room. That brought a smile to both Miss Olivia and Miss Simpkins, as they made eye contact. Even the boys showed interest if only to go along with the plan to get to the cookies!

"I'm very pleased to see you are interested," Olivia

praised them. "Do any of you like to cook or work in a kitchen atmosphere?"

Up went the hands again, and Miss Simpkins helped out with choosing students to tell of their experience. Many had helped at home, some had favorite recipes, and the stories led to holidays and family traditions. The classroom participation was impressive. The boys were as interested as the girls. The conversation then turned to the soup kitchen that El and Em open a couple weekends a month. Penny, one of the students, asked about the Thanksgiving dinner at CJ's Café. She had a neighbor that went last year. While visiting in the yard one afternoon, Penny heard her talking to her mom about the nice meal and plans to go again this year.

"Yes, CJ opens his Café on Thanksgiving Day, not for business as usual, but to offer a place for people that either can't travel or don't have a family to enjoy Thanksgiving dinner with. For a donation, whatever amount they can afford, he provides a traditional Thanksgiving dinner with all the fixings. Then he gives the money from that day to my charity, 'A Snug Around the Neck.' I can't begin to tell you how thankful I am to have a young man like CJ in our town. Last year he donated over six hundred dollars. I realize you don't understand how many families a donation of that size can help, just let me tell you, it provided Christmas dinner and gifts for many children in our own community. Again, that's where you come in. Will any of you be available on Thanksgiving Day that would like to help out by volunteering part of your day at the Café? We would get your parents' consent, of course, and don't expect it to work out for everyone. But it would be a start."

"That sounds like a fine opportunity for some of you to get involved in the community," Miss Simpkins added. "Does anyone have any interest in helping out that day?"

Some hands went up. As they discussed the options, several of the students had out of town plans but questioned if there would be other opportunities later on. They were assured of the weekends at El and Em's again. Miss Olivia had copied a schedule of the next couple months and written an article for the class to take home, explaining the work they do there. This would help the parents understand what they were becoming involved in. As a family, they could make decisions on the extent of involvement they felt comfortable with.

As the handouts were passed around and a few more questions answered, Miss Olivia passed out cookies and thanked everyone for their attention. "I'm putting a sign-up sheet by the door so after you talk this over with your parents, put your name down, and the time you can come to the Café to help on Thanksgiving Day. My phone number is on the information packets I prepared so your parents can contact me with any questions. I look forward to seeing you at some of our upcoming events. Have a Happy Thanksgiving if I don't see you again before that."

Miss Simpkins praised the class for their participation and dismissed them to recess. They all stopped by for more cookies on the way out.

"Well, I think that went very well, don't you?" Annie commented.

"Extremely," Olivia replied. "I'd like to talk to CJ some morning. Would you be comfortable meeting me there for breakfast? Perhaps Eliza would join us. I can give her a call."

"That would be fine with me," Annie replied. "In fact, I would really enjoy that. Are you thinking this Saturday?"

"Time is short; do you think we will have any replies by then?"

"I sent a note home last week that you would be talking to the students, so the parents were aware of the subject at hand. I think they will be quick to reply. We could plan early Saturday morning, and I'll bring the sign-up sheet with me, so we know what we have to offer," Annie explained.

"Sounds like a plan. I'll stop by the shop and talk to Eliza when I leave here. Thanks again, and I'll be seeing you. Are you coming to the Girls Knit Out?"

"I believe I will," Annie said with a smile. "I may not have a project to work on, but I can talk! I am getting more comfortable here in Spring Forrest all the time. I'm actually starting to feel like I belong."

A quick hug and reassurance that she was right where she needed to be and Olivia was on her way.

Annie was quite pleased with the discussion that

took place after recess about the charity. They also had questions about the soup kitchen. She didn't realize how many kids didn't even know what a soup kitchen was. She could see the deep thought on some faces as they discussed the events and life changes that create such needs.

The rest of the week at school went smoothly. The fifth-grade class decided to set aside time after their last recess every afternoon to discuss topics related to Miss Olivia's charity and the needs of the community. Some had talked to their parents one evening and brought back ideas for ways to help. They decided to start a class newsletter so they could share the needs of the other students. This had become quite a class project with greater participation than most subjects warranted.

As the last bell rang on Friday afternoon, the class ran out the door with their never-ending chatter. The week flew by. One week closer to Thanksgiving. Annie gathered her work and the sign-up sheet for the Café. She couldn't wait to tell Olivia she had six girls and five boys signed up to help with Thanksgiving dinner. She wanted to tell CJ about the class involvement and how anxious they were to help.

Girls Knit Out was buzzing. All they could talk about was the excitement in Annie's class. If this can be instilled in the youth, think of what integrity the future generation of Spring Forrest holds.

"I can hardly wait to tell CJ about all the help he has for Thanksgiving Day. We need a schedule, so they don't all show up at once. There will be plenty of work throughout the day, that we can be sure of." Eliza was speaking from experience.

"I have to say, I'm looking forward to the busyness of the day. I was dreading Thanksgiving alone, and with the long weekend, I didn't know how I was going to survive. This gives me something to look forward to," Annie rambled as Annie often does.

A few projects were pulled out to work on, and menus and family recipes were discussed as the talk about the class settled down. Another pot of coffee, a few more cookies, and the clock was striking ten o'clock before they knew it. Another Girls Knit Out flew by. As they packed up their projects, Thanksgiving wishes were shared. No Friday gathering next week.

"It's hard to believe the holidays are upon us," Olivia said. "That's exactly what we say every year! But it's true."

"So we are meeting in the morning for breakfast at the Café around seven-thirty? Do I have that right?" Annie questioned.

"Fine with me," Eliza replied.

"I'll be there," Olivia said with excitement. "I can't wait to see the look on CJ's face when we tell him. Now, I've got plenty to do when I get home, so I'll see you tomorrow," she said with a quick hug, and she was on her way.

"Could I help you with any cleanup or do you need help for the morning at the shop since you won't have extra time like you usually do?" Annie asked.

"Thanks, sweetie, but I think things are in good shape. The weekend before Thanksgiving is usually somewhat quiet in the shop anyway. Everyone is home cleaning and grocery shopping for the big day. I'll be fine. Now you get some rest, and I'll see you bright and early," Eliza assured her.

Another quick hug and Eliza locked the door behind Annie as she left for home.

Saturday morning seemed to roll around as quickly as the holidays do. Eliza was the first at the Café and chose a table in the window so they could soak up some of the morning suns. She had just sat down when in walked Annie and Olivia.

"Well, to what do I owe this pleasure?" CJ said, as he walked across the dining room, a tray in each hand and balancing one on his head. "Expecting a busy day. Just thought I'd get in some practice."

The three laughed at his antics, and Annie asked him what he did for an encore.

Turning a bit red, he realized how silly he seemed. "Hey, a guy's got to have a little fun. Now, who needs coffee?"

All hands went up. He was back with four cups and the coffee pot. "Mind if I join you?" he asked as he poured. "What's up?"

"We have some great news for you," Olivia blurted out. "I'm sorry, but I just can't wait to share. We have eleven students from Annie's class lined up to help with

Thanksgiving Dinner at the Café. They are giving you their time on Thanksgiving Day. Can you believe it? Eleven!"

"Wow! That's great. I'm amazed that so many kids are willing to work on their holiday. How did you convince them? Was it cookies?" he asked with a big smile.

"Well, there were cookies involved," Annie said. "Good cookies! But the kids were anxious to learn more when they realized there was a need in our county. They had their minds made up before they came back with the permission slips."

"Not only that, but some that can't help this time want to see about helping at the soup kitchen on weekends. I'm very proud of the outpouring of concern these kids are showing. We're hoping to instill some real values in them," Olivia went on and on. "I'm sorry, but I just have such a passion about this," she apologized.

"No need to apologize," CJ chided her. "We applaud you for your lifelong efforts in our community. Many of us have learned from you, and now we want to give back."

"Well, I just think it is wonderful," Eliza spoke up. "Do you want to put a schedule together for times and duties. Annie brought the list of names and times they're available. Get that back to her, and she will send copies home with the students next week so the parents can plan transportation."

"Not a problem. I'll get it in order tomorrow and drop it off at the school first thing Monday, if that is all right with you, Annie?" CJ asked.

"Fine with me, or I can stop by here on my way to school Monday if you can't get away."

"There'll be a chocolate chip waffle in it for you if you could. I don't like leaving Uncle Ben by himself for breakfast. You never quite know what to expect this time of year."

"I'll take you up on it," Annie smiled. "Now, I would like some of the French toast I have heard so much about. My stomach is growling just thinking about it."

"Coming right up, and what about you two? Are you eating?"

"Is the sky blue?" Eliza replied. "Of course we are eating. I'll have the same."

"Me too," Olivia added. "We'll make it easy for you."

CJ picked up his cup of coffee and refilled theirs, then off to the kitchen whistling a cheerful tune to start the French toast. "Nothing but the best for you ladies," they heard him mumble as he walked away.

After a wonderful breakfast and good conversation, everyone went about their business. Annie and Olivia walked home together so they could continue with plans and Eliza opened up the shop. CJ finished with the morning crowd and told Uncle Ben all about the plans for Thanksgiving Day dinner and the help they would have from the kids.

"Fifth graders?" Uncle Ben said with a smirk on his face. "Ought to be entertaining!"

They both laughed as they put more thought into what the day would likely bring. One thing for certain, the dinner crowd will appreciate the company of the youngsters. It should be an experience for all ages.

There was much to do over the next few days to get ready for Thanksgiving. CJ, Uncle Ben, and Molly were at the Café late most evenings getting the prep work done. There was bread to be cubed and dried, vegetables to be diced and chicken stock to make the dressing. The turkeys were roasted and picked from the bones, then covered in gravy making the serving much easier, unlike at home when the roasted turkey is carved at the table. A lot of thought went into an offering of this size. Eliza was busy making pies, baking six at a time in CJ's ovens. She used Mimzie's favorite recipes for Pecan Pie and Pumpkin Pie. The pie crust made them extra special, also Mimzie's recipe. Mary kept busy making her famous Apple Cranberry Relish. Eliza took some home for breakfast. It was filled with loads of fresh apples, cranberries, oranges, and pecans. She looked forward to this treat every year, maybe even more than the turkey.

Wednesday afternoon Annie brought her classmates to the Café to meet CJ and learn what their duties would be. After introductions to Eliza, Uncle Ben, and Molly and the discussion of which kids belonged to which parents in town, they gathered around to finalize their schedule. Annie and Lily would help to oversee. Olivia would arrive in the afternoon. She planned a noon meal at home to free up some hours later in the day.

CJ stood up after the plans were in place and thanked

everyone for the help. "This is a very important day in our town for those with a need. Take time to listen and converse with our guests, not just hurry through to do a job. You will have the opportunity to learn some very interesting history of this town and life lessons from our guests. There will be a wealth of information at your fingertips."

"Wow," Annie exclaimed. "This is going to be as educational in history as it will be with general life experiences. I hope it is worth the trade-off for the shenanigans you are in for. And please, don't resort to the child within and encourage them!"

"Well, you are just the funny one!" CJ snarled at Annie, with a boyish grin. "I guess we'll see how hard you can work! Did you think about that? Are you up for the full day of physical labor, or will a couple of hours do you in?"

"I'll be here, right beside you for the long haul! Just wait and see, CJ, I can keep up with the best!"

"Well, doesn't this feel like home!" Eliza said as she sat and shook her head at the two big kids and their colorful banter. "Hope we don't have to put the boss and the teacher in time out tomorrow in front of the class. Now, we have work to do."

"Ok," CJ said. "We will all be back here at seven-thirty tomorrow morning, lots of tables to set and last minute things to finish up. And just in case I don't get a chance to say it tomorrow, thank you all so much for helping me. I have learned from experience, I can't make this happen on my own. I may have the Café, but the people are what make it special. Now, before I get too sappy, let's get going."

Everyone kept busy well after midnight with the food preparations. They planned for about a hundred people. As CJ went over the sign-up sheet from the church, he noticed names that he didn't recognize. The Pastor relayed feedback from families that knew of people who would be alone for the holidays. They were referred to CJ's so they could have a good meal and enjoy companionship during this important holiday. He knew they had their work cut out for them, but at the same time, he could see that it was going to generate a lot more for Olivia's charity.

Thanksgiving morning started at daybreak, everyone working on last minute preparations. Ten o'clock rolled around, the sign was flipped to open, and the class, along with their families, arrived sporting their clean white aprons, ready to serve. Annie took some of the kids and set the tables, drink stations, and trash stations. Eliza was in the kitchen with a few girls slicing pies and dishing them up. They were having such a grand time, talking and laughing. It didn't seem like work at all. But then, they weren't really busy yet.

Uncle Ben and CJ were setting up the food line on the counter. It worked much better to serve the meal buffet style, and thankfully there were extra hands to help carry trays and retrieve drinks. Everyone knew what they were going to do, and who to ask if they ran into problems.

"Is everyone ready?" CJ asked in a loud voice. "There

will be a crowd here before we know it. Can I get a 'ready' from everyone?"

The 'ready' was much more enthusiastic than he expected. Seemed this crew was psyched! Followed by a cheer and round of applause, it was time.

"I'd like to take a minute for us to gather, join hands, and give thanks by offering a moment of silence for each of us to reflect on our own blessings. By doing so, we will gain strength, making this day a positive experience for all of us."

CJ and Eliza had previously discussed how to handle the situation, not wanting to upset anyone, not knowing each of the students' beliefs or parents' concerns.

"And... We're off!" CJ shouted as he unlocked the door and stepped out to the chalkboard to write in bold letters: THANKSGIVING DINNER IS SERVED

They were off to a slow start at 11:00, but by 11:30 there was a line forming at the Café door. CJ noticed a look of anxiety on a few of the students' faces, and quickly went to them for reassurance and encouraged them to relax and enjoy the task at hand. Annie was also quick to respond when she noticed an uncertain look or someone making menial mistakes.

"This is a learning process for each of us, and for our guests. Relax and enjoy the company. You are doing a wonderful job. The people love you," Annie said to Penny and Sydney, the two girls taking drinks to the tables and offering refills. They both had a look of relief on their faces from the encouragement and continued on with confidence.

Annie heard the students talking with guests about subjects ranging from the great depression, the wars, how much they paid for their first cars, to what was on television last night. She just smiled. What an opportunity this class is getting; a first-hand look at history and how the daily lives of such interesting people can be so mundane.

From time to time, the laughter got rather loud in the back. Oddly enough it was Eliza starting out with the girls quick to follow. CJ could only smile when he imagined what was taking place. They talked about growing up at the Homestead and how it still looks today. Many of them showed interest in visiting Slipknot Farm.

"Well, let's make it through today, and I will talk to Ms. Simpkins about a weekend visit for those of you interested in seeing it first-hand. How does that sound for a thank you for all of your hard work?"

The girls helping with the dishes were on board. They seemed genuinely excited about it.

"Do any of you know how to knit or crochet?" she asked.

No one did, but Kerri spoke up, "Sydney's mom does. She goes to Girls Knit Out, Sydney talks about it a lot. She says her mom makes some really neat things. Is it hard to learn?"

"If you spend some time at the shop, I could teach

you. Did you know that in her day, Mimzie, my grandmother, raised sheep at the Homestead and sheered them for their wool? She then dyed it with natural dyes from vegetables and plants and spun it into the wool she used to knit for her family. I have the old spinning wheel. We need to see about getting a group together. There's a lot of history to be passed on, more than just in the classroom."

CJ stood quietly outside the doorway for a moment, eavesdropping on the conversation. He was so proud of Eliza for taking an interest in the students and encouraging them in such a positive way. He pulled Annie aside to listen for a bit. She too was pleased by the conversation between her and the girls. They warmed up to her instantly.

"I'm going to need another stack of clean plates," CJ said as he made his way into the kitchen. "Everyone is doing a great job back here. I'm impressed at how you are keeping up. You all look like pros at dishwashing."

The girls started to laugh, in a charming, shy kind of way. CJ was just old enough to make them blush.

"If any of you get tired of dishes, feel free to ask someone if they want to trade duties for a while. You could go out front and talk with some of our guests if you like," he said as he went out with another large stack of plates.

"Do any of you want to trade places for a while?" Eliza asked.

"I'm fine here," said Kerri.

"Me too," followed Tracy. "Could you tell us some more stories about the Homestead or your business?"

"Well, I'm sure I can come up with something to talk about," Eliza smiled. "I'm not going anywhere, and it certainly makes the time go by faster. Now, let me think!"

Out in the dining room, the tables were full, and people were coming and going in a steady stream. They had been very generous with their tips this year, knowing the kids were volunteering their time.

The classmates were so thoughtful, helping with the doors and carrying things for the guests. From time to time, someone would recognize a student just by the way they favored their parents. Many of the guests had watched the parents of these kids grow up. With a gap in time, it was as if they were watching history repeat itself with the new generation. Their tip jar on the counter was filling up fast. CJ and Annie talked about the incentive it must be to the students there. They were all keeping busy and looking for ways to help. Some clowning around took place from time to time, but no one got carried away. It was more like entertainment for the elderly crowd.

A conversation was going on at a table full of ladies telling stories about their gardens. One captivated the group with her zucchini squash story. She had taken some fried zucchini squash to the new couple next door. The couple brought back her plate, asking how she made the tasty dish. She went on to explain she had grown the squash and shared the recipe that was handed down along the way from Mimzie. They were newly married, and this being their first home, neither had ever put out a garden. They asked a few more questions and thanked her again for the treat. They became very good neighbors and the following spring, she noticed they were putting in their first garden. When she asked what all the mounds were, they admitted they were so fond of the squash, they planted six hills of zucchini. Explaining one hill of squash was more than enough for a couple, they just nodded and decided to see what they could grow. That summer proved to be a great garden season. Early one morning, she saw her neighbors with a little red wagon, filled with zucchini squash, cutting across her back yard. She watched out the window, and they went quietly into her garden and placed their overflow into her single hill of zucchini. While focused on their mission, she stepped out the back door and stood quietly watching. As they turned to leave, they were as startled as she was tickled, and the three of them stood laughing at the situation. After chatting a bit, the couple said their goodbyes and turned to leave. She reminded them they forgot something. She took their wagon and loaded their squash. Then she asked them if they had visited the neighbor's garden across the street? The table roared.

"Remember Mimzie's Fried Zucchini recipe?" Uncle Oliver asked.

"Oh, do I ever, we haven't had that in such a long time. I could make a meal on it," CJ replied. "Why don't you plant a half-dozen mounds next summer?"

"Hilarious," he chuckled. "Don't you have work to do?"

"How are things going in here?" CJ asked in the kitchen. "Is anyone ready to go out and take over at the tables for a while?"

"Oh, dear, we are having such a good time in here, we aren't even looking at our fingers that now resemble prunes! We're enjoying each other's company. Right girls?" Eliza went on. "I think we have some girls with interest in learning more about the Homestead and the treasure trove of history it holds. They may even be interested in learning to knit and crochet."

"Really!" CJ exclaimed. "That's great. I'm sure we can get together with Ms. Annie and make some plans for a field trip sometime."

"I've heard a lot from Sydney about the shop, too. She told us her mom goes there. Maybe we can plan a field trip there as well," Kerri said.

"I'll certainly see what we can come up with," Eliza promised. "Now, do you want to go out and see if they can use some help with the tables? Ask Miss Simpkins if she wants to send someone in to help in the kitchen. I'll stay back here and get the next bunch busy when Miss Simpkins sends them in, and in the meantime, I'll fix some fresh water."

Uncle Ben was in his element, meandering around the dining room from table to table, taking the time to visit with the guests and reconnect with some of the townspeople he hadn't seen in ages. The afternoon continued to be as enjoyable for the guests as it was for those there to serve.

After the guests were gone and the Café was in ship-shape, everyone sat around in the dining room for a cup of cocoa and piece of pie. CJ couldn't thank the class, teacher, and his family enough for their help, making this Thanksgiving another success. He took the tip jar and set it on the table where the students were settled.

"Looks like you have some counting to do here, and then split your tips equally. Does that sound fair to you, Miss Simpkins?" CJ asked.

"I think that is the fair way to do it," she quickly agreed.

Seth picked up the jar and dumped it in the middle of the table. As they started to count, half the table separated the coin while the other half sorted the currency. The tally came in at two-hundred and thirty-six dollars and fifty cents.

"Wow!" exclaimed Ms. Simpkins. "That's a lot of money, divided by eleven is what?" she challenged them.

Seth, being the math whiz, quickly came up with twenty-one dollars and fifty cents each.

"Very good, Seth, now let's see if we need to make any change or if we can divide it up with the money we have," Miss Simpkins instructed.

"I want to donate my share to A Snug Around the Neck," Sydney quickly spoke up. "I didn't plan to get money for spending the day volunteering. Isn't this day to help the charity?"

"That's what I thought we were doing," Kerri joined in. "I want my share to go to them too."

In no time, it was unanimous. After all, that was the reason they helped. It was amazing to see what they could do when they worked together.

Everyone in the Café gave the class a standing ovation, clapping and cheering them on! Miss Simpkins was holding back tears, she was just so proud of her students.

As parents stopped by to pick up the students, they were welcomed into the Café for a piece of pie and cup of cocoa. The students continued to amaze their families while talking about the day.

As they were locking up, Eliza praised Annie on her very special students. They needed to talk about getting a field trip planned to Slipknot and an agenda for some history lessons and demonstrations of how things were done back then.

"I'm sure we are all going to sleep well tonight!" Uncle Oliver announced as he started out the door.

"I'm with you on that," Eliza said. "My bathtub is calling my name."

Before she was in the front door of the shop, the Café was dark, and everyone was heading home.

"I believe Uncle Oliver is right, we will sleep well tonight," CJ said to himself as he locked the door and started home. "Ah, what a Thanksgiving!"

Chapter Nine

The best surprise ever just pulled up in a VW Convertible...

ᎨᎦᎤ

The week after Thanksgiving was certainly busy. It was only Tuesday, and Eliza felt as if she had been on the go non-stop. After restocking a few racks and sweeping the shop, she only had an hour to go. She enjoyed seeing many of her old customers on return visits. Some brought finished projects from the goods purchased the year before. She admired their works as much as they loved showing them off. This is where many ideas are started. You see someone work up a pattern, and just holding it and looking at their stitches, a new idea comes to mind. She hadn't had much time to work on any of her projects over the last few weeks. Spending time with Annie's class gave things a fresh approach. Sharing the history of Slipknot, and the simple basics she grew up with had made her feel like she was passing on some very important values. They were all so eager to learn, which surprised her. It was amazing that young students would be interested in old-time skills.

Eliza was excited to see how involved the girls would be in learning to knit and crochet. They would have to put some effort in beginning patterns and set aside time one on one, so the girls didn't get discouraged. Knitting and crocheting can be like learning to read music. Some have the knack, and some struggle to learn. She hoped to eventually see a good size group that cultivated a lasting circle of friends.

Eliza planned to go to Slipknot on Saturday afternoon and spend the night so she could do some heavy cleaning. She needed to freshen the linens, arrange the bedrooms, and start with some of the Christmas decorations while the weather was still mild. The fall décor needed to be put away. She wanted to decorate the stable doors and put some lights on the gates to make the animals as much a part of the celebration as the visitors. Suddenly, the sound of a motor and tooting horn outside the shop brought her back to reality. She walked to the door, and as she looked out, she spotted a pearl green Volkswagen Beetle convertible, top down, and an old-fashioned hat with red curls spilling out all around. She snickered, thinking the car reminded her of a June bug at first glance. Then she saw a familiar smile and this jovial woman begin to wave and shout when she spied Eliza standing in the door. Could it be? This was so surreal, Eliza couldn't believe her eyes.

"Aunt Mildred, could it possibly be you?" Eliza shouted as she ran out the door toward the car. "I can't believe my eyes. What on earth are you doing in Spring Forrest?"

"It's me all right!" Aunt Mildred shouted as she

hurried from the car, grabbed Eliza, hugging her, and laughing out loud as they danced around in circles on the sidewalk. "I'm seeing the US of A. Enjoying every minute and every mile. Taking in the sights and taking the time to visit everyone along the way. I've been on the road for three-and-a-half months now. My Winnebago is parked just outside of town. It's my new home. As Bill always said, it's a great life if you don't weaken! After he had passed, I didn't think I'd find the strength to continue on, but by the grace of the good Lord, I have!"

"Oh, Aunt Mildred, I was so sad to hear you lost Bill. It must be quite an adjustment, especially after running a business together for so many years, raising your kids in the back of the store, and the trips you took together; your treasure hunts for the antique, estate sales, and flea markets. What an amazing life you shared." Eliza went on as her voice began to crack. "It must be difficult without him."

"No, not really," she replied, "I'm never without him."

"That's so sweet," Eliza replied. "I know he has a special place in your heart."

"No, no," she replied, shaking her head, and laughing at Eliza's sentiment. "He is always with me. I have his ashes in the Winnebago."

Eliza gasped with surprise and at a loss of words stood there staring at Aunt Mildred.

"Relax honey. Bill always wanted me to scatter his

ashes in North Carolina, on the ocean. We went there on our honeymoon and visited from time to time on buying trips to the store. We took the kids there for family vacations on several occasions. He loved it there. Having the heart attack so suddenly, we didn't have a lot of time to discuss things, but after spending the first year without him, the Antique Shop was no longer my passion. Besides, the sign that read 'If you can't find it, Bill & Mil will' just wasn't the same without him. That's when I decided to sell the business and travel. The kids didn't want to run an antique store, and they agreed with me when they realized I was serious. So, my dear, here I am! Another stop on my excursion from coast to coast!"

"Come in. Let's go in the shop and relax a bit. Do you want a cup of coffee, or need to freshen up?" Eliza said as she opened the door. "My apartment is just upstairs. You are welcome to anything you need. I'm just so glad to see you."

Aunt Mildred followed her into the shop and immediately started to look around. "I knew your shop would be a sight to see, dear, and always had good intentions of visiting you someday. This must be that day! Tell me about the yarns and some of the projects I see on display. Did you create these? You get your talent from your mom and Grandma. Being your daddy's little sister I know there was not one ounce of talent like this passed on from our side."

"We were very fortunate Mimzie took the four of us in to raise after we lost Momma and Daddy. We learned so much from her and Papa I guess I was so young when that happened, I remember more from hearing everyone talking than actually being there. Mimzie and Papa did a good job of instilling memories of them in all of us. I'm just so glad to see you." Eliza stood shaking her head. "It just hasn't sunk in yet that you are really here. How long can you stay?"

"Until I wear out my welcome I suppose," Aunt Mildred answered with a wink and a smile. "I have nothing but time. Oh, and money. I'm loaded! Sold the shop and home and things we collected for years that I couldn't live without. Come to find out, all that stuff wasn't what I needed. Bill was. Then, I realized I could pick him up and go anywhere we pleased. My cell phone keeps me in touch with the kids and grandkids if they need me. We talk a few times a week just to keep tabs on each other. They were raised to be independent, and we obviously did a good job. I'm going to miss him when we make it to the ocean. He is a lot of company to me in the evenings. Never thought I could sit and talk to a vase for hours on end. Later in years, he mostly sat and listened to me jabber anyway, so it isn't much different."

"Tell me about Alex and Lauren. I know they are both married. I'm sorry I've lost track after that. Where are they?"

"Well, Alex married a local girl, Celia, and they have Henry and Katie. They live in Colorado. He is an architect, and Celia has a catering business. Lauren married Sam, and they have the twins, Max and Lucy. I can't believe they're already fifteen. Lauren has a quaint shop in a small town just outside Portland. She has a wide variety of vendors that maintain their own areas, so that pays her rent, and Lauren designs and makes clothes for children from newborn to toddlers. She recently started collecting and painting kids furniture. She has an amazing shop. You really should go out there sometime and see it. Her husband, Sam has a construction company, mostly renovating and repurposing old town buildings in and around the area. They chose to settle close to his family and having grown up there, he has an attachment to the integrity of the old towns. The grandkids are such a blessing. I have pictures I'll show you as we catch up," she bragged.

"Well, I have an extra bedroom in my apartment and would love for you to stay with me as long as you like. We can take your motorhome to Slipknot and leave it there. Oliver lives there in the old summer kitchen he remodeled after Mary passed away. He'd love to see you. This is going to be so much fun!" Eliza said as she gave Aunt Mildred another hug. "I'll be closing within the hour. If you want, go upstairs and freshen up a bit and put on the kettle. I'll be up shortly and fix supper, and we can just settle in for the evening. Do you need to go to your motor home tonight?"

"No, I think it will be okay for the night. It is just a few blocks away from the church parking lot. Is that a problem?"

"Not at all. I'll call the pastor. I'm sure it will be fine. Now go on up and make yourself at home. Cody can go up with you if you'd like the company." Eliza showed Aunt Mildred to the door. "I'm sure you will recognize a few things up there. Enjoy yourself."

Eliza was a bit busy with a couple of in and out

customers, mostly browsers. Not much into the craft. Before she knew it the sign was flipped to closed, she locked the door, checked on the fire and swept up a bit and called it a day.

As she topped the stairs, she could smell something wonderful. It reminded her of something familiar, but she couldn't say what it was. In the kitchen, Aunt Mildred was at the stove.

"What is that wonderful aroma?" Eliza questioned as she walked over to the stove, looking into a pot of potatoes simmering in broth, and in the pan was thinly sliced onions sizzling in bacon drippings. A few pieces of bacon lay cooling on a paper towel.

"It's a pot of potato soup for our supper like my Grandma used to make it. She taught Alexander and me when we were big enough to peel potatoes. I'm sure he made it for the family. It was always his favorite, and he could make it perfect every time. I hope you don't mind me rummaging through your kitchen like this. I thought it would be comfort food, good for our souls as we settle in and talk. I doubt either of us will be going to bed early. I know I won't. Do you know how long it has been since anyone answered me, or joined in my conversations as of late?"

Eliza got tickled at her. Aunt Mildred was always outspoken, but never said a negative thing about anyone. She knew the good Lord didn't like to hear anyone grumble or complain. Ever want to get stuck in a bad situation, just keep grumbling, that will surely keep you there until you have learned your lesson. Then the Lord will move you on. It's the trials in life that make us stronger, even if we don't realize it at the time. She had heard Aunt Mildred say that more than once. And thinking back, Eliza knew she was right.

"So, can you teach me how to make the family recipe?" Eliza asked, "I'd like to share it with CJ."

"Why sure I can, dear. I want to pass on everything I can. I've been thinking, if it works out for us, I may stay on for a week or so. Now CJ, is that Rachel's boy? Where is he by now? He must be in his 20's."

"He is," Eliza explained. "Did you see the sign across the street, CJ's Café? That's his. He spent a semester away at college, and then returned home to start his own business. College just wasn't for him. Since he always loved to cook, the Café was a perfect opportunity for him. Ben helps him out, and I love having him so close by. He is going to be excited to see you. I'm sure he was a baby last time you saw him, don't you think?"

"Well, let me think about this a minute. I believe we stopped by Rachel's one year around Thanksgiving, not for Thanksgiving, but around that time. We were on a buying trip and heard she just had a baby that fall. That's right, we saw CJ, such a puny little thing at the time. Has he grown up to be a substantial young man?" she questioned.

"He has grown into a very nice looking young man. Of that, you can be assured. And he loves to cook, creates a lot of his own recipes, and of course, I share my family recipe box with him. You'll have to go over for breakfast and surprise him. You won't be disappointed. Now tell me how you make this wonderful soup and all about the family secret," Eliza went on. "But more important than that, when can we eat?"

"Soon, dear. It will be ready in about fifteen minutes. Now you do as you told me, and go rest a bit before supper. Are there any dishes or linens that are off limit? It has been so long since I had the chance to entertain, I'm going to set the table for company, and we can both feel special tonight," she said with a giggle. "There are still times that I miss my home very much. Oh, we should have invited Bill. I could have gone out and picked him up. But that is okay. Something tells me he is enjoying the peace and quiet tonight. He knows I'm having a ball."

Eliza couldn't do anything but smile as she picked Cody up and headed for her comfy chair. This is an unusual way to spend a Tuesday evening, she thought to herself, but what a special gift, for both her and her Aunt Mildred. She was anxious to taste the Potato Soup and get the recipe, another family recipe, from her dad's side this time. Very special.

As Eliza sat in her chair with Cody curled up at her feet, she went through today's mail. Nothing special. She looks forward to December. Christmas cards are such a joy to send and receive. It's one way to connect with friends and family at least once a year.

"Now what am I smelling? Not soup. It smells more like bread or pastry," Eliza thought out loud as she shuffled about in her chair. Add that to the aroma of the soup and Eliza's stomach was beginning to growl uncontrollably. Even Cody looked up at her from his nap.

"Supper is ready!" sounded a voice from the kitchen.

Eliza was anxious to see what was awaiting her. The table was set with a simple elegance. There were her favorite dishes and napkins she rarely used. Aunt Mildred lit candles, had the soup in a tureen, and a fresh batch of biscuits coming out of the oven.

"Wonderful!" Eliza exclaimed as she came through the kitchen door. "What a delight. I never take the time to do this for myself, and seldom have company in my apartment. I always invite my guests to join me at the Homestead. I'm so pleased to have you here." Eliza felt her eyes welling up with tears of joy. She hadn't connected like this in quite some time with family. It was a blessing.

As they pulled up to the table, Aunt Mildred reached for Eliza's hands and held them as she said, Grace. They both took a moment to reflect on what this day had brought them. Enjoying their meal, they discussed the soup and how it was prepared by the family in the early years. As they finished, the coffee was ready, and they had one more biscuit, this time with fresh apple butter, for dessert.

"After all, no meal is complete without a sweet-stopper!" Aunt Mildred said as she passed the knife to Eliza. "That is a rule I live by. It was passed on to me by my Great-Grandma. The whole family lived by it. So, you cannot pass up dessert. It's a family tradition, and don't you forget it," she coached Eliza as they remained seated at the table for another hour talking and sharing stories from their heritage.

It was getting late. Eliza didn't feel the least bit tired, but she could see Aunt Mildred was starting to mellow.

"I bet you are exhausted. I'd forgotten you've been traveling. You must be ready to get comfortable. You cooked. I'll clean up, and while I do, how about I draw you a nice relaxing bath. You can soak as long as you like. I'll get you some pajamas and show you to your room."

"I suppose I could use a nice long bath. Being on the road is a great experience, but I have missed some of the comforts of home, and my bathtub is one of them. The shower in the Winnie does the job, but that is all I can say about it. Are you sure I can't help you clean up first?" she asked reluctantly.

Eliza shook her head and led her down the hall to the guest room. She laid out PJ's and a robe, cracked the window open, and put an extra quilt at the foot of her bed.

"The bathroom is down the hall. It's all yours. Nothing off limits in there either. Stay in the tub as long as you like, and I'll check on you before I go to bed. I'm so glad you're here," Eliza smiled.

"Eliza," Aunt Mildred called to her as she turned to walk away. "You are an amazing young woman. Your dad would be so proud of you. I know I am. Let's make plans for the rest of the week over coffee in the morning. I know you have a shop to run. I'm sure you could use help with something around here. This time of year, there must be plenty to do. I love you, dear, and thank you so much for making me feel welcome. I'm sure I'll sleep like a baby! I just hope I don't snore too loud!" she said as she started down the hall. "Oh, and could you put this somewhere the cat doesn't attack it?"

Eliza turned and reached toward Aunt Mildred, then gasped, and let out a scream. She was dancing in place in the hall, shaking her arms trying to get her wits about her! Then, as she realized what it was. They both stood there looking at each other and burst out laughing. There was Aunt Mildred with her red curly hair in her hand, asking for a place to park her wig. Looking at her, Eliza recognized the familiar image of her Aunt. Her white hair was cut in a very attractive bob, classic. Eliza asked, "What happened to your long hair, you always wore it in a ponytail, or up in a bun. I love the new look, much better that the curly red hair-do, although it was cute."

"I had my hair cut to donate to Locks of Love. One of our choir members was going through Chemo, and we all got together and cut our hair short for her. I liked it so well, I kept it this way. The wig, I just wear that when I drive with my top down. It holds my hat on!" she said with a giggle. "So can you put it somewhere for me? I may need it later this week. I thought we'd take a ride with the top down this weekend and you could show me the sites. I haven't been in the area for quite some time. I'm curious as to what has changed, and what has remained the same."

"We certainly can, we'll take a drive Sunday, on the way out to Slipknot. I go every Sunday. The work out there is therapeutic for me. We can go out to church and cook a nice pot of soup, maybe bake something comforting and enjoy the day. I want to show you the treasures we found in the attic. I'm sure you'll enjoy them. We'll talk more in the morning, and I'll park your red curly friend in a safe place. Enjoy your bath!"

"Sleep well, just in case I'm not out before you turn in. I'm looking so forward to the soak, and your home is so inviting, I may just wander around looking at your treasures before I turn in."

"I get up early and go down to the shop, so I plan on letting you sleep in. Sleep tight."

Eliza kissed her on the cheek and went down the hall carrying the red curly friend as if she had a new pet. As she flipped on the light in her bedroom, Aunt Mildred heard a squeal!

"Forgot you were carrying my wig, didn't you dear? Nightie-night!" Aunt Mildred said as she closed the bathroom door.

Forgot, indeed, Eliza thought to herself as she perched the wig over an old oat tin she kept on the top shelf of her closet. She didn't want to wake up to that staring at her in the morning. Propping open the window and turning down the bed, she knew she was too wound up to fall asleep. She decided to call Rachel and tell her about the surprise. It had been so long since any of the family had seen Aunt Mildred. She was nearly ten years younger than their dad, his baby sister, and more like a cousin to them than an Aunt. They had so much fun with her around on summer visits. After she met and married Bill, her life went in a different direction, same as everyone else, and before they knew it, decades had passed. Christmas letters kept them up to date with family happenings, but that was it for communicating.

Rachel was so excited, they talked for nearly an hour, the conversation turning toward Christmas, and hopes to include Aunt Mildred in the plans. Soon, they said good night with Eliza promising to have Aunt Mildred call her one evening.

Still wide awake, Eliza went out to the kitchen to finish the cleanup and brew a cup of Sleepy-thyme Tea. Aunt Mildred was still in the bathroom, but Eliza could hear the water draining. She put on enough water for two cups, knowing they would be up for hours yet, catching up.

When the alarm sounded in the morning, Eliza moaned, sat up on the side of her bed, fumbling for her slippers, and yawned. Short night, she thought. But she wouldn't have traded sleep for the time spent reminiscing about everything from Aunt Mildred's childhood to her grandchildren. Many lost years were covered over tea at the old work table in the kitchen.

Quietly she readied herself and went downstairs to brew a pot of coffee, being careful to let her Aunt rest. The time on the road alone had to be tiresome. She stopped on the landing and gazed out at the sunrise. Perfect. The day is going to be just perfect. With that, she continued on her way to start another busy day in A Simple Stitch.

She looked out the front as her coffee finished brewing. CJ was on the sidewalk, putting his menu on the chalkboard now being held by one of Santa's elves, curly-toed shoes and all, reminding us that Christmas is just weeks away. Eliza walked across the street to catch him up on the exciting news of Aunt Mildred's visit. He didn't remember her, just of family conversations about her and Bill. Knowing Eliza would be busy in the shop, CJ said to send her over to the Café for breakfast. He was looking forward to getting acquainted with her. After chatting a bit, they both went back to work.

The morning was somewhat busy, having several familiar customers. The holidays were on everyone's mind. Olivia came by, dropping off a batch of cookies and a new flyer for needs over Christmas. Donations are good this time of year. Everyone has a giving spirit. It was already quarter after ten and no sign of Aunt Mildred. Eliza assumed everything was fine upstairs and she was just catching up on some long needed rest. After all, Eliza felt as if she could take a catnap herself if she sat still. The bell on the door clanged and in came a group of ladies, laughing, and talking, definitely in the Christmas spirit. As Eliza welcomed them, she heard footsteps coming down the stairs. The customers were occupied with the new yarns and patterns, so Eliza met Aunt Mildred as she entered the shop.

"Sleep well, I hope?" she greeted her with a quick hug.

"Just lovely, my dear," she replied. "I've been up for about an hour but took my time getting ready and enjoying my morning. It has been a very long time since I had such an inviting home to get familiar with."

"I saw CJ changing his menu this morning. He is anxious to get re-acquainted with you. Seems he has memories of you, mostly from conversations. He has been focused on the strength of family lately. You'll have to ask him about our holiday plans at Slipknot." Eliza explained as she walked her to the door. "He'll fix breakfast for you, take as much time as you like, and try and get him to sit down and join you. He could use a break."

"It sounds wonderful," she smiled. "Slipknot, I always forget that you called the Homestead that. Do you think we could take a drive out there this evening? That is if you have time. I know you are busy, dear. I would like to take the Winnie out to be sure she is safe though. It is my home, and I miss Bill. Haven't talked to him for nearly an entire day. Oh, how I'm really going to miss him when we get to the ocean. Well, I'll see you in a bit dear. What time do you close?" Aunt Mildred asked as she started out the door.

"I'm open until five, and I don't have any group coming in this evening, so we could drive out. Ask CJ if he has time to ride along if you like," Eliza encouraged her as she closed the door and turned her attention back to her customers.

"So, you have to be CJ," Aunt Mildred said as she walked into the Café.

He put the tray on the counter and ran to give

her a hug. Something seemed familiar, but he still didn't remember her. If Eliza hadn't told him she was in town, he would not have recognized her at all.

"Aunt Mildred, how nice to see you. I'm thrilled you're here. Hope you are hungry. I still have my French toast special left, or do you have something else in mind?" he asked as he pulled the chair out for her by the window.

"Oh, the special on your darling sign, that sounds wonderful to me. Could I start with a cup of coffee if you don't mind? My, you have grown into such a nice looking young man. I can't wait to see if you cook as good as you look!" she giggled. "You'll soon find that I just crack me up! I learned that laughter keeps a person young, and eases what life throws your way. Now, I take my coffee black, and you hurry back. I want you to join me. We have a lot to learn about each other, and I want you to tell me all about these Christmas plans you have in mind for Slipknot."

He was back in an instant with her coffee, Uncle Ben right behind him, and they had a grand reunion. He knew she had lost Bill, sent a letter to her, but hadn't seen her since. He was quick to invite her for supper with him and Molly the next evening.

She, of course, was thrilled. "Give Molly my best, and tell her not to go to a lot of trouble. It will be great catching up. Can I bring anything?" she offered.

He assured her they just wanted to spend time with her and she should plan on staying the night. Then he hurried back to finish with the last customers at the register and told CJ he could handle things while he visited with Aunt Mildred.

They spent half the day talking and laughing, and nearly in tears at times, first about the antique store that she and Bill started and then about their kids and grandkids. They also talked about how she decided to pick up and travel, and how she ended up here. She wanted to know details about CJ, his choices and how he became such a wonderful chef. She asked how he developed his recipes and menu. They discussed his strong need to have a family gathering this Christmas and where these feeling were coming from. Aunt Mildred was so easy to talk to. CJ felt as comfortable with her as he did with Eliza. He loved her natural curiosity for details.

"Oh, my, look at the time," she said as she noticed the clock. "I've kept you the biggest part of the day. Where did Ben go? You sure don't have much of a crowd." she exclaimed.

"Ben went home some time ago. Lunch was light today, and he had it all under control. I don't know what I'd do without him. The Café is closed, so nothing to worry about," he reassured her. "I've enjoyed this so much. I just cannot imagine that you wouldn't be able to stay on for Christmas. You would definitely liven things up and share so many memories. Won't you please consider staying on?"

"I will," she said as she cupped his face in her hands, gave him a kiss on the forehead, and looked out the window toward A Simple Stitch. "Do you think Eliza is extremely busy today? She had a few ladies there when I came down.

Should I go make her some lunch? The poor dear has to be starving." Aunt Mildred asked with concern.

"No, don't worry about her, she always keeps fruit and nuts at her counter and has a friend that brings in baked goods at times. If she's hungry, she gives me a call, and I pack her a to-go box." He walked Aunt Mildred to the door. "I'm going to get a few things lined up for tomorrow, and I'll come over before Eliza closes. I think I'd like to ride out to Slipknot this evening, if it's okay with you, that is," he said, waiting for Aunt Mildred's reply.

"I would love it. Give the three of us a little more time to catch up. I want to take the Winnie out there anyway. Maybe you could drive my car."

"We'll plan on it," he said as he gave her a hug. He just stood watching her cross the street, thinking to himself how much history she brings to the family.

That evening CJ got to drive the VW Convertible out to Slipknot, with Aunt Mildred following behind in the Winnie and Eliza leading the way in Bittersweet. He laughed out loud, thinking what anyone seeing this small parade must be thinking. After all, it was quite a sight for this small town. He hadn't seen Aunt Mildred in her red curly wig and hat, but he enjoyed driving the convertible more than he imagined. The evening was so clear, and although cool, he insisted on driving with the top down. As they entered the lane, they heard Eliza start honking her horn, and all followed suit! Uncle Oliver came running out of his cabin, not knowing what was going on. No one had told him about Aunt Mildred coming in. He met them as they parked side-by-side in front of the corral where the animals gathered, as curious as Uncle Oliver.

Hours were spent as they poured over the finds from the attic and the plans for Christmas, those expected to show, and even the recipe box from the old jelly cupboard.

Aunt Mildred asked Eliza if she could bring the recipe box back to the apartment with her so she could read through the family history.

"You know, I have always wanted to write a recipe book," Aunt Mildred said. "I loved to cook when the kids were young, even decorated cakes and cookies for every occasion. Then they grew up, and we got so busy with the Antique Store, cooking became a necessity, and all the creativity was gone. I do so love the holidays though."

"Well, it's settled then," Uncle Oliver spoke up, "there is no way we are letting you leave before the New Year's celebrations are over, and things back to everyday life here. Now, am I getting an argument, or are you going to make this easy and just let your family know where you are spending your lovely holiday?"

"It sounds inviting. I haven't had an old time holiday in years, and I know my kids have family plans this year since I was going to be traveling. We were planning to gather together next year."

"Sounds like it's a plan if you ask me," CJ said with a big smile on his face. "This just keeps getting better and better!"

All Eliza could do was smile.

Chapter Ten

So, you say this WAS a chicken house...

୨୦

As the sun came up, Eliza and CJ were feeling the late night. Aunt Mildred went on for hours. So many stories were shared of her childhood and growing up with Alexander. Eliza and Oliver were excited to hear stories of their dad's younger days. He and Mildred were inseparable growing up. Even though they picked at each other constantly, it was always in fun, the way brothers and sisters do. Oh, how they all could relate to that.

She told them of their horse, Lulu, that they rode double on. She was very gentle.

One day when they were in the pasture playing a game of stickball with some schoolmates, Alexander's temper got away with him after striking out. He had quite a tantrum, throwing the stick and stomping around shouting "I quit, I hate this stupid game, and I'm leaving!" So with that, he, went over and got on Lulu. When he took the reins and shouted giddy-up, she just stood there. He shook them again and repeated his demand, and there she stood. Finally, he shouted and slapped her on the hind side. That's when Lulu took off running, Alexander holding on with all his might, and she didn't slow down until she reached the far end of the pasture. She stopped. Aunt Mildred and their friends who were playing ball watched. Lulu stood there with Alexander on her back in the pasture, and they could hear him yelling at her to giddy-up, kicking his feet, wailing his arms, and acting as big a fool as he did during the game. She waited him out. He finally got down and came stomping across the pasture, grumbling as he walked back. When he got close to the gate, Lulu came racing back right past him, and there stood looking at him as he walked up to the gate. They glared, eye to eye. It was as if she were teaching him a lesson about his behavior. After that, he managed to control his temper, especially when Lulu was around.

The stories went on and on until Eliza and CJ had to say goodnight and drove back to town in Bittersweet. Aunt Mildred assured them she would make it home. Eliza heard her come in after midnight. She stopped at Eliza's door and whisper her a 'good night, dear' as she passed by.

The next two weeks seemed to breeze by. Eliza continued to enjoy every minute with Aunt Mildred. Girls Knit Out was totally taken with her wit and charm. They listened to her stories, and all grew to love her as Eliza and CJ did. She was a constant joy to have around. Between her and Eliza the story telling was better than ever. Aunt Mildred hadn't given a second thought about needing to be anywhere else but here for the holidays.

Another Friday was done! Aunt Mildred had a

light supper ready, so when the shop closed, they could eat and leave for Slipknot. The business in the shop had been hectic up until now. Getting so deep into the holiday season most people are focused on ready-made items by now. Aunt Mildred had picked up on the business and was a tremendous help with the customers even though she could not knit or crochet a stitch. Her sales ability from the years of the Antique Store came shining through. Eliza dreaded the day she would wave good-bye watching her driving away in the Winnie. But for now, Christmas was coming, full speed ahead.

The Girls Knit Out group didn't meet the last two Fridays before Christmas. Everyone was busy getting ready for their holidays, parties, and final shopping. Annie was excited that her dad was really coming in for Christmas. She could hardly contain herself. She offered to help Eliza and Aunt Mildred get things ready for the family gathering. She loved spending time at Slipknot and felt she was learning so much from them. They were the family she had been missing. She actually felt at home.

Bittersweet was loaded and ready to head to the Homestead. They planned to spend the entire weekend there cleaning and decorating inside and out. CJ drove out earlier to get a head start.

The drive was pleasant. Uncle Oliver and CJ were on the front porch hanging Christmas lights. They brought boxes of the old fashioned big bulb strands from the attic that were lit in red, yellow, green, blue, and orange.

As they parked the truck, they were so excited they couldn't wait to get out.

"It is like I remember it when Mimzie and Papa put lights out for Christmas!" Eliza ran up and grabbed Oliver and hugged him, dancing circles around him. "What a wonderful surprise!"

"Just want to give back some of the joy you've given me. You've made the past few years good for me, when I didn't think I had anything to look forward to," he said with a wink. "Now, I have one more thing to show you before it gets any darker. Come with me," he said, taking Eliza by the arm.

Aunt Mildred and CJ followed, not saying a word. He led Eliza around the house toward the old chicken house. There was light coming from the windows. This was odd. There hadn't been power to that building before.

"Oh, you ran power to the shed. Is that what you wanted to show me? Why did we need that?" she questioned as they kept walking.

"This is why." As they got to the front of the shed, Eliza noticed a new old door at the entrance.

"Where did you get the door, is that from the pile of used lumber and building surplus from the barn? I found that along the roadside years ago. Good thing I rescued it like Mimzie taught me, isn't it?" Eliza went on. "And you painted it red, an old barn red, just like I would have done. How thoughtful."

As she opened the door to the shed, she stepped back, startled. "What on earth have you done, and when did you take on such a project. This must have taken you months. It is absolutely amazing!" She grabbed Oliver and hugged him, nearly spilling them both backward into the yard.

"I have been piddling with it for months but wanted to make it a gift to you. The gathering just gave me a push. Now, quit your blubbering and come in and look around. Oliver held the door and followed as they all went inside.

He had worked for weeks restoring the integrity of the old shed. He wired it and put in an old woodstove for heat. There was a small kitchen area, with a counter and nook by the window overlooking the pond. He installed a bathroom with an open shower, three sides encased in the old brick that he uncovered behind the wallboards. It was very primitive and just perfect for the shed; a small sitting area, and plenty of room for a bed and chest. One great room created the perfect guest house. The old pine plank floors were white-washed, and the walls had been painted in a comforting creamy neutral.

She was speechless. That did not happen often. Overwhelmed by the generosity of the time invested and astonished by the workmanship she continued to praise Oliver until he spoke up, pulling CJ in front of him.

"This young man has been out here most evenings, working late into the night helping me."

"CJ, is that so?" Eliza started toward him. "I can't thank you enough. I don't know what to say."

Aunt Mildred stepped up, "You both should be proud. I haven't seen this quality of workmanship in many restoration jobs. It really is amazing. You know, the fun part is ahead of you; furnishing this guest house. Eliza, do you have any ideas in mind?"

"I haven't had time to think about it. I don't even know where to start. I doubt I can find enough time to go out searching for the right pieces, and there aren't any auctions coming up until spring. The furnishings in the house are going to be used for the gathering. I just don't know." Eliza replied, still feeling overwhelmed.

"Well, Eliza dear, I have an idea. You've been so gracious to take me in and make me a part of things around here, if you trust me, I would like to spend the next week gathering the perfect furnishings for the shed. I know plenty of places within driving distance. I could use Bittersweet to bring some of the finds with me and have the large pieces delivered. It would be therapy for me, back to doing what I loved. It will be my gift for your first Christmas gathering at Slipknot. I'm sure after this year it will be a tradition."

"Aunt Mildred, that is too much. I would love for you to go on the hunt, but you can't furnish this entire guest house. That's just too much," Eliza scowled.

"Nonsense, dear, don't you remember what I told you. I have more money than I know what to do with. My kids are fine. I want to do this for you. It will make me happy.

Please, let this old woman be happy. Don't make me beg." Aunt Mildred continued, "You may as well agree with me, I know I can wear you down! Anyway, you have a business to run next week, so I can easily do it with or without your blessing. So you see, dear, it is easier just to agree with me, and be happy."

"I don't know what to say. I knew I had a wonderful family. But all of this is just too much." Eliza continued.

"Just humble yourself and say thanks," CJ spoke up. "Let us give back to you. It'll be our Christmas gift to you. You're giving us the best Christmas present of all, bringing us all together. We'll have memories of this gathering the rest of our lives. I feel the same as Aunt Mildred. This is going to be the start of a new tradition."

"I give up. You win! I can't thank you all enough. Oh, the workmanship and hours you must have put in, I can't wait for the family to see this. I know I won't get any sleep tonight. Not after all of this excitement. Who wants coffee?" Eliza turned, starting to the door. "Let's go back to the house. I brought a Sour Cream Coffee Cake!"

Bringing in supplies from Bittersweet, they each took a load in on the way by. Eliza still felt weak in the knees. All she could think about was the shed. She couldn't wait to plan the decorating style and discuss the furnishings with Aunt Mildred. She was hoping for something simple, primitive, but comfy.

As the coffee finished brewing, Eliza got out the

Sour Cream Coffee Cake. This evening warranted something special. They gathered at one end of the old work table.

"Why can't I think about anything but the shed," Eliza said as she shook her head, almost as if trying to shake her thoughts around in there. "My mind is overrun with ideas. I think I'm going to walk out and look at it again before bed, whenever that might be! I can't even think about sleep."

"Hmm, you are starting to sound like Annie Simpkins. She rambles on and on like that when she gets nervous. Are you nervous, Eliza, because I have never seen you nervous before? I have seen you angry and excited, and I have seen you nearly falling asleep on your feet, but nervous, this is a new one for you ...oh, my... was I rambling?" CJ began laughing. The others joined in, and Eliza followed. Soon the laughing was over, they sighed, simultaneously, and sat staring at each other.

"Well, that was fun, now here are we going to start this evening?" CJ spoke up. "Did you like the lights on the front porch? We found them in the attic."

"They're perfect!" Eliza replied. "I want to cut some greenery from the tree line tomorrow and make garlands to put around the windows and surround the doors. I have some large pinecones that we can wire in the garlands, and it will bring back the integrity of the original holiday charm when Mimzie and Papa decorated it years ago. Does that sound like anything you had in mind CJ, or did you have other ideas?"

"I'd like to put a small fir tree with ornaments made to feed the birds on one end of the porch, opposite the swing. It would be a great place to sit and watch what comes up for a snack. They're simple to make. I have some pages I pulled from a magazine one time. I thought we could put them together late in the evenings when we need to wind down. We can wait to hang them, so they are fresh for Christmas. I think some simple white lights on the tree will be nice, don't you? And what about plain green wreaths on the shutters, hanging by a simple red ribbon," he finished.

"Sounds charming to me," Aunt Mildred spoke up. "It suits the period of the Homestead. Somewhat primitive, but welcoming and cozy, that is very important. Your guests must have comfort. They traveled and will need to rest and refresh their first evening here. We'll make them feel welcome. I'd like to make gift baskets for the bedrooms and bathrooms. I have extra supplies in the Winnie. I pick up things on the road when I stop for a break to walk around and explore a town or shop along the way. Is that all right with you, Eliza, don't want to seem like I'm trying to take over."

"Not a problem, that sounds wonderful. I'm so blessed to have such a thoughtful family," Eliza said, still visibly shaken. "I had no idea this year would take the path it has taken. Please, don't hesitate to offer your ideas or just take over and do what you know will be good for the gathering," she smiled. "This is OUR Christmas at Slipknot, and we are going to make it amazing!"

Uncle Oliver spoke up. "I do have one request, and I hope it isn't selfish of me to ask."

"Well, I hope it is selfish," Eliza jumped right in. "All you have done for me over the years, a selfish request from you would make me nothing but happy. Now, what is your request?"

"I was hoping we could offer the shed to Carson and Julia since Jaxon is only a few months old. It may give them the quiet time they need to get him settled. Unless you had something else in mind, that would be fine too. It just crossed my mind when we were out there looking it over. I'm starting to feel the excitement that this really is happening."

"Of course they can have the guest house," Eliza replied. "I had planned to offer them my apartment if they needed to distance themselves from the family at times, just hated the idea of them constantly driving back and forth. This is perfect. I think there is an old cradle in the attic if I'm not mistaken. We could get that down and clean it up if you think it would suit them."

"Oh, we already have. It's out in the barn," CJ replied. "Uncle Oliver and I brought it down when we found the Christmas lights. He had the same idea, to put it in by the fireplace for Jaxon to rest in while they were here. And it isn't too heavy to bring back and forth if they need to."

"Then that is settled," Eliza said. "Now, let's see how that farm set cleaned up. I'd like to get the fireplace freshened up and decorated tonight. I think that could be our kick-off, just enough to inspire us. Each time we walk by, we'll see how festive it looks, and it is something we can finish tonight without working too hard."

"Sounds like a plan. What farm set are you talking about?" Aunt Mildred asked.

CJ brought the box over from the back door. He had taken it home with him and cleaned each piece. Nothing was broken, and it all seemed to be there.

"This is it. It was in the attic. Eliza and Uncle Ben used to play with it."

Aunt Mildred gasped, then she started to giggle, an excited but strange noise coming from her. She had tears streaming down her cheeks.

"That was mine and Alexander's when we were kids. We played for hours with it when the weather kept us inside. We got it for Christmas one year when we were both very young. I think our Poppy even made the fences. I didn't think I'd ever see the likes of it again! And it is in perfect condition. Oh, my." She sat at the table staring at the set in disbelief.

"I had no idea," Eliza said. "I remember Ben and me playing with it. I thought he would become a farmer when he grew up. We wanted to surprise him with it when he comes out for the gathering. Are you going to be okay?"

Eliza brought Aunt Mildred a tissue and rubbed her shoulders.

"I'm fine dear. Not to worry about me. It just brought back a swarm of memories. I'm fine. Now, let's get started on that fireplace."

It took them nearly an hour to get the fireplace and mantel cleaned, and the farm set arranged. They found a piece of an old horse blanket to set it on, leaving room behind the arrangement for fresh greenery and white lights to line the length of the oversized hand-hewn timber that was used for the mantle when the cabin was built. They stood in awe of such an amazing piece of their heritage, now even more important than before.

"We'll let the kids string cranberries and use them for a garland to hang across the front of the mantle," Eliza planned. "We can hang Mimzie's stockings across the front, don't you think?"

"I have some of my own family heirlooms in storage back home. No one seemed to be too concerned about things when I sold the house. It takes a while to appreciate what was once taken for granted," she explained. "It was the same way with the antiques. The kids were raised around them, so they had no special meaning, just a part of the fixtures. Some day they will realize what memories they hold. Mark my word, they'll be pleased."

"Just how much did you save?" Eliza asked with caution.

"Oh, I sold everything in storage for the business, and the store building sold as the business itself. I put everything from our house in storage for the kids. I just hope I'm there to see their faces. They are going to be speechless, but I know they will appreciate it. It was part of their heritage. Now, this is getting way too serious in here.

How about you and I go back out to that new cottage and map out how you would like it furnished. Come on dear."

Aunt Mildred took Eliza by the hand and started for the door. "You boys finish what you want, it's getting late. We can pick up in the morning."

"It is getting late? I think I will turn in. Morning comes early for me," Oliver spoke up. "CJ, would you like to bunk with me tonight, or are you going back to town?"

"I thought I'd go on home tonight. I plan on coming back tomorrow afternoon when the Café closes, and spend Saturday night and help out through Sunday. We may have a nice crowd in the morning. At least I hope we do. I'm about ready to take off, too."

He gave Eliza and Aunt Mildred a hug and shook Uncle Oliver's hand. "I hope you all realize what this means to me."

CJ walked out with them. Eliza took a notebook and pencil with her. Cottage. Eliza liked that idea. It would make a wonderful cottage. Perhaps they could find a nice piece of wood and paint a welcome sign to hang above the door, even name it something comforting. That would take a bit of thought.

As they opened the door and flipped on the light, Eliza just stood there is awe again. It was still hard to believe her eyes.

"Ok, I need your help on this. You are the expert. What did you have in mind?"

"Well, dear, I was thinking about a combination of white painted and light wood furniture. Somewhat distressed, a true cottage style, with overstuffed chairs for the sitting area and a nice lamp and table to read by. There isn't room for a couch, or really a need for one with the bed right in the room. A nice wardrobe that could offer closet space on one side and house a small TV in the other. No matter how much people say they want to get back to basics, the guys can't live without a television. Is that to your liking, or did you have other ideas dear? It's your call."

"I think it sounds like what I had in mind, but I don't want it to seem too girlie, it has to be cozy. I was thinking a simple headboard, no footboard, and a big soft down mattress pad. And sage green for the bedding. Instead of a chest of drawers for clothing, I was thinking an old buffet or sideboard. That would help to blend the rooms. Will that work?" Eliza questioned.

"I like it. I like that idea! And a small table and couple of armchairs in the nook. It would be a great place for coffee or a snack, and some shelves above the small counter. I want to find some dishes, just a few things to accommodate early mornings and late nights. Meals will be at the Homestead. I thought a small china cabinet of sorts, also painted white to use in the bathroom for linens and necessities, and a small stool to sit on while drying off. Oh, and I will shop for linens, too. Sage green in there as well, don't you think? We want to keep things uniform, with a nice flow," Aunt Mildred said. "You have no idea how excited I am about this. I haven't been able to shop in so long. The Winnie is small. I can't buy anything to bring in without taking something out, so I have avoided the things I loved to look at, knowing I can't splurge. Well, this is perfect. I have an excuse to stalk the shops and treasure hunt like a pro. Come on Monday morning!" Aunt Mildred then took Eliza's hand, and they did a little dance.

"Aunt Mildred," Eliza stood there looking her in the eyes. "You are such an inspiration. And a real hoot. I haven't laughed this much in ages, and I consider myself to be a happy person. But you, you have given me a whole new look at things through your eyes. I thank you for that."

"Well, thank you, dear. I feel you have given me a great deal as well. I have to say I was dreading this Christmas, spending it without Bill, and knowing the kids had their own plans. I didn't encourage any change, didn't feel like sitting around having them pity me, but now, I feel like I'm a part of things. And that, my dear, is the best gift anyone could ever give me. Would you like a cup of tea? I feel like tea, and perhaps we could have another slice of that coffee cake. It just may give us a second wind. The kitchen could use a little attention, so I've noticed."

With a wink, Aunt Mildred turned toward the door, and Eliza followed. Lights out, door closed, and excitement about the furnishing for the old, new cottage, they made their way back to the Homestead.

"Did you bring your suitcase in yet?" Eliza asked.

"CJ brought it in for me. It is in the hall. I thought I'd have you show me where to sleep."

"I have a basket of clean linens. We'll need to freshen

a couple of beds yet tonight. I thought if it were okay with you, we could sleep in the twin beds in the first bedroom. We might need to talk each other to sleep tonight. I'll put on the water for tea. I think Sleepy-thyme may be the tea we need. Did you know it is already twelve-forty-five! We'll be saying good morning before we know it."

With a few more boxes of supplies unpacked, and a couple cups of tea, soon they were ready for bed. After all, there was much to be done this weekend. The fun work. Almost like playing house, only this time, the company really was coming.

Chapter Eleven

Yes, there is room in the stable for one more...

᠙᠔ᡒ

"What?" Aunt Mildred cried out from her sleep. "I thought I heard a rooster crowing. I must be dreaming. Wait, where am I? Oh! Eliza, that's you over there? For just a moment I thought I had died in my sleep and was not only in heaven but back in my childhood. There goes that blasted rooster again. I didn't dream it."

"Morning Aunt Mildred," Eliza replied wishing she was still asleep. "What time is it? Are you wearing a watch?"

"The sun is up. I know that much. Let me go see, you just go back to sleep for a while if you like, dear." Aunt Mildred shuffled into the other room.

Eliza went right back to sleep. She had been so busy lately, sleeping in was a real treat.

A good hour passed when the aroma of coffee drifting under her nose accompanied by the smell of cinnamon and fresh bread woke her from her sleep. She jumped up not knowing what time of day it could be. The sun was shining brightly in the window. As she went into the kitchen, she saw Aunt Mildred taking a pan out of the oven.

"Is that fresh cinnamon rolls I'm smelling?" Eliza asked, startling Aunt Mildred. "The coffee smells wonderful, too. How long have I been sleeping? And what time did you get up? I vaguely remember talking to you about a rooster."

"Oh, I've only been up an hour or so, dear. I cheated on the cinnamon rolls. They are made from biscuit dough, that way I didn't have to wait for them to raise. I hope I didn't use anything you had plans for. I wiped out the cabinets and put away the supplies while I was piddling around in here. Is that all right? Don't want to overstep my boundaries and a good way to do that is messing with a cook's kitchen."

"You don't have to worry about that. You are spoiling me. I love what you do. Now, may I please have a cup of coffee?" Eliza smiled, holding out her favorite Christmas mug.

"Let's take breakfast out on the porch, shall we? The sun is shining bright, and we have a busy day ahead of us. A nice slow start may be just what we need," Aunt Mildred said as she picked up the cinnamon rolls and pointed Eliza toward the tray she had ready with the small plates and napkins. She had already been out and swept off the porch and had a couple of quilts draped over the chairs by a small table. There was a tea towel draped over it with a pair of bluebirds embroidered on it and outlined with a delicate crocheted edging.

"Where did that towel come from?" Eliza questioned.

"Oh, I had it in the Winnie. Just a few of the special pieces I packed to travel with. It reminds me of the home before everything changed. I hope you don't mind, dear. I just wanted to share some of my favorite things with you."

"This is a wonderful treat. You know, I don't do the special things for myself, only when I have company. I'm learning a valuable lesson from you. I'm going to start treating myself as if I were company. That is a lesson we should all take to heart."

They enjoyed their morning over coffee and conversation. As they made plans, Eliza noticed a car coming up the lane. She knew it was too early for CJ and wasn't really expecting anyone. Then it stopped by the barn.

Annie got out and walked toward the fence. JoJo and the three sheep headed her way in a line as if they were going to board a bus. Annie had a few carrots for the sheep and an apple for JoJo. She stood there chatting with them and scratching their ears for quite some time. Then she spotted Eliza and Aunt Mildred sitting on the porch and waved whole-heartedly, and pulled over and parked in the drive by the VW. She got out and bounced over to the porch in a noticeably good mood. "Hi, I hope it is all right I came out uninvited again!" Annie said.

"You, my friend, are always welcome at the Homestead if I'm here or not. I want you to feel as if this is your second home," Eliza stressed. "Aunt Mildred and I spent the night, and she surprised me with this wonderful breakfast. Are you hungry? Have you had coffee yet?" she offered.

"Oh, actually, I'm fine. I had breakfast at home this morning. Then I finished a few things in my apartment. I'm so excited about Dad coming home for Christmas. I'm way ahead of myself for the holiday. I need a distraction to help me get through the weekend. I thought you might need some help out here. Please tell me if I'm intruding." Annie rambled in her usual way.

"Isn't she such a darling little thing," Aunt Mildred stepped in. "I don't know about where you come from, but where I come from we never call free help and good company an intrusion. Now, not another word about it, and you settle in for the weekend just as if you were one of us." Aunt Mildred rushed over and gave her the biggest hug. "I think you are adorable. Just adorable! And I hear you make a wonderful prize winning Chocolate Raspberry Cake. I would love that recipe for a book I'm going to write someday."

"I'd love to share it with you. My momma would be proud of that," Annie said with a warm smile. "What can I do to help around here today? I'm in the mood to work!"

"Well, guess we better get out of our PJ's and down to business," Eliza said, as she picked up the tray and gathered dishes. "Have I ever got a surprise to show you!" she said, thinking about the shed. She was anxious to go out and look it over in the daylight anyway.

In no time they were in the 'cottage,' as Aunt Mildred

dubbed it last night, and were discussing the decorating style. They explained it all in detail to Annie and asked her opinion. They were in agreement with the ideas. There was so much energy in the air. They were giddy, like a room full of school girls.

The air was crisp, the sun bright with a slight breeze. This was a perfect day for hanging out bedding. The washing machine went non-stop for hours. Pillows lined the porch railings and everything that was flat. Rugs hung over the corral fence and gate, and quilts were opened and draped over a ladder between two chairs, as not to soil them, but freshen them in the fresh air and sunshine. While the beds were stripped, they swept and dusted, flipped mattresses, and washed windows on the inside. Uncle Oliver had washed the outside last week, not knowing how perfect the weekend weather would be.

The four bedrooms were sparkling clean. The bedding was folded crisply and stacked at the end of each bed, then covered with a plastic drop cloth to keep all fresh until a few days before the guests arrived. Lunch time went by without notice. It was nearly two o'clock. Cleaning house had never been so much fun while being so productive.

"I have some white lights and greenery planned for the outside of the windows and doors," Eliza explained. "What do you say we find a little lunch and then work outside while the weather is still mild? It will be a pleasant afternoon for decorating."

"That sounds great," Annie agreed. "What kind of greenery are we using?"

"There are pine and fir trees out back in the wooded area. They can be trimmed without any noticeable damage, and the greenery will last well through the New Year. I love the fresh smell. This will be the first time I've decorated like this out here in many years. But then, we haven't gathered here at the holidays until this year. Our reunions are generally in mid-summer," Eliza reflected. "I do put up a small Christmas tree by the fireplace every year, so when I spend Sundays here, I enjoy the season."

"Okay, if you have some clippers and a basket, I'll get started gathering branches. I love being out in the woods and living in an apartment, I don't spend as much time outdoors as I like. At least not until I became familiar with your family," Annie went on. "Are we doing all the windows? That may take a few trips."

"I thought we would do the front and side windows, the back windows I would like to just lay a few smaller branches in the window sills inside the bedrooms, rather than outside. When we crack open the windows at night, the rooms will fill with the fragrance of the holidays. Walk out to the barn with me, and I'll get some gloves and clippers. I think it may be easier to take the wagon to bring the clippings back in. It may take you a couple of trips. If it gets to be too much for you, let us know, and we'll help."

Eliza and Annie walked out to the barn and gathered the tools. They stopped and gave JoJo some long overdue attention. She just didn't understand why no one came out and brushed her and saddled her up for a ride every day. They could see in her eyes that she missed the attention.

"Would you mind if I took her for a ride later on this evening?" Annie asked. "I think it would do both of us some good. I miss Pete so much. I hope they are taking good care of him. I know he is being fed and kept healthy, but I don't think anyone rides him anymore. That was his favorite time of the day. And mine."

"Come on, this is getting you down-in-the- dumps in a hurry. Do you want to take a ride before you go out to clip the branches?" Eliza offered. "We aren't in a hurry to finish. We have all day tomorrow, and if you would like to spend the night, you're more than welcome to join us.Your decision."

"I'll be fine, I'm starting to feel like a big baby," Annie apologized as she picked up the gloves and clippers. "I would love to go for a ride this evening, but right now, I'm going out to do the job I started to do. I'm really excited, and want to see how you put the branches and lights up." There was a smile on her face once again as they turned to leave the barn, Eliza pulling the wagon behind her.

As they walked out to the tree line, Eliza explained which trees would make the best trimmings. Annie got right to work. Eliza started back to the Homestead, and as she walked away, turned, looking back just to be sure of what she already knew in her heart. Yes, Annie was wearing her red cowboy boots! She smiled and kept walking.

Aunt Mildred had tidied up the kitchen after breakfast. Stacks of dishes lined the counters, and she was pulling out the old shelf lining. It was a job that had been put off far too long but didn't take priority when a day was spent in the country. Aunt Mildred's energy was amazing. She missed the job of homemaker. She had perfected that joy while raising her family. Being a business woman was second priority in her life. As Eliza stepped through the door, she was in awe of the progress that was being made. She couldn't have accomplished this on her own.

"So, you have the kitchen under control, Annie is busy cutting boughs for the outside, I think I will start on the dining room unless you need help in here."

"Oh, no dear, I'm enjoying this. If I have any question, I'll ask. I hope I'm doing a good enough job for you," she said with concern. "I love working in a cook's kitchen."

"You're doing just fine, organize as you would if you were setting it up in your own home," Eliza encouraged. "After all, you will be helping with as much of the cooking for the holidays as you want to."

Just then, she heard a car coming in. It was CJ. As he walked in, he was amazed to see how much progress had been made.

"I'm impressed!" he exclaimed, giving out hugs. "I guess I could start on the outside since things are well on the way in here. Would you like me to get started cutting some greenery for the windows, or did you have something else in mind for me to do?" he asked.

Aunt Mildred and Eliza's eyes met. They both smiled. CJ had no idea Annie was already out in woods.

"I think that is a delightful idea, dear," Aunt Mildred

quickly spoke up. "If you could go out back and clip some greenery, we could get the windows lit up before dark."

"Not a problem," he said. "I'll just grab some clippers and head that way."

As he went out the door, Eliza turned to Aunt Mildred, and they burst out laughing. "Aunt Mildred! I cannot believe you did that. I'm proud of you. You remind me of...well, me!"

"Oh, those two will have a good time out there once they get over the shock. I'm just wondering who will fluster who the most. We'll have something to talk about over dinner now, won't we?"

"They did spend quite a bit of time together at the Café when Annie volunteered to help with her class for Thanksgiving. They're getting more comfortable around each other. CJ's confidence is stronger than it had been in the past, and they are so cute together," Eliza commented. "I would like to be a mouse out in the brush when they bump into each other, wouldn't you?"

Looking out the window, they watched CJ heading straight for the same area Annie was working in. He had been to the barn and spent a few minutes with JoJo. This reminded him of when he was young and had chores to finish before he could go for a ride. As he went around a corner into the area he knew offered the best cuttings, he ran right into Annie as she bent over, clipping some lower branches. The bump startled her, she jumped up and screamed, the scream startled CJ, he dropped his clippers and basket and screamed back at her, and there they stood, eye to eye, mouths open, and neither able to speak a word!

As the moments of silence passed, Annie got herself settled down and asked him, "What are you trying to do, scare me half to death, sneaking up on me like that? I was already a bit shaken, thinking I heard something, and then this!" she scolded him. "You're lucky I'm clipping branches and not hunting rabbits! You could have been blasted!"

They stood there staring at each other and then both started to laugh.

"So, did Eliza send you out to check on me?" Annie asked.

"Actually, I think they may have set me up. Seems they knew you were out here and sent me to gather clippings anyway. They'll do anything for a new story to tell."

They continued to clip and gather and soon had the basket and wagon full. "I think we may have plenty for the inside and out," CJ said, as he put his clippers in his pocket. "If you want to pull the wagon, I'll grab the basket."

As they walked back, they talked about the gathering. Annie had never been part of such a big family holiday. She was excited for them. She was almost envious, although looking forward to her dad's visit for the holidays. As they passed the cottage, they talked about the surprise for Eliza. Annie thought she deserved it.

"I think this cottage would make a wonderful first home," Annie commented as they passed the front door.

"A home? What are you talking about," CJ questioned her as they stopped for a moment. "It isn't much bigger than a closet in there."

"Oh, but it would be so cozy, just imagine, and so romantic," blushing as she realized the direction the conversation had taken.

"Romantic!" CJ snarled. "Don't see how two people tripping over each other while living in a closet equals romance. But then, I'm not a girl!"

She slapped him on the arm and started on her way up the path.

He laughed, thinking wow, what muscles. "So, how long are you planning to stay out and help?" he asked.

"I hadn't really thought about it," she replied. "I have things ready for the holidays at my apartment. I guess I got so anxious since my dad is coming in, I got ahead of myself. I didn't decorate as elaborately as you are here, and I didn't have near as much cleaning to do. My apartment is like living in a 'closet,' so I guess I'm lucky that I am a girl!" she laughed. "I hope he's comfortable there. I think he's as anxious for the visit as I am."

"I'm sure he will be fine. The company is what he is coming for anyway. Have you thought about bringing him out here for dinner with us on Christmas Eve? You are more than welcome to join us."

"Oh, I couldn't think of barging in on your family holiday like that. The conversation never came up. I just wanted to come out and help, and by doing so, I knew I would learn a lot about the traditional way of decorating a wonderful place like this. Someday, I hope to live in the country and have a place for Pete and a few animals of my own. I would love to have a small garden. Well, I'm certainly getting carried away, aren't I?"

"Nothing wrong with talking about your dreams. I remember when I was away at school, all I could think about was having my own restaurant. I missed home. I knew after the first semester it wasn't for me. I just prayed for guidance, and it all fell into place." CJ assured her.

"That's a nice story. I had no idea that you found your dream by following your heart," she smiled at him gently. "Now who sounds like a girl?" Laughing, she took off running, pulling the wagon behind her, squealing down the path, knowing he would be right on her heels, and he was.

Aunt Mildred and Eliza came out the front door to see what was going on as they reached the porch. CJ grabbed the back of her jacket, and pulled her to the ground, pinning her down until she said, uncle.

"Now, who's a girl?" CJ said as he took her hand to help her up.

They brushed off and stood innocently looking at Eliza and Aunt Mildred standing there watching them. The ladies turned and walked back into the house, not saying a word. CJ and Annie burst out laughing.

"Guess we better straighten up before we get grounded," Annie said with a big smile.

"Yea sure would hate to get sent to my room and miss out on all this work," CJ joined in. "Come on, I'll teach you how to wire the branches and lights and decorate the windows. That is if you want to learn."

"Just show me the way," she replied. "That's what I'm here for."

They worked together for the next few hours. All the windows and doors were dressed in greenery. The Christmas spirit was alive and well at Slipknot.

"Ok, come on out and see if this meets with your approval you two!" CJ yelled from the front porch.

As Eliza and Aunt Mildred stepped out the door, they were in awe of the showpiece the two had created.

"Wow, this is amazing. You make a good pair. It looks just like I hoped it would. Thank you for all your work," Eliza said as she turned to hug them. "How about I put on a pot of coffee and bring out a snack. We can sit out here and admire your work. You must be starving."

"I am hungry, guess it is later than I thought," CJ spoke up. "Do you have soup?"

"I have potato soup. Won't take but a few minutes to warm it up. There is a loaf of crusty bread to go with it. You and Annie have a seat on the swing, and I'll bring it out."

"I was hoping to go for a ride yet before it got dark," Annie spoke up. "But I suppose I could do it another time if it doesn't work out."

CJ could see the disappointment in her eyes. "Come on, I'll help you saddle up JoJo, and you can get that ride in. There is plenty of time. I can wait and eat with you when you get back if you like."

"I'd appreciate the help, but you don't need to wait to eat," she said. "By the time I get back, I'll need to start home anyway. I can just eat a sandwich or something at my apartment. I would really like to take that ride."

They went to the barn, and Aunt Mildred went in to help Eliza. They chatted a bit while they got everything ready, and as they came out they found CJ sitting on the swing with a far–away look on his face. He hadn't been this somber since he decided to talk to Eliza about planning the gathering.

"My, oh my, what is with that face?" Aunt Mildred asked. "You look like a dying duck in a hail storm!"

CJ started laughing. "What is that supposed to mean! I have never heard that expression before in my life. Did I really look that bad?"

"Well, not quite, but I can see you are troubled. Now, you may as well spill it, because you know we won't let you rest until you do," Aunt Mildred continued as she set the tray of soup down on the small table by the swing. Leaning over she gave him a quick kiss on the forehead and smiled, adding, "I'm going back inside to finish the kitchen. You know where you can find me if you need my advice."

Eliza came out to the porch with a cup of coffee and

some warm bread and sat beside him on the swing. "Now, what's on your mind?"

"I was just thinking about how excited Annie got when she climbed in that saddle. It was like she was genuinely happy. She looked so natural, riding off, talking to JoJo with such a tender voice. I know she misses Pete something terrible."

"She really does," Eliza agreed. "She was talking about that earlier when we were in the barn getting the clippers and wagon."

"I know her dad is coming in for Christmas. She is so excited. And she worked so hard at the Café when we served Thanksgiving dinner. The kids think the world of her. She fits in as if this were her hometown. I think she'll stay. I wondered if we could call her dad and ask him to bring Pete here to live at the Homestead. If that is okay with you, that is," he said, looking at Eliza for her blessing on the idea. "It would be the best Christmas present anyone could give her, besides her dad."

"I love that idea," Eliza said. "It's just like you to come up with something so thoughtful. Pete is more than welcome to live here. I think JoJo would love the company, and maybe you would come out and ride more often if you had Annie and Pete to ride with."

"I might. I just know I'd like to try and reach him and see how he feels about the idea. Do you know if he is flying or driving?" CJ asked Eliza.

"I think he is driving. Annie mentioned he was

bringing up a few things she wanted for her apartment, and he will have presents no doubt. I don't have his number though," Eliza said, worrying about how they would be able to find it.

"That won't be a problem," CJ assured her. "I can find it online easy enough. Would you be comfortable talking to him? You would do a better job of explaining than I would," CJ continued with a bit of anticipation in his voice.

"I'd be happy to. We can talk about the ranch she worked at in the summers so I can get the name of her hometown for you. I don't think she will get suspicious," Eliza finished. "Now, are you ready to eat?"

"I'm more than ready, I'm starving. It smells wonderful. Is this the recipe you were telling me about, Eliza?" he questioned.

"It is, and you are going to love it. Aunt Mildred made it for me the first night she arrived. I could eat it every day."

He finished his soup as Eliza was bringing out a coffee cake for a sweet stopper as Aunt Mildred taught her. The evening was cool. It felt like winter was in the air. They weren't sure if the weather had really changed, or it was just the atmosphere. It was close to dusk, and no one made so much as a move to go inside.

Annie and JoJo rode up to the barn. CJ walked out to help Annie put the saddle away and close things up.

"Well, did you have a nice ride, you two?" CJ asked as he came through the door.

"Wonderful," Annie replied, with new energy in her voice. "Thank you for letting me ride her. Eliza told me that she has pretty much been your horse as long as she could remember. I appreciate you sharing her with me."

"No problem," he said. "You must be starving. That potato soup is great. It's just what you need after all the hard work and long ride. There's some left. You go on. I'll bed her down and close up. Go on," he insisted.

"If you're sure," she hesitated. "I am hungry."

"Won't take me long, and of course I don't mind."

As Annie got to the porch, Eliza had a tray ready for her with a warm bowl of soup and a fresh cup of coffee.

"Sit right down here young lady, here's your tray. I hope it is ok."

"Smells wonderful," Annie said as she took the first bite. "I guess I was hungrier than I thought. This is delicious. No doubt another one of your famous family recipes. I love it here more and more each visit."

CJ made it back to the porch and joined in the conversation. A good hour went by when Annie realized the time.

"I guess I should be getting back to town. Unless I can help with the dishes or anything else this evening," she offered.

"Don't think you have to be constantly working while you are here. It is up to you, what do you feel like doing?" Eliza asked.

"I'm open to suggestions," Annie replied. "Got any ideas?"

"Why don't you spend the night here tonight," CJ spoke up. "They can keep you busy half the night if you let them, and with most of the cleaning done, you're just getting to the fun part. They'll be decorating half the night. You don't want to miss that. I am planning on sleeping over at Uncle Oliver's. He asked me to keep him company, and I told him I'd be over around nine. He turns in early, and I've had a long day, too."

"Well, sounds like that is settled," Aunt Mildred declared. "I have an extra gown in the Winnie. We can make you comfortable. And CJ is right; we are getting to the fun stuff now. We may even bake something before the night is over."

"Doesn't sound like you are going anywhere," Eliza said as she gave Annie a hug. "I'm so glad you are here. You are one of us now, there's no getting away."

"I like that!" Annie said, and she hugged Eliza right back.

The evening was pleasant. The house was coming together nicely. Aunt Mildred finished organizing the kitchen cabinets. She put out some Christmas dishes she found a way in the back of the cupboard. They had aged to them. Eliza vaguely remembered the pattern. As they talked about the kitchen being so festive, Eliza brought in some greenery to lay in the window sills.

"These will be just enough to offer a little fragrance to the kitchen blending nicely with the aromas of the baking and holiday dishes we'll be preparing," Eliza explained as she stepped up on the ladder to reach the sink. "I don't remember this crock with the holly leaves and berries. Where did you find this?" she asked Aunt Mildred as she shook it, not hearing anything rattle, but could tell it had something in it.

"Oh, I had that with me in the Winnie," she casually replied. "It's Bill, in his Holiday urn. I was feeling guilty that he was isolated out there and we were all having such a good time in here. He loved the holidays so much. That's why I brought one of my favorite holiday crocks to change him over into for Christmas. I knew I probably wouldn't make the coast before the New Year."

"OH NO!!!" Eliza exclaimed. "I'm sorry I was shaking him that way. I had no idea. Honestly, I had no idea. If I had, I would have left him to sit on the sill and not disturbed him at all. I'm so sorry, you should have told me, Aunt Mildred, you should have told me!" Eliza repeated.

"Settle down, dear. I'm sure he didn't feel a thing. I never gave it a thought. I'm so accustomed to having him close by, it's like second nature for me. I hope I didn't upset you," Aunt Mildred said, rubbing Eliza's shoulders. "I would never do anything to upset you. If it bothers you, I will take him back to the Winnie. He will be fine."

"No. It's not a problem, not at all," Eliza assured her. "We will just set him back up here among the greenery, and he can enjoy the company, same as the rest of us. No one else has to be the wiser unless you want to introduce him or something?" Eliza looked to Aunt Mildred for the answer.

"No, dear, that won't be necessary. We will just put him way over here in the corner where no one will think anything of the crock. Just look at it as another antique in this lovely Homestead."

Annie stood there with wide eyes, having a difficult time understanding the conversation she just witnessed. "Who is Bill?"

Chapter Twelve

Mr. Simpkins was my dad. Call me Jon...

৽৽৽

O ver the course of the next week, Aunt Mildred didn't see much of Eliza at all. She was at the top of her game furnishing the cottage. She wanted it to be all Eliza hoped for. The daily treasure hunts were what she had been missing since Bill passed away and she sold their business. Often times she wondered if she had made the right decision. Loneliness played a part in that. Perhaps the trip to the coast gave her time to search for what would make her feel necessary and productive again. One thing she was certain of since she had been involved with family again, she felt as if she had her life back. It would not be easy to move on after the holidays. Her focus, for now, was Eliza.

After long days working on the cottage, Aunt Mildred turned in at the Homestead. She didn't want to spend the time traveling back and forth to the apartment. That was her excuse, but she knew this was the only way she could keep the secret of her progress. It was exciting to see the plans come together.

The shop had been slow as expected. Eliza worked during every spare moment knitting scarves for everyone that was coming to the gathering. Something handmade was a must under the tree. She might actually get them finished. As she sat and knitted, she went over the past weekend in her mind. Not only were their accomplishments exciting, but she enjoyed the time spent with CJ, Annie, and Aunt Mildred. She felt the bond strengthening as time went on. Oh, if only things could remain as they are. Life goes on; nothing can be taken for granted. That she knew too well.

Annie dropped by the shop just before closing on Wednesday afternoon. The holidays were getting so close, and she was so anxious. Her dad's visit had her wound up. She wanted to see when the Café would be open during the holiday weekend so she could take her dad there to meet CJ.

"Well, he is usually open Christmas Eve morning for breakfast, and then he closes until the twenty–seventh," Eliza explained. "I suppose your dad is just as anxious as you are. Do you think he'll do all right on the drive?"

"I think so," Annie replied. "He is comfortable traveling, and I'm sure he will take his time getting here. I told him to allow plenty of time to stop and get out to stretch."

"Is there someone to watch over things at home while he is gone? And who will care for Pete while he is away? What about the ranch just down the road? I remember you telling me of the time you spent there while growing up. Was it on the same road as your home?" Eliza pried.

"Well, yes, it is just down the road, I'm surprised you remembered. It's on Sundown Lane in Golden, Texas. I always loved to write out my address," she smiled. "Seems so long ago. Not even a year has gone by, and it feels like forever."

"I'm glad you are happy here. We feel blessed to have you in our lives. Thank you again for all your help this weekend and the wonderful company. Aunt Mildred was dreading Christmas. This has made her so happy." Eliza said as she took Annie by the hand.

"We're all taking away some wonderful memories from experience. I wouldn't trade it for anything," Annie assured her. "I want you to know that."

"I hope you have a good evening. I'm not doing much except working on a few more Christmas gifts. You can call me anytime you want to talk."

"Thank you. I don't want to wear out my welcome. I always worry about that. I don't want to be in the way." Annie started to dwell. "I've always been taught to wait until I'm asked before inviting myself along. Do you think I have been butting in?"

"No, you haven't, and as I said, you are always more than welcome. You know, if we don't get to meet your dad during the holiday, we'll all be very disappointed. Unless you don't want to share him with us, that is. I never thought you might want to keep him all for yourself."

"I've talked so much about all of you, he honestly can't wait to get here and put faces with names. Those were his words exactly." Annie was smiling again. "I need to hurry along now, I have a few errands to run, and I know you are busy whether you will admit it or not." She turned, gave Eliza a quick hug and out the door she went.

Annie hadn't even cleared the sidewalk and Eliza had CJ on the phone giving him the name of the street and town. He had the phone number before she hung up.

"Be sure to explain to him that we will take very good care of Pete, and he won't be a burden at all. He will actually keep JoJo company. I hope this works out Do you think he has a horse trailer?" CJ stammered all over himself.

"Just don't worry so much. I'm sure he can get a horse trailer. If he doesn't have one, there is a large ranch down the road. Now just keep your cool and let me get things lined up. I'll call you as soon as I talk to him."

"Thanks, Aunt Eliza, you're the greatest!" CJ said just before he hung up.

She flipped the sign to closed and ran upstairs. She grabbed her phone and plopped down in her comfy chair. Suddenly she remembered she hadn't seen Cody. Oh well, she can check on him when she finishes. This was more important. She dialed the phone. After several rings, a strong voice with a definite Texas draw answered the phone. Reality set in and Eliza found herself at a loss for words momentarily. The second hello and she got her wits about her. "Is this Mr. Simpkins?" she replied.

"Well, this is Jon. Mr. Simpkins was my dad," he

replied with a robust laugh. "Now just what can I help you with Missy?"

That Texas voice and sense of humor, Eliza liked him already. "Are you Annie's dad?" she asked.

"Annie, is there something wrong? Is she okay? She lives so far away now. She hasn't been in an accident, or anything has her?" he asked frantically.

"No, no, it is nothing like that. I'm Eliza, and Annie has become very dear to me. We are here in Spring Forrest. I didn't mean to startle you." Eliza continued to try and calm him down.

"Thank God!" he replied, sounding so relieved. "I just worry about her like she's still my little girl. I'm sorry about that. What can I do for you? I've heard a lot about you if you are the same Eliza Annie is always talking about."

"Well, I'm the only Eliza that I know of in this part of town, and we do spend quite a bit of time together, so it must be me," she went on. "That's why I'm calling. I have a special request."

"Oh, just what could that be?" he sounded curious.

"Did she tell you about Slipknot Farm, my old Homestead that we spend weekends at?"

"Every time I talk to her. She called me last evening so wound up about the fun she had helping get ready for some holiday gathering your family had planned. She couldn't tell me fast enough. I finally had to stop her and tell her to take a breath. Have you noticed how she tends to ramble when she gets excited? Gets it from her mom, I reckon."

"Yes, I have noticed, and I'm not so sure it is from her mom," Eliza said with a giggle. "Anyway, CJ and I were talking this weekend while Annie was riding JoJo, my horse at Slipknot. She has some years on her, and she doesn't get as much attention from CJ as she used to. We wondered if it would be possible for you to bring Pete here when you come for Christmas. Annie doesn't have any idea we are calling you, and it would be a wonderful surprise for her if we could work it out. Pete would be well cared for. My brother Oliver lives on the property and cares for the other animals. Annie would be close enough to come out and ride anytime she pleased. It may even get CJ interested in coming out and riding JoJo with them." She waited patiently for a response.

"CJ, is that the young fellow with the Café?" he questioned. "The one I have heard so much about from her, your son or nephew or cousin or something?"

"He is my nephew. They have become involved in several projects together, and yes, he is the one who owns the Café. In fact, she and her class helped him with a Thanksgiving Dinner for charity. They had quite a turn-out. Did she tell you about that?"

"Yep, she sure did. Said it was one of the best Thanksgivings she had in a long time. Annie always was generous with her time. This CJ, is he about her age? Is he a good boy?" he asked Eliza without hesitation.

"The very best," she replied without giving it a second thought. "I'm sure you will like him. I'm expecting you to come to Slipknot and join the gathering while you are here. We were hoping to invite you and Annie out for Christmas Eve. That way you could come here first when you get to town and drop off the horse trailer. We can get Pete situated, bedded down and comfortable. Then when you and Annie come out on Christmas Eve, you can surprise her. She has worked so hard helping us get ready for our family, we want nothing more than to have her family join us. Do you think any of this is possible?"

"You know, I've been a bit concerned about the old horse anyway. He seems to be grieving for Annie. Funny how an animal notices change. He hasn't been the same since she moved away. Kind of like me, I guess, just hasn't been the same. Not the same at all. I think I can round up a trailer, and bring him. Wouldn't be a problem. I know I can make the trip easy enough. Sounds like this may be just what he needs. Is she still wearing her red cowboy boots?" he asked.

"Almost every time I see her when she isn't teaching. Is there a story to them? I know she is adorable and it has become her trademark around town." Eliza replied.

"Her mom gave them to her for her birthday the year before she passed away. Annie holds them dear. She misses her momma so. She would never be without her red boots. Has a part of her momma with her all the time. Least that's how I see it. Glad she has kept true to herself in that way. Wasn't sure how she would handle it out east. Give me your number, Eliza, and I'll keep up with you on the plans, but as far as I'm concerned, I think we can figure it done. Sure was nice talking to you and I am relieved knowing Annie has people who care so much about her where she lives. I'll be talking to you soon. Take care now, and thanks again for calling me."

Eliza assured him Annie was in good hands and told him to call anytime he wanted to. They all looked forward to spending the holidays with them. They said their good-byes. A quick sprint down the stairs and she was out the door heading to fill CJ in. He was outside changing his menu sign for tomorrow morning when he spotted Eliza almost running across the street. Either something was on fire, or she had news. He hadn't seen her move this fast since, well, he didn't know since when.

"You move pretty well for an old woman.

What's on fire!" he yelled across the street.

"Do you want to hear the news or not?" she yelled back. "Cause I can go back where I came from and just let you wonder!" Not that she could ever do that. She would burst if she couldn't share the news. "I just got off the phone with Annie's dad about the trip. Such a nice man. His name is Jon. We had a great conversation about Christmas. He is all for the idea of bringing Pete. Seems Pete is grieving for Annie, and I think he is as well, but didn't admit it. Anyway, he is going to keep in touch, and we can plan the surprise for her on Christmas Eve. We just have to invite them out to celebrate with us. Doubt that will be too difficult." Eliza was so excited.

"So, he won't have any trouble getting a horse trailer and pulling it that distance?" CJ questioned. "If it weren't this time of year, I could probably fly down and ride back with him, or figure out a way to be of some help."

"No, that isn't necessary. He said he would take his time and travel safe, and thought the trip would be easy enough on Pete. He has a neighbor with a horse trailer. And I gathered from the conversation that he is really anxious to meet us. He and Annie have detailed conversations about her new home and friends here. Puts his mind at ease anyway, knowing she is around people that genuinely care for her." Eliza smiled at CJ. "She has even told him all about you!"

CJ's eyes got big! "Good I hope! Sure would hate to get off on the wrong foot with him. Don't know why, but I have a feeling he is a big man, maybe the Texas thing, but seems like he will be built like John Wayne. Hey, maybe that is where he got the name, Jon? You think?"

"Calm down there little buddy. You are letting your imagination get the best of you. It's going to be tough to keep this secret. And her mom gave her the red boots on the birthday before she passed away. That makes them extra special. Her dad really misses her. I suppose the house is very quiet."

Eliza felt a little blue for him. She spent plenty of time alone but had never had a family of her own to lose or move on. That would be a difficult life change. This holiday just keeps getting better and better. Slipknot has celebrated many special occasions, but this gathering may just top them all. How nice it would be if Mimzie were here to join in the fun. Somehow, Eliza felt she was.

As the week finished, time went a bit slower without many customers. The regulars came by to wish Eliza happy holidays and get an update on the gathering. Seems the town was buzzing with the excitement. In a small way, it seems to have them in the mood to do more for their own families this year. Everyone needs to look at the holidays in a different aspect from time to time, Rosie told Eliza on a quick visit. She wanted to show her the bag she finished crocheting for her husband's secretary before she gave it as a gift. They sat by the fireplace and chatted a bit before Rosie left. The excitement builds, but Eliza and CJ pinkie-swore not to tell anyone in town about Annie's gift. If it had leaked, it surely got back to her through her own classroom if not somewhere else.

Eliza wondered how Aunt Mildred was doing. She hadn't seen much of her, even less as the weekend grew near. She was so anxious to go out to Slipknot and see the cottage. Knowing how Aunt Mildred loved to search for the treasures in unusual places, she could hardly wait to see the finished product. It has to be magnificent. That Eliza knew for certain. What work this had to be, so much to accomplish in a week. She hoped Aunt Mildred didn't wear herself out before the gathering. Somehow, she knew Aunt Mildred was enjoying every minute. She just wondered if she was missing her, too.

Finally Friday! One more day to get through and then out to Slipknot for the weekend. Eliza had been working steadily on the scarves, one more to go, and done. She had such a nice variety and made each scarf with a special person in mind. That made it fun. She had come across some old wrapping paper in the attic at the Homestead, fashioned in the primitive homespun style, so she picked out some woolen yarns to make embellishments and chains to use as ribbons. Each gift tag cut and hand written and had old Christmas Seal stamps for decorations. She just loved having the time to spend on gifts.

As she finished the last scarf, she still had plenty of time to get the shop swept and tidied up before it was time to close. CJ came by to drop off a sandwich for her and get an update on her weekend plans.

"What time are you going out to Slipknot this evening?" he asked. "Just wondering how Aunt Mildred is doing? I bet she is having the best time. She was so wound up about that cottage. Must be a woman thing. Annie said she thought it would be a great first home! Have you ever heard such nonsense? Like living in a closet if you ask me." CJ went on and on.

"Take a breath, CJ. You seem to be wound up now. Yes, I suppose it is a woman thing. We love cozy, comforting surrounding, and the men, although they enjoy the comforts of home, don't usually know what goes into making a house a home. Have you ever thought about that?" Eliza waited patiently for an answer.

"Well, not really, I guess. My own place has all the necessities. What more do I need?" he replied sharply.

"A woman?"

"Enough said," CJ replied, quickly changing the subject. "Like I asked, when are you going out to Slipknot?"

"I plan to leave soon after I close shop. I have most of my chores done. Just need to throw a few clothes in the truck, and I'll be on my way. I do need to stop at the market. We'll need food for the weekend."

"I want to come out for a while so we can make a list of the groceries we need for the gathering. I can get larger quantities from my suppliers. Buying in bulk will be a big help on the budget. I've put aside some money since this was my idea in the first place. All the extra work it has caused, I want to furnish the food. It is the least I can do." CJ just smiled at her.

"That is a big burden for one person to take on. You don't need to be responsible for that. Your mom sent me a check for food. I haven't done anything with it yet. How about I give it to you, and when you order you can use it how you see fit. That'll take a lot off of me, and it will go for what she intended."

Eliza went to the counter and pulled out a card that Rachel sent.

"You may as well take the card and read it too. That way, when you start to feel like this has been a burden, you can see how it has touched everyone. This entire family is so excited that you came up with such a tremendous idea. Boy, are you going to get the hugs and kisses this Christmas!" Eliza reached over and tickled him. "You CJ are, well, like our hero!"

"Okay, that's it, I'm out of here! You're driving me crazy, and I don't see this attitude of yours getting any better until spring." CJ headed for the door. "Make your list, I'll be out around seven tonight if you have time for me."

"That'll be lovely," she replied.

He slammed the door. She finished her work and was on the way up the stairs to pack. "Come on Cody, we're off to the Homestead for the weekend!"

Chapter Thirteen

Driving down the lane right into Slipknot past...

As Eliza made it down the road, she felt as if she had just driven into Christmas past! The Homestead lights were lit on the outside and inside. The windows were dressed in greenery, and the tree on the porch made it all feel so welcoming. The large wreath was on the barn and lights on the fence surrounding the corral, even Uncle Oliver had put lights on his home. He hadn't done that before. This holiday is going to be good for everyone, she thought to herself as she parked. That is when she saw it. It made her gasp. The cottage. It was all lit up, and the same greenery adorned the windows and small porch as the Homestead. She noticed curtains and could see bits and pieces of furnishings through the windows. The cottage looked full. Almost as if it had been lived in for years. There were even window boxes on the windows facing the driveway. They, too, had greenery and white lights filling them with holiday warmth. She couldn't move. Never would she expect someone to go to these lengths for her.

Just then, Annie, CJ, Aunt Mildred, and Oliver appeared on the front porch. They looked like Mr. and Mrs. Clause and a couple of elves standing there. Well, if you have ever seen Mrs. Clause in a red curly wig and an elf in red cowboy boots, that is! That just made them all the more special. Eliza suddenly realized she was looking through a hot blur of tears. Trying to shake it off before they got a good look at her, she picked up Cody and tossed him out the door, then gathered her bag of gifts she had wrapped along with her purse. CJ started her way to help.

"What's the matter now? Nothing much to say all of a sudden?" CJ mouthed at her as he gave her a quick hug. "I've got this bag. Do you have anything else to bring in?"

"Actually, I have a satchel with my clothes and a box of food in the back. If you can't get it, I'll make another trip. I didn't expect to see you and Annie here. The Homestead is just breathtaking. I'm a bit overwhelmed."

"I don't think I've ever seen you like this," CJ replied with a genuinely concerned look on his face. "I'm not sure you're going to be able to handle going in. I'm a manly-man, and it brought a tear to my eye!" he said, consoling her, all the while holding back laughter and trying so hard to control the little boy in him that wanted to tease her.

"Nice," she snapped at him. "I can't help it. I'm a bit emotional right now. I'm just so stinkin' happy!" She slapped him on the back. "Now quit dragging your feet and carry this stuff in. It isn't exactly warm out here. Besides, I have plenty to do."

"Well, there's the Eliza I know!" CJ said, as he loaded up his arms and followed her to the porch.

As she walked up the steps, she met Aunt Mildred with a hug. "I have missed you. You haven't been in touch this week. Glad to see you're all right," Eliza whispered in her ear before letting go.

"Well, dear. I did have a few things on my plate. And just so you know, I cannot tell you how much I've enjoyed every minute. I feel like I'm ten years younger!" she said with a smile. "Perhaps part of it's the red hair!" laughing while she primped in the door glass. "Been spending a lot of time in the VW. By the way, remind me when I go to bed that you brought that cat of yours, so I park my friend out of reach."

"Be glad to. Now, is there anything you would like to show me, or do I have to wait until morning?" Eliza said wringing her hands. "I've had a trying week. It was very difficult not to drive out and peek."

"Okay, dear. Let's take a walk. I'm as anxious to show off your cottage as I believe you are to see it. Let's put your stuff inside." Aunt Mildred opened the door so Eliza could step in.

As she walked in, she was mesmerized by the aroma of something wonderful; a fragrant blend of herbs and spices that filled the Homestead.

"What is this wonderful aroma that has me by the nose?" she turned and asked. "I can't say I've ever smelled the likes. Have you been cooking all day?" she asked Aunt Mildred.

"Hardly!" she replied. "Do you think I have had time on my hands? Have you forgotten about the cottage?"

"Sorry, I just can't believe how wonderful it smells. What is it, might I ask? And who is responsible?" Eliza waited for a reply.

"Well, the school was out, and I didn't know what to do with myself this afternoon, and I saw Miss Mildred go by in her VW. I waived. She stopped. We chatted a few minutes, I offered to come out and prepare dinner. I hope that was okay. Here I am just inviting myself out and butting into your lovely weekend." Annie finished.

"Are you kidding me?" Eliza asked, walking over to Annie, giving her a hug. "When will you realize that you are a family? Now, what are you cooking? It smells wonderful."

"I'm making Dinner in a Pumpkin like my momma taught me. It was one of my favorites growing up, so I thought I'd share it with you. I also made Butterhorns. I found the recipe in your box and tried really hard to do it like you taught me on my first visit. I'm sure they won't be as good as yours, but I tried. I really tried. Just wanted to contribute," she smiled. "Now, I want to see the cottage as bad as you do. What do you say, Miss Mildred? Can we take that walk?" Annie asked.

"I thought you'd never ask. I'm ready when you are. What do you say, Eliza? Want to see the cottage?"

"Lead the way. It's the moment I've been waiting for all week!"

As they started out the door, Oliver said he had a couple of odds and ends to finish up before he turned in. He had some busy days lately, and it was catching up with him. He was going to have a bowl of leftover soup and call it a night. He gave Eliza a hug, a quick handshake with Annie and CJ, and a wink at Aunt Mildred, and he was on his way.

Eliza actually had butterflies as they walked down the path. The cottage seemed to say 'Welcome Home.' The windows were warmly lit, and the outside so festive.

"You even landscaped. How did you manage this? My, you must have been busy every minute and spent a fortune."

"Come on around to the door, dear. The best is yet to come." Aunt Mildred reached to open the red door that was decorated with a simple strand of greenery all around and tiny white lights. She had hung an oversized Christmas stocking on the door with several old toys tucked inside and a vintage mailbox beside the door, lid open and filled with an assortment of Christmas Cards. She hadn't left out a single detail. As the door swung open, everyone gasped. Even CJ! It was unbelievable.

The first thing they spotted was the bed. An antique sleigh bed, white-washed wood, and layered with quilts and throws; pillow with shams and what looked like old lace curtains used as a dust ruffle. It was dressed in sage green and shades of taupe with some dark red for accent. There

A Simple Stitch, A Common Thread

were braided rugs in shades of greens and reds; a large one under the two overstuffed chairs and small white table in a sitting area off the kitchen, and a similar one under the bed extending out each side to cushion the early morning floors. The curtains were simple white cotton, left open to enjoy the view of the lake in the mornings and the Christmas lights adorning the Homestead and outbuildings at night. The kitchen was furnished with a small island and a couple of stools, perfect for breakfast. Open shelves above the small length of the counter were well stocked with colorful dishware and special coffees and teas. Baskets held snacks and flatware, while a granite dishpan held kitchen linens.

They went into the bathroom, and it was even more amazing. There was a large white chenille rug softening the brick floor. The window and shower curtains were made from a worn chenille bedspread that had been cut and repurposed. An old cabinet that Eliza recognized from the barn had been painted red and stood near the shower with the door left open, exposing stacks of fluffy white towels. Matching bathrobes hung from old wooden spools mounted to the inside of the cabinet door, and another granite wash pan atop the cabinet was well stocked with shampoos, lotions, body washes, powders, and everything imaginable. The sink was mounted on yet another old cabinet from the barn. There was a large round mirror hanging above it with a white- washed frame and a pair of lights on either side made from a pair of old porch lights with blue mason jars for shades. The soap dish and toothbrush holder, as well as the towel holders, were reproductions in graniteware, and a rectangular baking pan housed washcloths and facial wipes.

212

The lighting throughout the cottage was unique. An old floor lamp with a marble base stood between the comfy chairs in the sitting area, while a mismatched pair of old bed lamps hung on each side of the headboard for late night reading. The island in the kitchen was built from old barn wood, and a small chandelier hung above it.

The vintage wardrobe in the bedroom was painted sage green with white porcelain knobs. The inside was painted white, one side storing an extra set of bedding and pillows, and on the other a small television with a DVD player and nice assortment of movies from new releases, old classics, and of course many favorite Christmas movies that were a must. Extra quilts were draped over the backs of chairs, and a small bookshelf was filled with an assortment of hardback books and several board games. There were old mirrors in unique shapes and sizes with mismatched frames hung throughout to reflect light from the windows. Old prints, many farm animals, and scenes were tucked in just the right places. There was a space left open for the cradle found in the attic for Jaxon.

Everyone just stood there, utterly amazed. Who wouldn't love to call this home for the holidays? There was an antique feather tree by the door. It was adorned with miniature blown glass ornaments and a small tree skirt fashioned from scraps of an old quilt. It stood on a fern stand from a shop close by where the furniture is built by local craftsmen.

There was a small stereo in a corner cabinet near the sitting area by the wood stove. Aunt Mildred had a soothing assortment of Christmas music playing softly.

There were no candles, she explained, due to the location of the Homestead and cabin. She didn't feel comfortable with an open flame. Instead, she opted for old crock bowls filled with pinecones, fir branches, and cinnamon sticks to offer the scents of the season.

"How? How on earth? How on earth could you accomplish this in a week?" Eliza stammered. "Aunt Mildred, it's awesome. I can't begin to put my feelings into words. I don't know what I am trying to say. I just never want to leave. It couldn't be more perfect."

"Hearing your voice and seeing how much you love it means more to me than any gift I could ever receive. This is going to be such a memorable holiday. And I was worried about being depressed, spending my holiday on the road, alone. Now I'm a part of this. This is just where I want to be." Aunt Mildred went on. "I talked to my children and grandchildren this week while I was out and about. I told them what I was doing, and shared the plans for the gathering. They told me that I sounded more like myself than I have since Bill passed away. They're so thankful I'm back, and wanted me to pass on thanks. They asked if you are making this gathering a tradition, and if so, could they please be invited next year."

"I'd like nothing better than to have them gather with us. It's too bad they have plans in place this year. They would be more than welcome, right CJ?" Eliza turned to him for reassurance.

She looked around and spotted him with Annie sitting in the overstuffed chairs with their heads together, talking up a storm. Although she couldn't hear what they were saying, she could see one of them point at something, and the other agree, sparking another idea. They were so involved in the conversation they didn't even hear her.

"Oh, I told them that, dear," Aunt Mildred smiled. They've had plans in place for months now. We came to an agreement on their plans long before they made reservations. I assured them I would be fine, and now, low and behold, I really am fine, fine as frog hair!" she chuckled, her entire body jiggling.

"Just what are you two discussing so intensely over there?" Aunt Mildred questioned.

It caught them by surprise.

"We're talking about the ideas you had for the cottage," CJ said. "I know I've seen the cabinets you used in the bathroom and for the island. They were in the shed as long as I can remember. I would have never thought of using them like this. I thought my apartment was nice. Now I feel like I'm going home to a motel room. It just never occurred to me to look at things in a different perspective like you have."

"Me either," Annie joined in. "I love my apartment, but now I'm looking at it differently, too. I hope Dad feels at home here. He may not think much of it at all. Looking back, Mom really made our house a home."

"All right, the both of you need to settle down over there. Don't be hard on yourselves. You have homes that suit your needs for this season in your life." Aunt Mildred comforted them. "And when you need more, call me. Our sign didn't say 'If you can't find it, Bill and Mil will' all those years for nothing. I have a sixth sense about seeking out Antiques and Uniques. It's my God-given talent. Remember that!"

Annie and CJ shook their heads and just smiled.

"Now, what are you doing with your dad when he gets here? Do you have big plans for him on Christmas Eve?" Aunt Mildred questioned. "Because we are anxious to meet him. Should we count on the two of you for Christmas Eve dinner?"

Annie was so excited. "I really didn't have much planned for Christmas Eve, actually. I thought we could have dinner at my apartment, and maybe take a walk. We won't have that many presents to open. I haven't been able to come up with anything very special for him. That would be a great plan. I can't wait to tell him," she giggled.

"How are you planning to sleep at your apartment? Have you thought that through?" Eliza asked. "Don't you only have one bedroom?"

"Yes, but my couch is a hide-a-bed, and I can pull it out and sleep on it and give him the bedroom. I know he will argue, but that will be more comfy for him, and give him some privacy. It will be fine."

"As long as you have it figured out. If you need anything, just ask. As far as I know, my apartment may even be vacant. You know you have options," Eliza assured her again. "Now, I know we have things to do, fun things, but I just hate to leave."

"You know, dear, there isn't any company coming for a week. You could be the first to sleep out here tonight. It is only fair. It's your gift, you should be the first to enjoy it," Aunt Mildred reminded her.

"Wonderful idea," Eliza said. "I wouldn't have thought of that. You know, I'm going to do it.

I'm going to spend the night out here. Then I can take it all in as I drift off, and sleep as long as I like. Now, we have things to do so let's all put on our elf hats and curly-toe shoes and get to work. Don't want to disappoint Mr. Claus now, do we?"

"I'm going to have to object," CJ spoke up. "I draw the line at hats and curly toe shoes!"

The ladies went skipping back to the Homestead, arms locked, singing "Santa Claus is Coming to Town." CJ, walking a safe distance behind them, was grumbling and shaking his head, but on the inside, his heart was smiling.

"Oh, it's a good thing we are in the country," Eliza said as they went in the door. "People would think we were hitting the eggnog early! Now, let's have that dinner in a pumpkin and rolls. I like to start with my signature recipe, Toasted Almond Fingers if that is all right with everyone else. But first, I need food!"

CJ and Annie had set the table earlier and had everything ready. The meal was as delicious as it smelled.

And Annie didn't let anyone down with her first solo try at Butterhorns. By the time they finished, everyone was stuffed.

"Annie, you out-did yourself. What a great meal," Eliza praised her. "Now, you and CJ took care of the meal, why don't the two of you take a walk out to see how JoJo is doing and I'll clean up the dishes. Aunt Mildred, I'll fix you a nice cup of tea, and you can put your feet up for a while. I have so much energy swirling around inside me, I couldn't sit still if you duct-taped me to the chair."

"Well, I was thinking about walking out to the barn to see what was left in your stockpile of goodies," CJ said. "Seems I will be looking at it differently now that I see what can be done. Annie, do you want to walk along? You might have some ideas, too."

"If you are sure you want to take on the dishes alone, Eliza," Annie asked, with a look of anticipation on her face.

"I wouldn't have offered if I wasn't up to it. Now you two go on, and you, Aunt Mildred, go over there and put your feet up, I'm going to set out some eggs and butter to bring to room temperature while I clean up, and then start the cookies. I'll ring the bell on the porch when it is time to start baking if you aren't back. Don't forget, JoJo could use some company too. And here, take these apples to the girls, the sheep haven't had much company lately either."

Off they went. Aunt Mildred headed for the rocker without argument, and Eliza went to the kitchen, got out the eggs and butter, turned to the window, looked up at the

Christmas urn and smiled. "Well, Bill looks like it will be just the two of us. So, Bill, tell me how you've been. Are you enjoying the Homestead?"

Eliza continued to work as if listening to the stories Bill had to tell. She felt wonderful.

Chapter Fourteen

**A full moon, a walk, a talk and a good start on
Christmas cookies...**

৵৵৵

Annie and CJ had a nice evening going through odds and ends of old doors, windows, bits, and pieces of hardware, and cabinets like had been used in the cottage. They searched piece by piece, making notes and talking about possibilities for each treasure. They noticed the patina of the original paint, and the character bits of rust or scratches added. They spent time with JoJo and fed the sheep. As they started out the barn door, Annie pointed out the full moon peeking up just over the roof of the Homestead.

"Wow, what a gorgeous picture," CJ commented.

"Yea almost looks like a Christmas Card. I wish I had my camera, we could use it as the picture for one next year," Annie replied.

Then suddenly, realizing what she just said, she stammered around, she tried to correct herself without making it obvious she used 'we' rather than 'I,' hoping CJ hadn't picked up on it. No such luck.

"We? Why Annie Simpkins, whatever do you mean? Are you talking to the horse or the sheep? We?" CJ egged her on until she turned red with embarrassment. "Calm down, you know I'm just teasing you. I hope you are here next Christmas. I could see 'us' as a 'we,' couldn't you?" he asked very casually.

"I never really put much thought into it," she answered with a nervous crack in her voice.

CJ could see she was starting to get a bit flustered. "Oh, I just wanted to give you something to think about. How about a walk before we go in? The old farm looks pretty in the moonlight, and after that supper, I could use a little exercise."

"Sure, I guess that would be good for us. Just don't get us lost or anything. I don't really know my way around here that well. You aren't planning on taking me out in the woods and leaving me are you?" she asked him with a smile on her face.

"No, I promise!" he replied. "Come this way first, I'm sure the reflection in the lake behind the cottage will be even better than the view over the Homestead," he said, reaching down and taking her by the hand. They walked for quite a while, neither saying a word. The silence seemed appropriate for some reason. They had a feeling of calm, of coming to a place where they both had been longing for.

Soon the bell on the porch sounded, echoing through the woods.

"We better start back as not to worry Eliza," CJ said. "It has been a nice evening. I'm glad we could spend a little time together tonight. Gave me time to think."

"What about?" Annie questioned.

"A new direction. I guess ideas were sparked by the feeling I got in the cottage, seeing that treasures can be right in front of you and go unnoticed. Does that make any sense? It's a bit hard to explain, really. It seems my need for the gathering, the thought of family together, all here to make lasting memories. Or maybe it was the need to start making some memories of my own before long. Okay, I have to stop talking now. I can see on your face you are about to tell me I sound like a girl again, and I don't know how many more times I can let you get by with that!" he smiled.

"Not this time," Annie was quick to reply. "I think I know how you feel. Looking to belong. Life is good for me now, but there is a piece missing. I was hoping when Dad got here I would feel as if my Christmas was complete. I know he will make it special, but I still feel a bit empty, too."

Just then the bell clanged even louder and longer.

"She's getting worried! I'll race you back."

CJ said as he grabbed Annie by the hand again and took off running. "Can you keep up?"

"Keep up? It's dark. The thought of being left in the

woods will give me the speed I need not only to keep up but pass you if I feel a fright," Annie replied, keeping side by side with him all the way back to the porch. "Thank you for the evening, CJ." Annie looked at him with a smile before they went in. "I needed this."

"Me too. It was good," CJ smiled back.

"Well, finally," Eliza said as she swung open the door finding them coming up the steps. "I was beginning to think something got the two of you. Didn't you hear the bell?"

"The town heard the bell!" CJ snapped at her. "We were out enjoying the full moon, walking off our dinner. We ran back as fast as we could," winking at Eliza. "You know, I had to take it easy cause I couldn't go off and leave the girl trying to keep up."

"You better watch your back, making remarks like that mister," Aunt Mildred said. "I think the girl you are talking about could easily keep up with you down most paths of life."

"Yeah, maybe so. Besides, I might just let her. Now, I'm heading back to town. I'll leave this batch of baking up to the ladies. Are you going to be at church in the morning?" CJ asked.

"I planned on it," Annie said. "Wasn't everyone?"

Eliza and Aunt Mildred both planned on joining them. After all, wasn't this really what Christmas was about? They would all meet at the Church in the morning and back out to Slipknot for a big brunch. CJ volunteered to make French toast and knew there would be plenty of good food to go with it. That should be the perfect start to another great day.

"Good night, then, I'll see you tomorrow. Annie, are you staying out here tonight, or do you need a ride back to town?" he offered.

"I'm planning to stay. I brought my clothes. I didn't really have anything else to finish up at home and hoped to help with baking. Thank you, though, for the offer."

"Have fun then."

They were up well past midnight, baking and talking, and sampling all the goodies. They finished two batches of Toasted Almond Fingers that Eliza had mixed up while she was working in the kitchen, then three batches of Pecan Tartlets, another family favorite.

"These are wonderful. They are just like eating little pecan pies," Annie said, reaching for a third one. "I love these. You have to teach me how to make these cookie recipes as good as you do, Eliza."

"Butter and practice," Eliza advised.

"What?" Annie questioned.

"That's my secret. Butter and practice. Always use real butter. Make lots of cookies, so you know the recipe and oven time well, practice, practice, practice. Besides, your friends will love you when you share the results."

They laughed the evening away, sharing so much joy

in baking together. Aunt Mildred and Eliza came up with more family tales, and before the night was over, Annie had even shared a story or two of her own, remembering her childhood in Texas and some of the times she cherished. They knew when her dad arrived they would see the genuine girl surface. There were many great days ahead.

"Well, one-thirty in the morning is plenty late for a Saturday night before church, don't you think?" Eliza asked as she noticed the time. "I had no idea it was so late. I believe it's time for me to make that journey to the cottage. This is going to be a perfect ending to a perfect day."

"Annie, you are welcome to stay in here with me, in the twin beds. I washed the linens today and hung them out. The beds are nice and crisp," Aunt Mildred offered.

"Fine with me," Annie said, as she picked up her bag from the corner of the dining room, and one more cookie. "May as well finish this before I brush my teeth."

One more round of laughs and they were all headed to rest. Aunt Mildred watched down the lane until she saw the light from the front door as Eliza walked to the cottage. She went into the bathroom, parked her red curly friend in the linen closet, letting Annie in on the plan as not to startle her in the early morning hours, and with a quick hug, bid her sweet dreams, and was off to bed. Annie wasn't far behind. She snuggled in the crisp bedding, pulling up a vintage quilt. The window was cracked open for fresh air and the room nice and dark except for the moonlight peeking through the window. As she lay there, she could not help but think of the nice evening she had, enjoying the walk she took with CJ most of all.

The morning arrived too quickly, but the sunshine coming in the window and the smell of fresh coffee helped. As Annie opened her eyes, she realized where she had spent the night. Thanking God for the blessings in her life, bidding Him good morning, she sat up on the edge of her bed. Miss Mildred was sleeping soundly, so Annie tip-toed out of the bedroom not to wake her.

"Good morning," Eliza greeted her. "How did you sleep?"

"Wonderful!" Annie replied, "I feel like a little kid, waking up excited that Christmas is coming. I have been so anxious about getting my apartment ready and working out here that it just dawned on me that it is less than a week until Christmas!"

Eliza smiled. "You know, you're absolutely right. I didn't think about that either. I have just been focusing on enjoying the company."

"How did you sleep in the cottage?"

"Well, once I closed my eyes, I slept like a log. But first, I just wandered around and took it all in again. I loved the particulars and the comforts that all the extra touches bring. I don't see anyone staying there and not feeling special, just like we want them to feel here at the Homestead."

The church was full. Everyone in and around town

was there, some with a company that had already arrived for the holidays. Eliza visited with folks she hadn't seen in quite some time. There were people that hadn't seen Aunt Mildred for ages either. It was quite the reunion. Everyone lingered outside the church to visit. Fellowship was a priority this morning, no one in a hurry to leave. This being the last Sunday before Christmas, the downtown shops were all open today from noon until three. It was more of an open house atmosphere, each serving something special to drink or snack on. CJ would have the diner open as well, but only serving soup and warm drinks. That offered a comfortable place to sit and eat while others kept on the move. The weather was perfect, sunshine, but a cold day so in and out was refreshing. A Simple Stitch was closed, as Eliza would see most of her customers and the group throughout the week. She liked having the day to mingle with others while out shopping for her own last minute needs.

She picked up a few little treasures along the way to compliment the gifts she had under the tree. Aunt Mildred had done such a wonderful job on the gift baskets for the bedrooms and cottage she didn't need to find any extras for the guests. Now she could concentrate on the actual holiday from now until Christmas Eve.

Annie knew the Café would be open for the afternoon, so she told Miss Mildred and Eliza she would like to go see if CJ could use her help. She, too, had already finished with her Christmas shopping and seen all the shops and owners over the last few weeks. Perhaps she could take some of the steps off of Uncle Ben. He had been picking up the slack for CJ while he was busy with the Cottage. Annie felt truly blessed to become a part of a family that was so kind and considerate of each other's needs. She couldn't wait until her dad arrived to be a part of it, if only for a short time.

The Café was busy, so the afternoon went by quickly. Annie and CJ made plans to drive out to Slipknot after they closed.

As they pulled up, Eliza was looking out the kitchen window. They could tell she was busy at the counter. No doubt, another treat for the guests.

"Hello there," CJ shouted, as he and Annie came in the front door. "What are you busy with already?" he asked Eliza as he opened one of the cookie jars and took out a couple Pecan Tartlets. "These have always been one of my favorites!" he announced as he popped one in his mouth.

"I finished wrapping the finds I picked up this afternoon, so I thought I'd make a batch of gingerbread men. That's Rachel's favorite. We made them together every Christmas when we were young. I still have the cookie cutter of Mimzie's that we used. It sure stirs up some memories. This is the rolling pin that Mimzie taught us to roll dough with, too. The one with the green handles, although now, there isn't much green paint left on them. This old rolling pin has seen its share of dough through the years," Eliza said with a smile and a wink. "A lot of miles, and like me, hopefully, we both have a lot of miles left in us."

"I remember something about Mom telling me when she made her first gingerbread man, she was so excited that she took a bite of it before it was baked, or something like that. Do you remember what that was about?" CJ questioned Eliza.

"Oh, I remember. It wasn't your mom that took the bite of the raw dough, it was me. That is a taste you don't ever forget. We had a sheet full, it may have been the first time I got to help. We put the icing on them. Mimzie taught us to use the kind that was put on the dough and baked right on, and I was so excited, I just picked one up and popped half of it in my mouth before Rachel could stop me. Well, needless to say, it came right back out onto the cookie sheet as fast as it went it. With my tongue hanging out, I grabbed a pot holder to wipe off the taste, and turned around to find a drink of water and fell right off the stool I was standing on," Eliza continued to tell with a chuckle. "A typical day in the kitchen at Slipknot!"

"What can I do to help?" CJ asked. "I'm in the mood to bake, not clean!"

"Okay, get that plastic straw and make some holes in the tops of this sheet full of gingerbread men. I want to hang them on the small tree on the counter. It can be set by the cookie jars, and they can be eaten right off the tree. I thought the kids would enjoy that. Another tradition I remember from Mimzie."

"How fun is that! I may use that idea at the Café next year if I can remember that is. I could set up a small tree by the cash register for the guests to take along. It can be a new tradition at the Café and give my customers something to look forward to."

"Okay, after you get those done, roll out that ball of dough in the bowl and cut them out. The icing is in the bag on the counter. Decorate them how you want, and I'll go check on Annie and Aunt Mildred to see what they are up to. I don't want those two overdoing it. After all, it is Sunday, and we all need a little rest. By the end of the week, we are all going to be running on very little sleep and busy every minute."

"No problem," CJ replied. "This is the kind of day I was hoping for. I feel festive! Must be the surroundings and the company I keep."

Eliza found Annie and Aunt Mildred in the bedroom, freshening up the beds they had been sleeping in. The three of them continued on throughout the other bedrooms, making up all the beds with the fresh linens and quilts. The smell of sunshine radiated from them since airing out earlier in the week. What a gift for everyone when they arrive. After that, they went to the cottage and changed the linens and freshened it for its next guest. They brought out the cradle, and Eliza found an old baby quilt that Mimzie embroidered one winter. It had been in the trunk and surprisingly wasn't brittle with age. It made the perfect welcome for Jaxon. Eliza brought out a jar of cookies for the counter to set next to the coffee pot for first thing in the morning when getting up and around.

"Well, ladies, I think we have it. I don't know of anything else that needs to be done around here now until the guests start arriving mid-week, beginning with Rachel. I'm surprised she hasn't already shown up on our doorstep. It has been trying for her not to be a part of the 'getting ready for company' stage. That is her favorite thing to do! This time, she gets to be the company and get pampered for a change," Eliza finished as she fluffed up the pillows on the chairs in the sitting area. "We can head back to the Homestead and see how CJ is coming with the gingerbread men."

The smell of gingerbread cookies was drifting out the door as they stepped up on the front porch. The holidays were in the air. Eliza found herself humming a favorite Christmas hymn from this morning. Aunt Mildred began to sing along, and Annie whistled quietly as they entered the dining room. The gingerbread men were amazing. CJ had decorated them so that they looked as if they stepped right out of the 50's. Amazing how he seemed to do it just as Mimzie did. He did admit to seeing Christmas pictures when he was younger of the past holidays. It must have held a place in his memory. He was anxious to see if anyone else recognized them.

They sat on the porch with a cup of coffee and relaxed chatting about Christmases past and enjoying the brisk evening. The sunset was gorgeous, but there was a dampness in the air that brought a chill over the evening.

Everything was in perfect condition. They were ready for guests.

All they had to do now was wait.

Chapter Fifteen

Christmas Eve-Eve! Guests arrive, memories stirred, and Aunt Mildred steals the show...

Ꮀ᎐ᏪᎶ

Thursday morning was here before they knew it. Aunt Mildred and Eliza came out of their rooms at the same time with one thing on their minds. It's the morning before Christmas Eve. The guests should start arriving today. Rachel and Robert were due in with Beth early this afternoon, and Sophie and Jack planned to arrive with Celeste that evening. Carson, Julie, and Jaxon should be following them on that night. They hoped to make most of the drive while Jaxon could sleep.

Eliza planned to close the shop at noon. She had her sign on the door since Monday and would re-open on Monday, the twenty-seventh. Their clothes were packed and ready, suitcases lined up by the door. Aunt Mildred wanted to spend the morning around town looking for last minute extras for the weekend while Eliza finished in the shop. They'd drive out together. This would give them plenty of time to get the meal ready. Oh, how they were looking forward to preparing the first of many favorite recipes.

CJ planned to meet them out there after he closed the Café. Annie offered to go by and help clean up and close so he could be there when his mom and dad arrived.

As the day went on, they kept busy with last minute shoppers and regulars just stopping by to wish them a Merry Christmas. Uncle Ben went home early to help Molly gather gifts and load the goodies that she had been busy preparing for the gathering. They planned to go home at night, but their days will be spent at Slipknot with the family. Everyone was as excited as little children counting down the time until the first guests arrive.

CJ was bursting at the seams, knowing Annie's dad would arrive early in the morning so he could unload Pete before everyone was up and around. Several times, Annie caught him whistling while he cleaned the Café. "This may be the best Christmas gift of all," CJ' thought. And imagine, the secret remained safe.

As CJ and Annie arrived at the Homestead, a huge pot of Chicken and Noodles was simmering on the stove, and next to it, a pot of Vegetable Beef soup. There was the familiar smell of fresh Butterhorns in the oven and jars of favorite cookies lining the counter by the small tree sporting CJ's traditional gingerbread men. Coffee was ready, as was a jug of freshly brewed tea. The large table was set with holiday linens and a fresh centerpiece of cinnamon sticks, pinecones, and pine branches. Beeswax candles burned in mismatched cups, and the inside and outside lights were lit. Everyone was anxious, full of anticipation, waiting for the gathering to come full circle when the guests begin to arrive. The setting, it couldn't have been more perfect!

Suddenly the first car was coming down the lane honking the horn. Rachel had her hand out the window, waving and calling Merry Christmas. CJ was the first one out the door to welcome her. It was the moment he had imagined for the past six weeks. Let the gathering begin.

Eliza, Aunt Mildred, and Annie stood back, patiently, and watched CJ run out to greet them as if he were six years old again. He had Rachel's door open before the car had come to a complete stop. "Merry Christmas, Merry Christmas! I thought this day would never come," CJ shouted as Rachel stood up out of the car. He grabbed her and twirled her around in the driveway, and then hugged her. "The past few weeks seemed to take forever to go by!" he said, as he then gave her a big kiss on the cheek.

Beth opened the back door, jumped out of the car and hopped on CJ's back, hands across his eyes squealing, "Guess who, guess who!"

CJ turned, flipping her off his back, grabbing her, and hugging her as if he hadn't seen her in years. "Are you as excited about this Christmas as I am, sis?" he asked her as he gave her a second hug.

"Every bit," she replied. "I thought it would never get here! Almost worse than waiting to open gifts when we were kids."

"What about me!" his dad said as he slammed the

car door. "Are you going to give your old dad a hug and kiss, too?" he taunted.

In a split second, CJ ran around the car and did just that!

"Wow, you are in rare form!" Rob replied. "I think you are full of the spirit... or something! How about you get a grip and help with some of these bags?"

Eliza and Aunt Mildred came out onto the porch. Annie, suddenly feeling like an intruder, stayed behind in the doorway.

"My goodness, look at this family. It has been a long time since I got to see the four of you together," Eliza exclaimed. "I'm next in line for the hugs."

Aunt Mildred quickly stepped in front of her, "Now just one minute. I believe it has been much longer since I've seen them than you, missy. You just wait your turn." She nearly bolted down the steps, grabbing Rachel first. The scene was that of an instant replay of CJ's greeting. Eliza quickly joined in the circle, and before they knew it, everyone was carrying gifts and suitcases, all talking at once, headed for the steps.

"Oh my, this is such a wonderful welcoming," Rachel said. "It feels like we could open the door and see Mimzie standing there."

As she reached for the door, Annie, still standing in the shadows, opened it for her, and offered to take her bag.

Rachel, startled by Annie, squealed, dropped her bag as she jumped back, bumping into Beth, nearly knocking her down the steps. "Oh, my! For a second I thought you *were* Mimzie! I guess it really feels like coming home," she rattled, as she turned to see if Beth had regained her stance.

"Oh, I'm so sorry! I meant to stay back and not interfere. Now, look what I've done. Let me help with your bags. If you want to set the rest on the porch, I can bring everything in. I hope I didn't upset you. Eliza and Miss Mildred and CJ and everyone worked so hard to make this moment perfect, now I've spoiled everything. I'm so sorry!" Annie rambled on with her usual southern charm.

"Nonsense, young lady. I loved that for a moment Mimzie was with us. In spirit, we know she is, and always will be. But you brought her to life, if only for a moment. And you, why, you are just charming. From what I have heard, and looking at your red boots, you must be Annie," Rachel said as she reached out and gave Annie a hug.

CJ gave her a big smile as he walked in the door. "That was quite an introduction, one I'm sure they won't soon forget!"

"I'm so embarrassed," she said, as she turned red again. "I was trying to blend in. Look at the chaos I created right off the bat. I hope Eliza isn't upset with me."

"First of all, Eliza doesn't get upset. And second, of all, you gave this family a greeting they will never forget. Everyone loves to see Mom get going, and that was a classic. So thank you for that. And as this weekend goes on, you are going to see our family's true colors shine. You'll fit in better than you've ever imagined. I'll just be glad to see what your dad brings to the table. Somehow, I think he is going to be as welcome as you are. Now, take one of these bags and let's see where we can help." CJ handed her a bag, put one arm around her shoulder, and they went down the hall.

Eliza had cards hanging from the doorknobs welcoming each guest and helping them find their way. The presents were piling up very quickly under the tree.

As Annie and CJ returned to the dining room, the door opened, and a robust "HO HO HO" rang thru the house. It was Uncle Oliver, coming in to greet the family. He had seen the car pull up, but wanted to let things settle down a bit before he came over. Rachel was the first to get to him for hugs. They hadn't seen each other lately or talked on the phone much for that matter. Not like they had when Mary first passed away. Time seems to heal, and as Oliver became busy at the Homestead, the calls became few and farther apart.

"Oh my, you look wonderful. It is so great to see you again," Rachel gushed over him. Being older brothers, Oliver and Ben were always protective of Rachel and Eliza. Growing up they were inseparable. Before anyone else could get to him, the tears began to flow, first Rachel, and then Oliver right behind her.

"Okay, now this has to stop!" Oliver demanded, reaching in his back pocket for his hanky. "We are going to spoil CJ's plans for the great family gathering. The boy has worked his tail off, and the tails off the rest of us for

that matter, so we all have to live up to his expectations."
With that said, the rest joined in razzing CJ, and the mood
lightened. Rob shook hands, and next was Beth, up for a big
bear hug from Uncle Oliver. "My, but you sure are growing
up too fast. Just don't know why these kids can't stay kids,"
he grumbled and shook his head, turned her loose and went
over to take a seat by Aunt Mildred. "Sure smells good in
here."

The soup is hot. There are fresh-baked Butterhorns
in the basket and coffee and tea freshly brewed. Help
yourself and sit where you like." Eliza instructed. "We are
making this as easy for everyone as possible. The dishes are
on the counter, and you all know where the dishwasher is,"
she laughed. "This is a self-service holiday!"

"Oh, a new tradition?" Beth asked. "I like the idea,
but I especially want lessons in Butterhorns before I go
home."

"Annie can teach you," Eliza stepped up and took
her by the shoulders. "She has made them twice now, and I
know any practice batches won't go to waste."

"Oh, no. I think you are giving me too much credit
here. I have only made them twice, and the first time was
with Eliza by my side. My solo attempt wasn't a pretty
sight," Annie graveled.

"But if you ate them with your eyes closed, they
were great!" CJ poked at her. "Give yourself a little credit.
You and Beth will have such a good time you won't even
notice if they aren't all the same size."

"I'll put that on my list, if it is all right with you, Annie," Beth smiled.

"I'd love to bake with you, just don't get your hopes up for any miracles," Annie said smiling back. She was starting to relax and enjoying the family so much, she almost forgot to be anxious about her dad's arrival tomorrow.

"I see headlights!" CJ was up and across the room before anyone else. "It looks like it may be Sophie and Jack. Uncle Oliver, would you like to be first out to greet them?"

"You know, I believe I would. Been a long time since I've seen them. Long time." He went out the door shaking his head, trying not to let anyone notice the tears welling up in his eyes.

They watched out the door and windows. It was an emotional homecoming, as expected. The holidays were still hard on the family without Mary. They did a good job keeping her memories alive. As they started unloading bags and gifts from the trunk, the door opened, and everyone trailed out to greet them, everyone talking at once. This was turning into the gathering CJ had hoped for.

"Oh, Eliza, the Homestead looks wonderful. Just as if it were thirty years ago. I just love how you keep the past alive," Sophie went on. "This is going to be a Christmas celebration none of us will soon forget. I can't wait for Carson, Julia, and Celeste to get here, and Jaxon. Oh, Dad, you aren't going to believe Jaxon. He gazes into your eyes, and your heart turns to butter. Carson and Celeste have been so excited. They both remembered stories about the

Homestead and the times they visited growing up. Carson and Julia haven't been here since they married so this will be a new experience for her with our family. They have been trying to fill her in on the things they either remember or repeating stories that have been passed on through the years. Julia is more excited than anyone to get here. Not only for herself but to start instilling these family values in Jaxon even at his very young age. She wanted her son to be close to his family, like his dad, Carson, has always been. She asked Celeste to ride along with them so they could continue their stories."

"Well, thanks for the credit, but what you are seeing was a joint effort. I must say the gang did most of the work. I don't know what I would do without them. After Aunt Mildred surprised me by showing up at my door, we put her right to work along with the rest of us. And did you realize the gathering was all CJ's idea? We just went along with him to keep him from moping around this Christmas!"

The room roared. "Go ahead, poke fun, but I'm not the only one that's been looking forward to this!" CJ snarled.

"You're right about that!" Aunt Mildred chimed in. "We salute you. You, sir, are a hero." With that said, she walked over and gave him the biggest hug, followed by a "Merry Christmas! Oh, look, more headlights!"

Oliver once again was the first out the door. The porch quickly filled with everyone lining the rails like birds on a wire. The first one back to the steps was Oliver, with Jaxon, to show off his Great-Grandson.

"He likes me, he really likes me!" Oliver chuckled. "Isn't he just the most handsome little guy since, well, I guess since CJ?"

"He looks like he has grown since I last saw him," Sophie said as she followed him in. "And that was just hours ago. I just can't imagine not getting to enjoy him as much as I do. I'm so fortunate to have them close by."

Shortly after Carson and Julia made it in, Ben and Molly followed. No one even noticed them pulling up, trailing right along with the crowd. "Oh my goodness, Uncle Ben, Aunt Molly, it has been so long," Carson exclaimed when he turned and saw them. "Let me introduce you to my wife, Julia. This is my Uncle Ben, Mom's brother, and my Aunt Molly. They still live in town. You are going to love them!"

"So pleased to finally meet you," Julia said as she quickly gave them both a hug and kiss on the cheek. "I have heard wonderful things about you from Carson. So many wonderful things."

"Well, I guess the gang's all here," Eliza spoke up as she spotted them. Everyone continued with their hellos and hugs, and necessary introductions.

Celeste was the last one in, but the first to grab CJ and then Beth. She had missed her cousins. Julia and Jaxon were introduced to everyone, and no one could forget Annie. The room was buzzing. Soon everyone broke apart into groups, and the feast became the focus. Rachel and Sophie were quick to remember the gingerbread men on the small tree displayed on the counter. Eliza got out the old cookie cutter of Mimzie's that she taught them with when they were kids. The cookie cutter was passed around the room for inspection. This prompted Aunt Mildred to get out the first photo album.

She and Molly soon had their heads together. Ben, Oliver, and Rob quickly joined them. Eliza, Sophie and Rachel went out to the cottage. Eliza couldn't wait to share every detail. Expecting to be there a while, they took their coffee with them. They found themselves snuggled in the comfy seating area and continued to catch up on family news.

CJ, Beth, Carson, and Celeste were busy telling Julia even more stories about times they spent as kids at the Homestead.

Annie stood up to bid them goodnight. "I really need to be going home," she said as she looked at the clock. "I know it is only eight, but Dad is coming tomorrow, and if I know him, he will get here at sunup!" she laughed. "It has been a great evening, and I'm so glad I got to meet all of you," she smiled.

"You're one of us now, Annie Simpkins," CJ said in an eerie voice. "You'll never get away! Once we let someone in on the family secrets, there's no escaping! Bah-ha-ha-ha-ha-ha!" He went on with an evil laugh.

"Well, I have news for you Mr. CJ, you couldn't throw me out of this family if you tried. Eliza likes me. So there." Annie wrinkled her nose at him, turned, and smiled at the girls and winked. "Would you tell Eliza and Miss Mildred that I'm going? I'll say my good-byes to the rest on the way out."

"Sure. Do you need anything before you leave? You and your dad are coming out tomorrow afternoon and staying for supper, aren't you? I'm sure everyone is expecting you. We can't wait to meet him." CJ led her on, knowing well they would be out.

"That's my plan unless Dad wants to do something else. If anything changes, I'll let you know. Have a great evening catching up," Annie said as she left the room. "Maybe tomorrow, some of the newnesses may have worn off, and I might get a turn at holding Jaxon. He is so adorable, I'm anxious to snuggle up with him."

"Not a problem," Celeste mumbled. "I'm just soaking him up now. I'll share him tomorrow. I want him to remember that I'm his favorite Aunt!"

"You are his only Aunt," Beth sounded off.

"I know! That's why I know I'm his favorite!" With that, the familiar sound of laughter filled the room again.

"Sleep tight, and no peeking under the tree!" Annie demanded in her sweet southern draw as she went toward the door.

From behind her, she heard Celeste shout, "You can hold him if I can wear your red boots!"

As the evening went on, everyone seemed to migrate

to the large worktable in the kitchen with old albums and
continuous cups of coffee. This wasn't coming to an end
anytime soon. Eliza, Sophie and Rachel came back from
the cottage with a refill and cookies in mind. They walked
in on the gathering, and soon, were right in the middle of
the excitement. There were so many memories in the pile
of albums.

"What about Mimzie and Papa's wedding," Celeste
asked. "Are there any wedding pictures?"

"There were only a few pictures," Eliza explained.
"Back then, a picture was a luxury, and not many were
taken. Let me see if I can find them. I'm pretty sure they
are in a drawer in the old sideboard. They are in sepia, that
much I am certain. That is pretty much all they did then, the
old brownish prints."

"I remember Mimzie talking about their wedding.
Nothing fancy. Right outside here where the Homestead
now sits. Caroline and Caleb, the couple that started it all
years before they become known as Mimzie and Papa. It
was a simple gathering. They did have a flower girl, one
of the neighbor girls if I remember right. She was not in
fancy dress, just Sunday best, and she got to hold Mimzie's
bouquet of wildflowers during the ceremony, at least until
Caroline's goat, Tootsie, decided to have a snack. When
she grabbed the middle of the bouquet, the flower girl
started screaming but refused to let go. She and that goat
went around and around. About that time, the wreath-
like headpiece that Caroline had made for the stupid goat
to wear for the wedding, slid down over her eyes, and
then she really threw a hissy-fit. Her hind legs were going

over her head, and the entire wedding party scattered. If Caleb hadn't grabbed Tootsie by the back of the neck and pulled the headpiece off, she would have been right in the middle of the wedding cake. I'll never forget that story," Aunt Mildred reminisced. "All Caroline bothered to do was calm the goat down, got the chickens out of the crowd and thanked Caleb kindly for rescuing Tootsie. She calmly nodded to the preacher to continue. To Caroline, it was as if nothing happened, just another day at the Homestead."

Everyone was so tickled at the story they quickly asked her if she remembered anymore from the early days. Aunt Mildred loved an audience. When Eliza heard the request, she laid the wedding pictures on the table and went to put on more coffee. She knew this would be an interesting evening. Long, but interesting.

"See, here in the picture, standing back over by the tree. That's Tootsie. After the ceremony, Caleb found a rope and much to Caroline's disliking, he tied Tootsie to the tree. Caroline didn't say anything, but chances are if it hadn't been their wedding day, that goat would not have been tied to that tree or anything else for that matter. And the chickens running around, they all roosted in the old shed out back every evening. There were boxes built along the walls filled with straw. They gathered eggs daily for their meals. More than once when anyone came out to visit, that old red rooster in this picture by Tootsie would chase them into the house, biting at their heels. One day, it got hold of the back of Mimzie's leg when she was hanging out clothes. The next day, she cooked up the biggest pot of chicken and dumplings they ever saw. The kids loved every bite, Papa was wise as to the treat, but just smiled and said, 'Good dumplins there Caroline...good dumplins!'

"They always had sheep and raised little ones every spring. Mimzie sheared the sheep and dyed and spun the wool into yarn. Then every winter, she knitted scarves, socks, and sweaters for everyone, out of necessity. Some of the warmest clothes they could want. Lasted forever, and was handed down as they were outgrown. That's why I was surprised when Eliza found the stockings in the attic that Mimzie made. Christmas stockings. She usually put effort into utilitarian needs, rather than something like that. Did everyone see them hanging on the mantle?" she asked, pointing to the fireplace.

"Oh, wow!" Ben stood up from the table, astonished and surprised as he noticed the rest of the keepsakes. "Can that possibly be the old farm set we played with as kids?" he turned to find Eliza. "I haven't seen that for years. It has been a long time since I even thought of it. See it, Molly? That is the set I've told you about. Eliza and I played for hours on end with it. We always dreamed of having a farm together some day."

Eliza stepped up behind and gave him a hug. "Aunt Mildred recognized that set, too. She said when she and our dad were kids, they had the set. She didn't know it was still around. They played with it for years, planning their farm just as we did. So many memories. Oliver spent hours cleaning and restoring it to display. We were hoping you'd be surprised."

Ben just stood there, eyes welling up, and looked

seriously at Eliza. "Do you think we could play with this tomorrow morning before breakfast?"

With that, Eliza couldn't help it. Tears streamed down her cheeks. "Yes, Ben, I believe we can. First one up will wake the other, just like we used to do when we were kids."

"You know, I think the mantle could use some strands of popcorn and cranberries. Anyone want to help?" CJ asked. "We thought we'd save that for a group project."

"I'll pop the corn." Beth got up and started to the cabinet. "I think there is an old hot air popper here somewhere. And I see the jar of popcorn. Do you have a spool of quilting thread here Eliza?"

Aunt Mildred put a granite bowl on the table with several large needles already threaded. "We were hoping to do this one evening," she said. "Should be enough for anyone inclined to join in."

"Only if you continue with your stories," Beth requested. "We aren't anywhere near ready to go to bed. It isn't even nine yet."

"Well, it isn't late, but I was up before daylight, so I'm going to start saying my goodnights if you don't mind," Oliver said as he stood up from the table.

He went over and gave Julia and Jaxon a warm hug goodnight, and then Sophie took him by the arm. "Come on Dad, I want to walk you home. But first, don't you think you should be the one to take Carson and Julia out to the cottage. Maybe Aunt Mildred would like to walk along as well, help them get acquainted with the surroundings. Show them where everything is. After all, I hear you had a major hand in getting that ready," she said with a smile.

"Good idea, dear," Aunt Mildred took his other arm.

Together they took Carson and Julia out to their guest cottage where they would spend their first Christmas at the Homestead. "After all, there are lots of memories to be made, and I'm going to need some new stories," Aunt Mildred added as she showed Julia around. They were overwhelmed by the work that went into that old chicken house.

"I'm so glad you told us the story of this old building earlier so we can really appreciate the efforts. Are you sure you want us to be the first guests to sleep here though?" Julia questioned.

"Of course, dear. We talked about it. This way, if you need to bring Jaxon out for some quiet time, you have the place close by. Eliza thought it was a great place for the three of you, rather than offering her apartment and you traveling back and forth from town. The cradle was in the attic from past generations. Jaxon will be making his own memories and doesn't even know it yet," she laughed. "Take lots of pictures! Now, is there anything else we can get for you before we walk Oliver home?"

"Couldn't think of a thing!" Carson replied. "We'll just walk back with you until bedtime. We're so blessed to be a part of this extended family. Grandpa, I think you are going to start seeing a lot more of us. Jaxon needs to know his family if that's okay with you."

"Nothing could please me more, Carson. Nothing I want more than to be a part of that little guy's life."

The table was alive with laughter while they strung the popcorn and cranberries. Aunt Mildred returned and continued with stories. Some stories were about her and Alexander growing up, but a lot of stories were about Mimzie and Papa that had been passed down through the years. Soon it was eleven pm. The group started winding down. Tomorrow being Christmas Eve, they knew it would be a busy day, so Eliza started showing everyone to their rooms. Soon it was just Eliza and CJ still awake. They cleared the dishes, put things away, all the while talking about the evening. Things could not have been more perfect. Eliza brewed them each a cup of peppermint tea. They sat outside on the swing with the lights lit, stars out and a bright moon just over the stable, each wearing a quilt around their shoulders to knock the late night chill.

"You know, it's believed that if the moon is full on Christmas Eve, the animals in the stable can talk to each other," Eliza explained.

"Well, too bad the moon was full a couple nights ago. Annie and I enjoyed it when we were out walking. She thought it would be a good picture for a Christmas card next year. So, no talking animals this year. But that's okay. If tomorrow evening goes as planned, there is going to be more than just talking going in that stable. Hope Annie's dad makes it here in the morning without any trouble. He's going to call me when he gets into town. I can't wait to see her face when she sees Pete standing in the stable next to JoJo. Oh, look, I just saw a shooting star. I'd make a wish, but I couldn't think of anything I don't already have." CJ put his arm around Eliza, and with a little squeeze and a gentle voice, he said. "I love you, Aunt Eliza. I hope you realize how much."

"I know you do, CJ, and I love you right back," she smiled and laid her head on his shoulder.

They sat on the swing relaxing for the next half hour, just taking in the quiet, admiring the lights and finishing their tea. As they got up to go inside, they glanced out to the cottage, spying only a night light in the window. Seems everyone has settled in.

"Sleep well CJ," Eliza said as she went down the hall. "Tomorrow is Christmas Eve! You are going to need plenty of rest. We have lots of memories to make and a special tree to cut down and decorate."

As Eliza closed the door to her room and crawled into bed, she couldn't help but lay there and smile. After all, the best surprises were yet to come. She finished her prayers, followed by a soft-spoken, "Merry Christmas to all, and to all a good-night!" She then drifted off to sleep with a smile on her face.

Chapter Sixteen

A Texan, a truck, and trailer, better than
Santa himself...

ৎৄ৽৻

"It is only four-thirty," CJ thought as he looked at the time on his cell phone. Rarely does he keep it at the bedside, but he had been waiting for the call from Annie's dad to get the final directions. He was nearly as excited about this as he was in anticipation of the gathering. It had been a very long time since he was this excited about the holidays. It felt good. Knowing he would not fall back to sleep, he got up and started the coffee pot. Walking out on the porch the air was fresh and brisk. He put on his coat and walked out to the stable with his coffee.

"Good morning girls, and let me be the first to wish you a Merry Christmas Eve," he laughed as he reached down to rub the ears of the eager sheep all lined up in a row. JoJo was reaching over all of them to nudge him on the shoulder, not to be ignored. "How are you doing today, JoJo?" he questioned her as he reached into his pocket and handed her a Christmas cookie. "I knew you would like a treat. Well, today you are getting company, a new roommate, Pete. He is coming here from Texas to join you so he can be closer to Annie. Maybe that will be the excuse I need to come out and ride you more often. Can't let her give Pete attention and leave you out, now can we?"

JoJo stood there eating the cookie and enjoying the long needed attention. She has always been here as long as he remembers. He got out the brush and groomed her while he had his coffee. It had been a long time since he spent a leisurely morning with her. Since he opened the Café, he spent early mornings preparing for the breakfast crowd. It felt good to start off slow and relax.

Just then his phone rang. Startling him, he dropped the brush, searching frantically for the phone to answer the call.

"Good morning," the robust voice with a familiar southern drawl sounded. "Are you up and around yet, or did I wake you?"

"Oh, no sir, you didn't wake me. I've been up and around for about an hour now. Just spending some long needed time in the stable with JoJo. How's your drive coming along?" CJ questioned.

"Well, I got going early. I couldn't sleep so I thought I might as well finish the drive. Got Pete some oats and fresh water, and we hit the road. We just stopped at a roadside park area. The sign said Spring Forest, twelve miles. Guess we are about there. Which way do I go from here?" he questioned. "I have pencil and paper and ready for directions."

CJ gave him directions around town to make it a bit easier pulling the horse trailer, even though there wouldn't be much traffic this time of morning. Knowing he would be to Slipknot within the hour had him all wound up. One last glance at the stable, filling the trough with a bit more fresh water and getting the girls fed, he went back to get another cup of coffee and wait.

Eliza was sitting at the table with a cup of coffee and a journal in front of her when CJ came in.

"Good morning. Wasn't expecting to see you up and around. What do you have there?" he asked, as he warmed up his coffee.

"Oh, this, nothing much. It is a poem I wrote when I was in college, the short time I was away from home. I get out this old journal and read it every Christmas Eve. Grounds me, knowing this was God's plan to put me where I am. There are still times I look back and question decisions I made. This just reassures me a bit. This and looking around at family and friends. What are you doing up, and where have you been? Did you just come in?"

"I woke up early and went out to the stable to spend some quiet time with my girls. I haven't had that privilege in a very long time. Felt good. Anyway, I needed to explain to JoJo what was going on. Didn't want her to think she was being replaced. Annie's dad just called for final directions, he'll be here within the hour. Can I read your poem? I had a lot of stuff swirling around in my head while I was gone from here, too. Often times I wonder if I'm where I should be at this stage in my life. It might help me clear some things up in my mind. And I want to see what kind of poet you are!" he laughed.

"You can read it, but I don't want any grief. I'm sure it's no prize. But it was how I felt at the time."

He pulled the chair out across the table from her and grabbed a few more cookies. "Did you sleep well?" he asked, reaching for the journal.

"As good as I expected with all of the company and anticipation of Christmas. How about you? Did you sleep at all?"

"I slept well until about four-thirty then gave in and got up. I'll read your poem to help pass the time while I wait for Annie's dad to get here?"

"Take your time. I'm just going to start a couple batches of biscuits before everyone gets up and around. More coffee?" she asked as she reached for the pot.

"Thanks, think I will. It's a great morning!" With his coffee in one hand and poem in other, he made his way to the swing and began to read.

> "My Christmas Eve Sunrise"
> Somewhere among the busy days
> As time goes much too fast.
> We misplace time for the simple things
> A moment that should last.
>
> This Christmas Eve morning
> Up early, as usual, to make use of every minute.
> So many obligations, each one more important
> Just don't know if I'll finish.

Then at a glance, totally unexpected
Much to my surprise.
A calm, the beauty, peace and still
Reflecting in my eyes.

A sharp thin line, yet such a glow
Breaking through the dark and cold.
The very beginning of a glorious sunrise
Just mine, to have and hold.

With a steaming cup of coffee in hand
Quiet, and all alone.
What's left to do is set aside
The morning is mine to own.

To patiently savor each and every second
Each memory better than the last.
The sky becoming more orange, the color so vivid
But the darkness, still not yet passed.

I refill my cup, and continue to dream
The darkness begins to fade.
Still the orange in the sky, so beautifully confined
Like the world, just opening the shade.

Christmas should be such a happy time
With the house decked out in good cheer.
But at times, even in the bustling crowd
It's the loneliest time of the year.

The sun is now up, back to reality I come
One last moment to have for my own.
Now deeply renewed for the time that I spent
Feeling the effects of the dawn.

The day is still cold, in a beautiful way
And I've seen there's a dream still to come.
Whispering to myself "Merry Christmas."
I now have the strength to go on.

Eliza busied herself with some early morning treats. She made a double batch of biscuit dough to roll out and cut into triangles, brushing them generously with butter and sprinkling with cinnamon sugar, then rolling tightly like croissants. They always called these Cinnamon Moons. Then she mixed another double batch of dough to pinch off in chunks and make another old favorite, Caramel Pecan Pull-Apart-Bread they loved as kids. Everyone would remember these treats. Just right with a cup of coffee to hold them over until time for the hearty brunch she planned. She had no idea how long before everyone would be up. She put the pans of bread in the oven, set the timer for thirty minutes, then wrapped an afghan around her shoulders and went out to join CJ on the swing.

"This is amazing," he said to her, holding up the journal. "I only read your poem, not your secret thoughts," he said smiling at her. "It's a lot like I felt when I was away from home. The only difference, I came home for the holidays but had these feelings rushing around in me. Still, do at times, I think, even though I feel like I'm where I want to be. There is something missing. Do you ever feel that way?"

"Once in a great while something will spark that mood in me, but not nearly as often as it did then. I think I'm well anchored now, have a tremendous group of friends, and my life is good. I love my work, maybe someday I'll end up like Aunt Mildred in a Winnie and a wig! Wouldn't that be a hoot, seeing the U.S. of A.?"

They had a good laugh to lighten the mood, each knowing just how the other felt. Suddenly, Eliza heard the timer on the oven beeping about the same time CJ saw a truck pulling a horse trailer coming down the lane. With that, he bolted off of the swing as if going to a fire.

He stopped, turned to Eliza as said, "Oh, guess that's Annie's dad, what was his name again?" he asked her, seemingly a nervous wreck. "Don't know why I'm so excited. Not like I never had a hand in surprising anyone before."

"Well," Eliza smiled, "perhaps this surprise holds more meaning deep down than you realize. His name is Jon. And CJ, relax. It's only a horse, the only thing as important to Annie as the man bringing it, and I think as the man planning the surprise, but that is just my opinion."

"Enough of that talk," CJ shook his head as he started toward the stable. "Got enough going on in my head as it is, don't need any more ideas in there from you."

The truck pulled over in front of the stable, a tall man got out wearing a red cowboy hat, gray hair peeking out all around. He was a stately man, carried himself straight and tall. He started toward CJ. "Well, howdy there young man. Not hard to figure out you must be CJ, the man behind the plans for Annie's big surprise." He held out his hand, and with a confident grip, shook CJ's hand. "Merry Christmas and glad to finally meet you."

"Same here, sir, and great to put a face with the voice. I can't tell you how much I appreciate this. I know Annie is going to be as surprised as the rest of the family. Eliza and I have kept this a secret to keep it from leaking. You know how tough secrets can be, especially at the holidays."

"Sure do, son, and call me Jon. I'm a working man; don't need to be hearing anymore 'sirs' out of you. Now, let's get this guy out of the trailer and give him a little room. He's been cooped up long enough."

Swinging open the door, Pete turned and looked eye to eye with CJ. He reached into his coat pocket he handed him a Christmas cookie and rubbed his forehead. "I think we are going to be good friends here, guy. You sure are a good looking horse. Nothing less than I expected."

As Jon pulled out the ramp, CJ took Pete by the reigns and led him out into the corral.

"We'll let him get a little exercise in here for a while before we put him in the stable with JoJo if that's all right with you. Do you think he'll be okay?"

"He looks like he's right at home if you ask me. Yep, going to fit in real well. Got a beautiful place here, son. Beautiful place. Nothing like Texas, mostly flat and not nearly this green. But it's home to me as this is to you."

CJ showed him where to park the trailer, not to be noticed as everyone came and went, and then parked the truck up by the house.

"Come on in, and I'll get you some coffee and introduce you to Eliza. She was the one who called you. She and Annie have spent a lot of time together. Lately, that's where I came in actually. My Café is across the street from Eliza's shop. Oh, and did I mention Eliza is my Aunt?" CJ rambled.

"Slow down son, you are starting to sound like Annie when she gets wound up. It's too early, and I've been on the road too long to try and keep up with you. Now, I'll take you up on that coffee, if you'll show me where I can wash up."

"I know, I even noticed it that time!" CJ laughed. "That's not good. You can go down the hall, bathroom on the right, and this is Eliza," he said in passing as they entered the front door. "Was that better."

"Much!" Jon replied. "So you are Eliza, glad to finally meet the lady I hear so much about. Both of you, actually, but I figured she'd be telling me all about a boy. Very nice to meet you, Miss Eliza," he nodded. "Let me wash up, and I'll take that cup of coffee if I'm not intruding."

"Not at all," Eliza replied. "Glad you made it in. Did you have any trouble on your drive?"

"Nope, none at all, back in a minute," he said, tipping his hat as he headed down the hall.

"Well, what do you think," CJ came over and whispered to Eliza. "Is he what you expected? He seems nice, down to earth. He says just what he thinks. No beating around the bush with him."

"I hope you're right, that's a great quality. Mimzie and Papa were like that. Sign of good people. He is a big man. Pretty much what I expected after talking to him on the phone. Could tell by his voice he was going to be a statuesque man. I'm glad he's here, and I'm especially glad your Christmas surprise is going off without a snag, so far, anyway. Now pour him a cup of coffee and get that coffee cake off the counter so we can be hospitable when he comes back. I'm sure he could use the coffee after the drive, and I'd enjoy getting a bit more acquainted before he hurries off to see Annie."

"This is quite a place you have here, Miss Eliza. Is it Miss?" Jon said as he pulled out a chair. "Annie never mentioned a Mr. Guess I shouldn't take it for granted that it's just you."

"Oh, it is 'just me,' but I seem to always be surrounded by friends and family, so that's a blessing," she smiled. "Help yourself to the coffee cake if you'd like. Or would you rather have some bacon and eggs?"

"No, this will be fine. If I eat too much, Annie will be wondering why I didn't wait for her. Was going to ask for a tour of the place before I headed to town, but thought that would be forward of me, and it will make Annie happy to be the first to show me around and introduce me to everyone. Can't let the cat out of the bag when we are this close to one of her best surprises ever!"

He sat and chatted with Eliza and CJ for about an hour, telling them stories of Texas and how things have been for him with Annie so far from home, and about her phone calls. They didn't realize that she had become so happy and content in Spring Forrest. They had all become family to her, more than they realized.

"Well, CJ, it's getting near seven. If you want to give me directions to Annie's I'll be heading that way. Does she know what time to come back out here today?"

"I told her we wanted you to come out midday and join us. We are planning for you to be here for supper and the evening if you don't have other plans. She wasn't quite sure what you might have in mind," Eliza explained.

"That shouldn't be a problem getting her out here, may be harder to keep her away," he laughed, as he jotted down the directions to Annie's apartment. "I'll give her a call when I'm almost there, let her direct me, that makes her feel good."

As they said their goodbyes, CJ told Eliza he should be back around eleven or so. He knew Uncle Ben had planned on opening the Café for a few hours to accommodate last-minute shoppers. The shops in town would be open until noon so he will have coffee and sweet rolls ready for those needing a place to rest and regroup. If he went in and helped with clean-up, it would give the two of them time to catch up.

Chapter Seventeen

A new tradition and the best-kept secret at Slipknot... almost...

ৎৡ৵৾

Everyone else started coming to life around nine a.m. Aunt Mildred was up shortly after CJ and Jon went to town. She and Eliza enjoyed the morning in the old kitchen, cooking breakfast for the crowd, making biscuits and gravy like Mimzie did, with chunks of sausage in the gravy. Her biscuits were cut with Mimzie's old biscuit cutter, and they got out some vintage stoneware bowls and granite pans to serve it up in. Christmas Eve breakfast was set out on the sideboard, looking so festive. Stacks of stoneware plates were waiting, with the silverware wrapped in homespun checked napkins tied with a chain crocheted of cotton thread and sprig of pine. They were piled in the drawer opened just below the plates. Of course, a mixture of mugs, some for the holidays and some old favorites waited by the coffee pot and big pitcher of milk on the counter. Cookie jars lined the counter, filled and waiting as a constant temptation. The tables were set with red and white linens. Simple centerpieces of pinecone and pine branches in old crocks and wooden bowls graced the settings. It felt as if they were stepping back in time. Aunt Mildred was given the honor of offering the blessing. That said, everyone fixed their plates and found a place to settle in, continue stories of Christmases past and make new memories of this great Christmas Eve morning. Everyone was certain their bedrooms offered more comfort than the others. They all agreed they never wanted to leave. Hearing that was the best gift Eliza could get. Satisfaction. She couldn't wait to pass it on to CJ.

Most were still in their pajamas and robes at noon. One by one they wandered away to take a shower and dress. Some helped with the dishes while others tidied up and made beds. It was like clockwork, no one feeling like company, just a part of the Homestead lifestyle they had been waiting to enjoy.

Just after noon, CJ and Uncle Ben returned with Molly and some goodies she had baked for Christmas Eve. The day was perfect for a walk through the woods or a cup of tea on the porch. It was wool sweater and neck scarf weather.

Eliza made sure there was plenty of each hanging on a long coat rack that Papa had made so long ago. Many times they recalled coming in from a cold day hanging up their coats, hats, scarves, and mittens, ready and waiting in anticipation of the next outing.

"Okay, who is up for a trip to the timber? Time to find the Christmas tree! Need someone strong to help cut it down and drag it back! Any takers?" CJ shouted loudly enough to hear it in town.

"Sure you do," Aunt Mildred quickly shouted back. With that she started pointing fingers and naming names. It wasn't long until half the crew was pulling on caps and scarves and getting ready for the mission.

"Thanks, Aunt Mildred, you made that simple," CJ smiled. "Let's grab the saw from the barn, and we will be on our way. Everyone keep up. Would hate to lose someone in the timbers this close to Christmas. Would be a real shame!"

"Oh, you scare us CJ," Celeste jeered back at him as she tagged along on his heels. "I'll take a head-count, that way we won't come back with any less or any more than we leave here with!"

They were all laughing as they went out the door. Another great tradition coming full circle.

"CJ," Eliza yelled. "Please keep in mind the amount of space we have for the tree to fill. Don't want any surprises when you drag it in the door. You know what I'm talking about!"

"Gotcha, and no need to worry, we're going for a small, old fashioned fir. I think I know where one is that will be just right!" he replied, waving at her and talking as he hurried to the barn.

Within the hour the group was coming down the lane, pulling a tree on the old piece of belting CJ drug along to keep it from being damaged. As they came upon the porch, CJ and Celeste stood the tree upright, shaking out any loose leaves and needles and secured it in the stand.

"We'll leave it to sit out here for a bit to relax and get back to shape before we bring it in. I'm sure Eliza knows right where she wants it."

Everyone came crowding into the kitchen for a glass of iced tea. The walk warmed them through, even though there was still a chill in the air. They were all talking about the experience.

"Another memory made. Don't you love it when a plan comes together?" Eliza chuckled.

All afternoon, there was a constant flow in and out of the kitchen. Eliza and Rachel were reminiscing about so many of the memories that this gathering sparked.

When they got out the old granite roaster that Mimzie had baked so many turkeys in, Ben was passing through the kitchen. He then started telling the story of the Thanksgiving that Papa took him and Oliver hunting for a wild turkey.

"We went to a densely wooded area," Ben began. "Neither Oliver or I realized that turkeys could outrun the three of us. We came upon a flock of more than two dozen turkeys, all running in a group, waggling in and out of the trees, and Oliver got so excited. He thought he could catch one with his hands. He took off running after the turkeys, and as he was gaining on them, he was yelling for me and Papa to hurry, help catch them. About that time, the turkeys made a quick turn, and Oliver was then being chased. Now he was screaming for Papa twice as loud as before. Papa quickly grabbed me up and put me on his shoulders, and we stood behind a tree, out of sight, and watched as Oliver and the turkeys continued the chase. Soon, they were going in so many directions, no one could tell if Oliver was winning or losing. He managed to grab hold of one of the turkeys, and the real fun began. The turkey was flapping his wings and squawking and pecking at Oliver's legs and Oliver was so busy screaming, 'I got one, I got one' he didn't even notice no one was there to help him. Suddenly, he was on the ground, the turkey on top of him, still beating him up and now winning. Having enough, Oliver knocked the turkey off him, jumped up and started running. He was back at the Homestead before Papa, and I could walk out of the woods. By the time Oliver got to Mimzie and started to tell her about the turkey, she asked him where it was. With that, he just dropped his head and turned to walk back to the woods.

You know, we never let him live that down. In fact, when he gets here today, ask him if he brought the turkey. He will know exactly what you are getting at," Ben smirked.

The room filled with laughter. Eliza knew Ben could tell a good tale. He just didn't do it often.

Everyone continued to come and go, tending to their business while anxiously waiting for the Christmas Eve celebration to begin.

Aunt Mildred gathered the ladies in the sitting room and told them all about the antique business she and Bill had built. She explained her trip across country and goal to end at the ocean. Rachel, Molly, and Sophie got out their yarn and crochet hooks and worked on projects they brought while Aunt Mildred continued to entertain. Eliza joined them, getting out her yarn as well. Oh, how wonderful it felt to sit and enjoy company and share their heritage.

Celeste and Julia spent time out in the cottage while Jaxon took a much-needed nap. They wrapped some last minute gifts they still needed to slip under the tree.

"When will Annie get here?" Julia asked. "I really enjoy her company."

"I know she is bringing her dad out for the evening, but not sure when. If CJ were here, he would know. He seems to know everything about Annie." With that, they both giggled.

CJ came in after finishing up a few last minute details. He stopped in town at Flora's Unique Floral Boutique and picked up a large red Christmas bow he had her tie for Pete's bridal. Not to leave JoJo out, she tied up a nice bright green one for hers. She also tied three ribbons for the sheep. Flora is thoughtful that way.

"Could I help you finish anything in the kitchen?" CJ asked Eliza as he came through the sitting room to say hello.

"Nope, I think we have everything under control," she told him as she gave him a quick hug. "What time are you expecting Annie and her dad?"

"They should be getting here anytime, I'd guess. I know they're planning on being here for supper. I think I'll walk out and check on things in the stable."

The day had been perfect. Relaxed. Everyone entertaining themselves and enjoying the holiday. Julia and Celeste came in and set the tables for the evening, getting out fresh linens. They decided to set the dishes on the counter, buffet style, for the meal later on. Jaxon took a nice, long nap so he would be pleasant for the evening.

Annie and her dad drove in just as CJ came out of the barn. He walked over to greet them, last minute remembering that no, he should not already know her dad. Great save, as she started the introductions, he reached out his hand to shake Jon's and welcomed him.

"Everyone is inside, relaxing and doing their own things right now. How has your day together been? Did you have a nice trip up, sir?" CJ asked Jon.

"It's just Jon, no sirs or Mr.'s or anything else, just Jon. You remember that and we'll get along just fine," he said with a wink, as they already had this conversation once today.

"I'll do my best," CJ assured him. "There is a chill in the air today, a dampness that makes it feel a bit more like Christmas."

As they went in, Annie started the introductions, going around the room with her dad trying to keep up. He shook hands and gave hugs until suddenly, he just threw up his hands and told everyone to remind him who they were and where they are from when they have their first real conversation with him.

Everyone agreed.

The wonderful aroma from the kitchen had supper on everybody's mind. Eliza called everyone together, thanking them for making the trip to spend this Christmas Eve at Slipknot. A special thanks went to CJ for suggesting the gathering and helping to make it happen, adding how nice it would be to start another tradition.

Just then, Annie spoke up. "I want to thank everyone for making me, and my dad feel like we are part of your family, and welcoming us into your home like this. We'd like to share part of our holiday tradition with all of you. So, if that's okay, after supper, we'd like everyone to gather outside. Our Christmas Eve tradition has always been fireworks at dusk. It makes up for not having any snow at Christmas. For us, the bright display against the dark sky lets us feel as if it were snowing. We always gather, make hot chocolate and sing Christmas Carols as they light up the sky."

"Sounds amazing!" Eliza replied. That's a welcome surprise. Another new tradition we can share at our Christmas gathering every year. I can hardly wait!"

Everyone agreed, then bowed their heads as Aunt Mildred once again led them in the blessing. The kitchen was alive with the sounds of family and friends, plates clanging, laughter, and compliments to the chef.

"Not many left-over's to put away this evening,"

Aunt Mildred said as she started to load the dishwasher. "Glad for that makes clean up a breeze, and we can get on with Christmas Eve. It is, after all, almost dusk. Time to gather out on the porch. I'll put on a pot of milk. We can start some homemade hot cocoa. Mimzie would never allow us to serve instant."

"Sounds like the perfect end to a wonderful meal. How about I give you a hand in here," Jon said as he came in the kitchen with the last of the dishes from the table. I sent all of the young ones out on the porch. They had the energy to burn, but not burning it off cleaning up. So, what else can I help you with?"

Aunt Mildred was taken back for a moment, not expecting him to come in and do kitchen work. "Well, Jon, if you want to wipe off the table and counters, I can finish up the dishwasher, and we'll leave the pots to air dry. We can take the kettle of cocoa and that tray of mugs and go out and join them. Oh, and we mustn't forget the jar of marshmallows. I'm as anxious as you are to get this gift-giving celebration on the way. Especially the fireworks! That will be one of the best gifts by far."

Jon just smiled, knowing that Pete would soon be the best surprise of all.

Out the door, they came with the cocoa. Everyone had pretty much settled in on the porch. Even Jaxon was snuggled up on Annie's lap enjoying the swing with Celeste and Julia. CJ had a place ready for the fireworks display. Eliza had been outside helping him. They had their heads together, both so excited, knowing they had pulled off the surprise for Annie. Not long now till she gets to see Pete.

"Oh, what a blessing this day has been. I can't remember a Christmas Eve that I've enjoyed or anticipated more. I couldn't have done it without you, or the heritage of Slipknot. Now, I have to stop rambling like this because if one more person tells me I sound like a girl, I may end up in counseling," CJ said, as he hugged Eliza around the neck. "Merry Christmas!"

"Move over, boy!" Jon said as he hit CJ on the back. "I'll get this show on the road. I know you and Pete are both chompin' at the bit to get Annie in the stable. Going to be a memorable ending to a perfect evening, and Christmas Eve, just a bonus."

He turned and gave a whistle toward the porch. It became silent. Annie quickly stood up with Jaxon in her arms and started to cheer. "I'm so excited that we can share our holiday traditions with all of you," she said. "And I just want to thank all of you again for letting Dad and me barge in and be a part of your gathering. Okay, let's get the show started!" she shouted and squeezed back on the swing with the girls. She turned Jaxon forward so he could enjoy the fireworks as well. "As young as he is, this being his first Christmas, he will think this is just a regular ole Christmas Eve," she said to Julia, and they all started to laugh.

The first rocket went up, whistling all the way, then exploded in red and green sparkles. The next one right behind, all white, resembling snow. Then three at a time, a red, a green, and another red, so festive, so beautiful against the evening sky, stars shining brightly in the background and an almost full moon coming up behind the stable. The show continued for a full twenty minutes, only enough time between to let the smoke clear. Then, just as they always fear, the rocket that was just lit, fizzled and spun around a bit, then smoldered.

"Well, there's our dud, one in every bunch," Jon shouted. "Is everyone ready for the grand finale`? I always save the best for last! Hold on to your hats!"

He sat out five rockets, side by side, then called to CJ to come and start at one end while he started at the other. As they lit the rockets they went up simultaneously, first white on both ends, filling the sky with a snowy delight, then a double dose of green, as if looking into the branches of a giant Christmas tree. The center stage soaring higher than all was a rocket filled with red and white rockets, exploding in every direction, with each leaving a long tail of sparkles, then just as they thought it was finished, a large rocket exploded, and silver and gold drifted down to the field. They all stood and cheered on the porch, then turning to each other, passing out more hugs and Merry Christmases! Then, they all went out toward Jon to thank him and share the joy.

"What an amazing tradition to add to our holidays!" Eliza said and gave Annie a crushing hug, then turned to Jon and gave him one of the same. "You have no idea how much we all enjoyed the show."

Suddenly CJ turned to Eliza and said, "Did you hear a noise coming from the barn? I bet the fireworks have JoJo and the sheep wondering what is going on out here. Do you think I should run out and check on them?"

He was so convincing that Jon winked at Eliza, thinking to himself CJ deserved an award for his performance.

"That's probably a good idea. They have never heard fireworks before, at least not at Christmas. I hope you can get them settled down. Let me know if you need help."

"It'll probably be okay. I can go check, unless, well, Annie, would you mind to come out and help me get them calmed down?" he said.

"No, I don't mind at all. I can walk out there with you. Let me grab a couple of cookies. I know they'll like that. Here, Julia, I suppose you might want to take Jaxon," she said, giving him one more squeeze.

As she ran toward the barn to catch up with CJ, Eliza quickly motioned to everyone on the porch, "Quick, gather around and listen, you are about to hear the best surprise yet! Let's all walk over toward the barn." Eliza was so excited she could hardly contain herself.

"Why Eliza, what on earth are you up to, you are almost giddy!" Aunt Mildred asked as she took hold of Eliza's arm. "Let me walk up here with you so I can see just what's going on. Is this some kind of secret?" she prodded. "And how on earth did you keep it from me?"

Eliza just smiled at her, explaining. "CJ and I have

been planning this for weeks, and so neither of us let anything slip. We pinky-swore not to tell a soul. Sorry!"

As CJ and Annie swung open the door to the stable, he stepped back and let Annie go first. He flipped on the light, there stood JoJo with her festive green bow on her bridal, the three sheep close under foot, them, too, sporting their Christmas bows.

"Well, you girls are just a bit shook up, aren't you," Annie said as she walked toward them. "Guess you haven't had the pleasure of Christmas Eve fireworks before."

Just as she reached to rub JoJo on the head, the reflection from the shiny red ribbon on Pete's bow caught her attention. She turned to look, asking CJ at the same time, "What's that red over there?" Pete recognized Annie's voice. He let out a whinny that could be heard all the way up to the Homestead, she looked closer and realized it was Pete! By this time she was screaming with joy, ran and grabbed him by the neck, her feet not even on the floor.

What an amazing reunion! Everyone had made their way to the barn door by this time, filling each other in on what was taking place. There wasn't a dry eye in the crowd.

When Annie turned loose of Pete's neck, she turned to CJ, dropping to her knees in total disbelief. "How did this happen?" she asked him, tears streaming down her face. "Did you do this?"

CJ just smiled, tears welling up, he nodded his head. "But I had some help from your dad and Eliza. Are you happy?"

"Happy doesn't begin to explain how I feel. I'm overwhelmed," she said, as she jumped up, latching on to CJ's neck, same as she did Pete. She was clearly shaking in her red cowboy boots. All she could say was, "Thank you, thank you, thank you. This is the best Christmas present ever." Annie didn't even notice everyone else was watching from the doorway. As she looked him in the eyes, she said Merry Christmas CJ and kissed him unlike the friend to friend kiss he had expected.

"Merry Christmas, Annie." he replied and kissed her right back.

Just then, the dud, still smoldering in the driveway, began to whistle. It whirled around in the dark, pointing first toward the crowd, then the house, then the cars, back at the crowd, it shot straight up into the air and showered beautiful red, white and green sparkles over the night sky.

Everyone was so excited, they didn't know whether to watch Annie and CJ or the fireworks.

All CJ could say was, "Wow"!

"What a great story they'll have to tell their grandkids," Aunt Mildred announced! "What a great story!"

CJ, totally unaware of the crowd, suddenly took a step back, looked in her eyes as asked, "Annie, did you see fireworks? I actually saw fireworks! I have heard of times like this, but could it really be?"

Annie just smiled, then began to laugh, wiped her tears and hugged him again, "Yes, CJ, you actually saw fireworks, there were honestly fireworks! It was our first kiss. Would you expect anything less? Now come on, I want to get Pete out here and introduce him to everyone. And bring JoJo, too. I want this to be the beginning of 'our tradition,' a ride on Christmas Eve, just the four of us, under the stars, tonight, and every Christmas Eve to come. That, CJ, is my gift to you."

CJ wiped his eyes, gave her a hug, and started for JoJo. "I like that gift, Annie. Nothing could please me more."

As they walked the horses out to greet the family, the crowd was clapping and cheering. Annie's dad was shaken, as was Eliza. She walked over and took him by the arm and led him to the horses.

"I believe we have started quite the tradition here tonight, Jon. Going to be hard to out-do the gift of family. I think we just witnessed a new beginning that will go on for generations. What do you think?"

He just smiled, looked down at her in agreement. "Looks like I'm going to be driving to Spring Forrest every Christmas Eve from now on, least as long as I have the drive in me. To see my Annie this happy, that is the best gift I could ever wish for."

CJ and Annie rode down the lane, side by side, enjoying the sound of the jingle bells Flora had hidden under the bows on their bridals. "Be back soon," CJ said as they both waived.

Everyone made it back to the porch in awe of them. Aunt Mildred went in to make some more cocoa and share this amazing tale with Bill, and Eliza and Jon sat on the swing in silence. Eliza couldn't be happier. Seeing the smiles on CJ and Annie as they rode away just melted her heart.

"Sure hope those crazy kids get back before midnight," Eliza mumbled.

"Why is that?" Jon asked. "Do you think they'll get out there and get lost in the dark?"

"No, it's not that," Eliza replied. "CJ knows the land better than I do. It's just that if they don't, as wound up as everyone is already, I'm sure someone will realize it is Christmas and want to open presents!" She laughed, shaking her head and said, "I'm tired! I want to save some of the excitement for tomorrow!"

There was a soft roar of everyone comparing notes about Annie and CJ, the surprise, the fireworks, cocoa, and the best Christmas Eve ever!

Eliza and Jon sat contently, in sync with the rhythm of the swing, looking at the moon and the stars lighting the sky.

Just then, Aunt Mildred came out with a big tray of cocoa and cookies. "Oh, my, it is feeling like Christmas. There is such a chill in the air. I believe I will go back inside by the fireplace. Here are refills, hope you all enjoy yourselves out here. Anyone that wants to join me is more than welcome to follow." With that said, she turned and went in and made herself comfortable on the couch.

Eliza lifted her mug to Jon, "I'd like to propose a toast," she said.

He lifted his, looking at her in anticipation. "To Christmas. This evening has reassured me of what I have always known. Gathering with those that are important to you is the best gift we could ever receive."

"Cheers. And I couldn't agree more. Thanks for making me and Annie a part of your family. It means more to us than you'll ever know."

Their mugs clinked. They both took a warm sip, and just then, as they looked back to the sky, it began to snow.

Chapter Eighteen

A wish, another surprise and it really 'Twas the Night Before Christmas'...

ᔮᨏᨏ

Eliza stood up from the swing. "I got another wish. I wished that it would snow. I knew it was next to impossible, but all day I felt the chill in the air. It's like a miracle. We have to get everyone out here to see this," she commanded Jon, taking him by the arm. "Look at the size of the flakes coming down against the moonlight! Why they are as big as chicken feathers!"

"Settle down. What on earth did Miss Mildred put in your cocoa? You seem a bit tipsy there Sis," Jon taunted her. "It's only snow."

"Only snow? Do you know how long it has been since we had a White Christmas?"

"Come on. Let's get the youngsters out here to see this. It really is quite amazing! I can't believe it myself. I haven't been in a snowfall since I can remember."

They went in the door, arm in arm.

"What would be the best ending to this day? Who has a suggestion?" Eliza shouted, getting everyone's attention.

"Is there pie?" Carson said, coming up out of his chair. "That would be awesome, although I'm stuffed!"

"Nice try, any other guesses?"

"Are we making homemade ice cream?" Celeste asked.

"Nope, but you're getting closer!" Jon replied.

"We give up! What's your best ending?" Julia asked. "Jaxon can hardly wait for another Christmas memory. I can see the excitement in his eyes!"

"Okay, enough of that. Everyone come out on the porch. It will only take a moment," Eliza ordered.

As they started trailing out to the porch, Jon and Eliza stood, one on each side of the door and took in every ooh and ah, all the squeals of excitement and exclamations of disbelief. As Aunt Mildred made her way out, she stood there, looking straight up toward the sky, watching the giant pillows of snow drift down on her face, as if she were but a child. As she turned back toward Eliza and Jon, they knew immediately what this meant to her. Such a blessing for her on this Christmas Eve among the extended family that had come to love her.

Just then, CJ and Annie came riding in, singing "In the meadow, we can build a snowman."

"This is just wonderful! Who'd have believed it would snow tonight, on Christmas Eve!" Annie squealed. "It's, it's like...magic!"

CJ rode by her side with a smile on his face, still humming their tune. "It's like the cherry on the sundae! Who would have expected snow?" He climbed down from JoJo and walked over to give Aunt Mildred a hug. "You look so happy. How long has it been since you played in the snow?" he said with a grin.

"Honestly, I can't remember. I think I was a child. And you know, dear, I feel like one again."

Everyone stood in awe. They hadn't seen this emotional side of Aunt Mildred, and CJ seemed to be humbled. Eliza and Jon stood in silence. They continued to watch the giant flakes drift gently to the ground as a soft blanket started becoming more obvious.

"Coffee anyone?" Eliza asked. "I don't think we're going in soon. I'll grab the scarves and quilts."

"I can give you a hand," Jon followed.

They all settled in on the porch, singing carols and watching the snow accumulate. Celeste brought her guitar and played along. Jaxon seemed to be enjoying the evening as much as the 'big kids.'

Annie and CJ bedded JoJo and Pete down in the barn and gave the sheep a bedtime snack then came back to join in the fun.

"It doesn't seem like it is almost midnight, does it?" Annie commented. "That means soon it will be Christmas! Are we going to trim the tree tonight?"

"I have the trimmings laid out in the living room if anyone wants to go in and get started," Eliza said. "As for me, I just want to sit out here, take in the night and watch the snow fall a little bit longer."

No one hurried in. The songs filled the air, and the snow continued to pile up.

Ben and Molly decided to sleep at Oliver's rather than drive back to town, so they weren't in any hurry to leave. Oliver was excited about the thought of company. Not waking up to an empty house on Christmas would be a gift in itself.

Just then, through the large snowflakes, headlights appeared in the lane. It looked like two cars.

"Are we expecting company?" CJ asked, being the first one to notice. "I thought everyone was here. Do you think someone has lost their way?"

"I don't know," Eliza spoke up. "I don't think we are expecting any Christmas strangers. Wait and see if they turn back." She sat there very relaxed.

"I'm a bit uncomfortable, dear," Aunt Mildred spoke up. "It is very late and not likely anyone would still be traveling on a night like this. I hope no one is having trouble."

They all stood to see what was going on. The two

vehicles pulled up side by side in front of the Homestead. The license plates weren't familiar.

"Jon, do you want to walk out with me to see what is going on here?" CJ asked.

"Sure thing son. Seems a bit odd. That's for sure."

As CJ and Jon started off the porch, the driver side door opened on one car, and the passenger door opened on the other, simultaneously, almost as if planned. A man stepped out from the driver's side, a woman stepped out from the passenger side, and they walked toward the porch. As they stepped into the light, they both started jumping up and down as if they were children excited at Christmas, both calling "Mom."

Suddenly Aunt Mildred recognized their voices and went weak in the knees. It was Alex and

Lauren, unannounced, and certainly unexpected by Aunt Mildred. She had told everyone about their family plans, explaining why they were unable to attend the gathering this year. They pulled up a chair and helped her sit down, and she instantly began to cry.

"Alex, Lauren! Is it really you? How can this be? I spoke with both of you just this morning. You were on your holidays? This just can't be." She mumbled as she wiped her eyes.

"That's the magic of cell phones," Lauren said as she wiped away her own tears. "Merry Christmas! Surprised?"

Alex held on to Aunt Mildred as if he would never

let go. "I missed you so much, Mom. It just wouldn't be Christmas without you."

Just then, everyone rushed from the cars. Lauren's husband Sam and the twins, Max and Lucy, were next to smother her with hugs and kisses. Then Alex's wife Celia had her turn, leaving Henry and Katie for last.

"I feel like I'm in a dream. How can this be happening? What about all of your plans?" she kept questioning.

"Mom, you are our Christmas plans. It has been a wonderful week. Our families haven't spent time together like this for as long as we can remember. And we owe it all to Eliza," Alex explained.

"Eliza!" Aunt Mildred gasped.

"Merry Christmas," Eliza said as she gave Aunt Mildred a long comforting hug. "After all the joy you have given me, given all of us, how could I give you anything less than family for Christmas?"

"But how? When? I don't understand. I thought therewere plans," Aunt Mildred stuttered, still obviously shaken by the surprise.

Lauren went over and put her arms around Eliza's neck. "She called us after you were with her a while. She wanted to give you a special gift for Christmas and felt we would be able to help her come up with something we knew you really wanted. Deep down, we all knew you said you were fine with our plans, but we could tell you had an emptiness in your voice every time we talked. It was your family. Not extended family, but your kids and grandkids. Alex called, and we talked about it, and both decided this trip would be the best gift we could give our own families, as well. So after a few calls and cancellations, then new reservations, we had the best time planning our journey. The surprise and the look on your face are priceless. And a bonus, we are in the snow on Christmas Eve!"

Everyone on the porch began to clap, then cheering broke out, just then someone started whistling. Then the sound of a guitar and a beautiful voice brought the night to silence.

Celeste was standing in the doorway and began to sing. One by one they began to join her until the porch sounded as if it were entertaining a choir.

CJ, feeling the need to lighten the mood when the song was finished, stood up, center of attention, began to sing in a howling off-key voice, "Oh, Christmas Tree, Oh, Christmas Tree, how empty are your branches...the kids are here, the lights are near, if they would stand, I'd fill their hand, and Christmas Tree, Oh, Christmas Tree, you could be trimmed and lighted..."

Laughter filled the air. "Well, what's everybody waiting for?" CJ said. "Everyone inside, I think we 'youngsters' can trim this tree and you 'grown-ups' can grab a quilt and stay on the porch and enjoy the snow."

"Great idea," Eliza said. "But am I a youngster or a grown-up?"

"Yea, what is the age limit," Carson chimed in. That

285

led to a crowd gathering around CJ asking if they belonged inside or outside. Soon, he just turned around, threw up his hands, shaking his head went inside and closed the door.

"Why don't we all go in, get something warm to drink and a snack if you like, and everyone go where they please. There is, after all, a Christmas Tree to be trimmed."

"Let me help you fix some coffee, dear," Aunt Mildred said as she took Eliza by the arm. "Rachel is showing Lauren and Celia around the Homestead."

"That will be great, so how are you handling the surprise. Is it a good thing?" Eliza asked.

"It is a wonderful thing, dear. Just one problem. Where are they all going to sleep? I know most of the beds are taken. And there are so many of them."

"Not to worry, we already took care of the particulars. Alex and Celia and Lauren and Sam have already dropped their things off at my apartment. They brought sleeping bags for the kids and plan to let them decide where they want to stay the night. Viola`. Everything in place. Now, do we want regular coffee or decaf? After all, it is past midnight."

"I don't think it would matter to me. I'm not going to get much sleep anyway. I am so wound up. It's such a wonderful feeling!"

Aunt Mildred smiled as she went to help supervise the tree trimming. Eliza busied herself, brewing a couple pots of coffee and setting out a big bowl of caramel corn she had made. There were still plenty of cookies and cake to satisfy the sweet tooth. Everyone helped themselves. The snow continued to fall, leaving a glistening white blanket under the light of the moon. It was a gorgeous night.

Annie and Jon excused themselves to go back to town, promising to come out for brunch. She had already planned an early morning ride with CJ, taking full advantage of her Christmas gift.

Alex suggested they follow them to town and get some rest, as well. Aunt Mildred went along to Eliza's apartment. They had lots of catching up to do. The twins decided to camp out in the living room, so Henry and Katie agreed to join them for the night. Little by little, everyone went their separate ways to settle in.

Noticing the time, one-thirty a.m., Eliza finished up a few things in the kitchen, stepped out on the porch to finish her coffee and gaze into the night sky and take in the still blanket of snow before she and Cody snuggled in for what was left of the perfect Christmas Eve.

At the same time, Aunt Mildred and her family had time to get settled in at the apartment. Bill had been placed on the table intermingled with the Christmas centerpiece, not to be too conspicuous, but to comfort Aunt Mildred in knowing he was a part of the celebration. They all gathered around the old kitchen work table for one last cup of tea before turning in. The stories of Christmas Eves during their childhood began to flow. Alex and Lauren confessed of the times they rummaged through closets, under beds, and in the basement trying to find the gifts that may be hidden around the house. From time to time they found a stash, then regretted it on Christmas morning when their surprise was ruined by their snooping. One year, when trusted to be home alone, they opened the gifts under the tree and carefully taped the paper back and replaced them. Then as the days grew nearer to Christmas, they shared their regrets. What they had done, knowing what their gifts were, once again they had no surprises for Christmas morning. That was the last year they snooped.

After several stories, Aunt Mildred spoke up, "Don't you kids know that your dad and I knew every time you two peeked at your gifts? It wasn't that we noticed a poor job of re-wrapping, or anything moved. It was the look on your faces. The excitement wasn't there. We first thought the excitement was fading because you were getting older, but soon we put two-and-two together and figured out your escapades. I can tell you exactly which year you grew up enough to quit peeking."

"And you didn't try and stop us? What kind of parents let their kids keep ruining their holidays like that?" Lauren spewed dramatically.

"Yea, we were traumatized all of those years, and you could have saved our holiday anxiety of getting caught and the guilt for peeking!" Alex added.

"Nice try with the drama," Aunt Mildred scowled. "I think it was a lesson well learned. The one I'm sure you have shared with your own kids, teaching them a valuable lesson before they make the same mistakes. That's what parents do."

They all had a good laugh. With that, another Christmas Eve came to a pleasant end. Each picked up their bags and meandered down the hall to see which room they would settle in. Aunt Mildred was already making a cozy bed on the couch. The tree was twinkling. Eliza had put it up earlier in the season. Now that too, made perfect sense. She had questioned Eliza's extra work, putting up a tree where so little time would be spent. She did it just for them. Before she turned in, she went back to the kitchen to clear the table and tell Bill good night. The gathering was off to a magical start. She couldn't wait to see what Christmas Day would bring.

Chapter Nineteen

**Faith. Family. Friends. THE COMMON THREAD
woven of blessings that hold us all together...**

‿❦‿

Christmas morning! Eliza wasn't the first to rise. The smell of fresh coffee and something baking got her out of bed.

CJ and Beth were up early. He couldn't sleep, so he woke her up to keep him company while he made Cinnamon Rolls, the good old fashion yeast kind, just like they had first thing Christmas mornings growing up. They would open gifts, then after church, they would have a big brunch with family. Amazing how the simplest of traditions are such an important part of their memories.

"Good morning sleepy head!" CJ said as he handed Eliza a cup of coffee. "You aren't the last one up, but then Jaxon is but an infant!" he poked at her. "I suppose you were the last one to give up and go to bed?"

"I was, and thank you for the coffee. I couldn't stop looking at the snow. It was just so beautiful. One-thirty a.m. How long has it been since I stayed up that late intentionally?"

"Probably the night you slept in the cottage, but who is keeping track."

"You're right! This has been an exciting gathering. And today is Christmas. We haven't even opened the gifts under the tree yet," Eliza said, winking at Beth. "No one has been peeking, have they?"

"Well, actually I woke to the sound of paper rattling and found CJ under the tree shaking packages," Beth replied. "Yep, he nearly knocked the tree over when I snuck up on him and yelled........**B-U-S-T-E-D**!!! Just like I did when we were kids."

They both jumped, Eliza splashed out her coffee, not expecting such force coming from that little girl she once knew.

"Gotcha!" She pointed at them and laughed. "Now, can we get everyone in here and open something?"

"I don't mind, but don't you think we should wait for Aunt Mildred and her family to get here from town?" Eliza suggested.

"I guess I forgot about them, and Uncle Ben, Molly, and Uncle Oliver haven't made it over yet either. I can wait," Beth whined.

"Don't know what the problem is," CJ said. "Not like anything under there is for you anyway!"

"Now kids!" Eliza stood up and physically separated them. "Santa is still watching you!"

Another good laugh as a few more stragglers made it into the kitchen to join in the fun, but more so, to join in the cinnamon rolls.

Soon, everyone was ready for church. They loaded up the cars and were meeting Aunt Mildred and her family there. Annie and her dad also had plans to attend. She and CJ had re-thought their plans of the early morning ride, putting it off until they were all together after church. After all, it was the most important message of all times.

The service on Christmas morning was always uplifting. Everyone fellowshipped a bit afterward, but then on with family plans. They were back at Slipknot before they knew it. A brunch menu had been in the plans for weeks. No one was particularly starving at the moment, so they gathered in the living room. Carson had the wood ready in the fireplace and lit it when they got home. It was definitely a white Christmas, not often seen in this area.

Molly and Ben went into the kitchen to start cooking, watching through the dining room as everyone gathered to start opening gifts.

"Come, Ben, watch Jaxon as he opens the gift we put under the tree for him," Molly ordered. Never having children of their own, they always enjoyed the little ones any chance they had.

They stood and smiled as he opened the toy horse they picked out. It reminded Ben of JoJo. Jaxon, of course, had no idea what it was, so it instantly went into his mouth to chew on.

"Looks like he likes it!" Julia said, as they all laughed at him, and snap, another picture for the first year album.

As everyone continued to pass out gifts the room was buzzing with excitement. It was really quite unorganized. Some gifts were the answer to a Christmas wish, while some were complete surprises. It seems that 'Santa' had left new blankets under the tree for Pete and JoJo. Funny how the writing on the tags strongly resembling the penmanship of Jon.

The gifts that Aunt Mildred had mailed to her kids and grandkids somehow made their way under the tree. Fortunately, they had arrived before the trip, so they loaded them up and brought them to Slipknot for Christmas.

Eliza was the last to pass out her gifts, all packaged in the tradition of the Homestead. As each opened the scarves, she had either knitted or crocheted, one by one they put them on, planning to wear them all afternoon. Eliza was pleased to see everyone enjoying the gathering. Once they settled down with their new treasures and the mounds of paper was picked up, it was just about time to enjoy the brunch Molly and Ben had prepared.

The tables were set in their Christmas best. Nothing spared for this special morning. The likes of which no one had witnessed in the Homestead for years. Family and friends, all joined together by a common thread.

Everyone gathered in the living room by the hearth,

hearts warmed by thoughtfulness, hands warmed by the fire, and they gave thanks for all the blessings surrounding them. CJ was overwhelmed as Annie quietly reached over and took his hand. He knew what he had been searching for. Jon thanked everyone for welcoming him in to share in the family gathering, Aunt Mildred thanked Eliza again for bringing her family home, and Uncle Oliver thanked Carson and Julia for Jaxon, a blessing in itself. He felt as if Mary were standing by his side, this time bringing a smile to his face rather than a tear to his eye. She would be at peace knowing he was full of life again. Ben thanked CJ for bringing his brother and sisters together, not only for a holiday but uncovering the history still tucked away at Slipknot, for everyone to enjoy. Rachel thanked Eliza for everything she had done to ensure their heritage remained intact and cared for in such a loving way. They would all be forever grateful for that.

Molly fixed a wonderful French toast casserole recipe perfect for a crowd, along with plenty of crispy maple glazed bacon. Uncle Ben made his famous country omelets with the crispy hash brown potatoes outside, and eggs, ham, and cheese filling the inside. A fresh grapefruit compote with rosemary syrup and maraschino cherries added to the festivities, as did a crisp batch of shortbread cookies and warm apple cider. Everyone seemed to get their fill then linger at the tables and talk about their gifts and plans, hopes and dreams. No one wanted this morning to end.

CJ and Annie excused themselves, bundled up and went out to the barn to take JoJo and Pete for the ride they promised. The morning was cold, the snow sparkling, but the wind was still, making it very enjoyable.

Julia took Jaxon out to the cottage for a nap, and Carson tagged along hoping to get one in as well. Seemed the late night and early morning was catching up with them now that they had full tummies and time to really relax.

Beth and Celeste volunteered to clear the dishes and clean up after brunch, encouraging Uncle Ben and Uncle Oliver to join Rachel in the living room by the fire. They needed time to catch up. Sophie snuggled up with her dad on the couch for a long overdue visit as well. Jack took a chair by the window to read the novel he found in the bookshelves, and the kids were all entertained with the new games they got for Christmas.

"Electronics!" Ben exclaimed, shaking his head. "What would the kids today do without them? Even at the Café they bring them along and sit at the table and play their games."

"Now Ben, if you don't understand what they are doing and how they work, you can't discount what the kids are really learning," Mary quickly scolded him.

"I know, I know, I'm always too quick to judge! At least that's what I'm told. Just don't understand it, that's all," he grumbled.

Meanwhile, Eliza joined Aunt Mildred and her family at the dining room table. They had been talking about the town, what had changed in the area and what had remained the same.

"I for one think we should take a drive around town. I've heard so much about it and would like to see the original architecture of the buildings. I enjoy visiting areas with great history. I have my camera in the car. Is anyone up for it?" Alex suggested.

"Well, dear, guess we can't fault you for that," Aunt Mildred quickly agreed with her son. "It's the architect in you. You always did have that curiosity!"

"I'd like to see what is for sale in the area," Lauren added. "Not that I'm looking to buy anything, just nosey!" she said with obvious enthusiasm. "What do you say we load up a couple of cars and see some sights?"

Everyone at the table seemed to be in agreement.

"As long as you have your camera, Alex, would it be possible to take some family pictures while we are out?" asked Aunt Mildred.

"That's a great idea. We'll get some of everyone here at Slipknot later, but there are no doubt some interesting buildings and scenery we can stop at while we are out for some nice candid shots."

Eliza invited Jon to join them, as Annie was out riding with CJ, and didn't want him to feel abandoned.

"Sure thing, and thanks for asking," Jon replied, quickly on his feet getting his jacket and hat. "I'd love to see more of what this town has to offer. It was dark when Annie and I went home last night, and she isn't much of a tour guide. We have different interests when it comes to what's worth looking at. Her head seems to be in the barn or in the clouds, one or the other, these days!" he laughed.

"Would you mind terribly if we stop by the apartment, Eliza?" Aunt Mildred asked quietly. "I'd like to pick up Bill. It is Christmas, and I hate to see him there all alone."

"Not a problem at all. That'll be our first stop," Eliza smiled and gave her Aunt a hug. "It is Christmas, and no one should be alone."

Aunt Mildred and her family easily fit into Alex's car. Eliza and Jon drove Bittersweet, just for the fun of it. She thought he'd get a kick out of touring around in her old truck. They stopped at her apartment, as Aunt Mildred requested, and with Bill settled in the truck of the car, they all got out for a walk around town. Several pictures were snapped in front of A Simple Stitch and CJ's Café. They walked along admiring the storefronts and window shopping, as nothing was open. Then they came upon the church and took a few more family pictures there. The snow in the background made the pictures even more beautiful, and what a great way to remember the Christmas it snowed in Spring Forrest.

"Why don't we walk a few blocks around the residential area? There are some unique homes, many nearly a century old and very well maintained," Eliza suggested.

"That's what I'm interested in seeing," Alex spoke up. "You lead the way."

They made their way a couple blocks past the church,

slowing down for Alex to point out some unique styles and trim work. He knew the technical terms and era of the woodworking that made them stand out.

"These homes are magnificent," Lauren spoke out. "Unlike the properties in Portland and surrounding areas. The cold winters and snowfall calls for different types of materials. These homes have such a traditional feel. And they are so well maintained, all of them. Many times we see a disheveled home amidst the pristine block so well cared for. The one in need of maintenance is due to a family member in poor health or left alone and unable to care for the property. These are truly amazing."

"Everyone looks out for each other around here. Many of the families have been here for generations and have life-long friends. Then there are the handymen around like Hank, from the hardware store. He has several retirees that help out with odd jobs around town. Everyone takes pride in their work to keep the integrity of Spring Forrest intact," Eliza bragged on and on about her hometown and the people she loved.

"Oh, let's cross the street at that corner," said Sam. "There are some interesting buildings over there."

As they crossed the street, Alex took pictures of the homes as they continued on. Crossing the next corner, back within a block of the church, Lauren pointed to a charming home with an iron fence outlining the front yard. It had a wraparound porch with bayed windows on either side of the front door. The gate at the end of the sidewalk that led to the front steps had a sign hanging from it.

"Can you make out what that sign says, Mom?" asked Lauren. "Is that some kind of business, a Bed and Breakfast or something?"

Aunt Mildred got a bit closer and said, "Oh, it just says 'Welcome' dear, but it is a charming place. Wait. There is a sign on the porch by the mailbox. What does it say?" she questioned.

Sam opened the gate and took her by the arm. "Let's go see what is says. This looks like a nice porch for a family picture. There is a bench that would make for a nice setting."

"We can't just go up on someone's porch, for heaven's sake, it's Christmas Day. What about respecting their privacy!" Aunt Mildred argued. "I'm for exploring as much as the next person, even nosey at times, but I have respect. There are limits you know."

"Oh, loosen up Aunt Mildred," Eliza laughed as she took her by the other arm. "It's only a picture."

As they went up the sidewalk, suddenly Aunt Mildred spoke out, "Why, I used to have a bench just like that, back home, when we had the shop open."

"I remember that bench," Sam said. "And didn't you have an old twelve-gallon crock like the one in the corner by the door?"

"Why yes, yes I did. I kept a huge geranium in it. I had forgotten about that. That's odd," she said as she walked closer to the steps.

"What does the sign by the mailbox say, there, by the door?" Lauren questioned again.

Everyone was quiet, waiting for her to read it.

"It says, 'Antie-tiques and Uniques.' Isn't that curious," she said. "But wait, it has something under it I can't quite make out." She took a couple more steps and then started to read; "It says, 'If you can't find it, Aunt Mil Still Will'! Why what on earth?" she said with a confused sound in her voice.

Just then Alex, Celia, Sam, and Lauren shouted, "Merry Christmas Mom! And welcome home."

She stood there staring at them. "What are you talking about?" she said, the surprise still not sinking in.

"It is your Christmas gift from us to you," Lauren spoke out. "That is your bench and your crock. Come inside, you'll see more of your treasures," she said as she unlocked the door. "Come in!"

"I don't understand," Aunt Mildred said again, sounding a bit feeble.

Alex took her by the arm and walked her through the door. "We wanted to give you a home. We don't like seeing you roaming from coast to coast. We know you don't want to give Dad up, even if he did love the ocean. We want the two of you to have a place to belong. And what could be a better place to settle down in than Spring Forrest. It's where you began. You have extended family here that needs you. This is for you," he repeated.

As she looked around she recognized every piece of furniture, her favorite dishes were set on the dining room table, her vintage linens and curtains she treasured, and they had even installed her favorite old chandelier she so carefully placed in storage. The three bedrooms were completely set up with her original bedroom sets from home.

"This is absolutely amazing," Aunt Mildred shouted. "Absolutely amazing, how did you do this?"

"You haven't seen it all, come see the garage," said Celia.

"The garage? Why on earth would I want to see a garage?"

As they stepped out the back door, the two car garage had a larger sign above it that said 'Antiques and Uniques.'

"Welcome to your new Antique Shop. Look inside, the rest of the pieces you had in storage are inside, just waiting for you to make it into your shop. We're leaving that up to you," Celia explained.

"We thought that would give you and Dad something to do the rest of the winter, and if you want to open this spring, that is up to you," Alex said. "If you never want to open, you don't have to, but at least you have your treasures where you can enjoy them."

"And if you want to travel, it will all be looked after by me and CJ, welcome home."

"Well, are you surprised?" Jon asked. "I am, and I'm not really sure what is going on here."

Everyone laughed.

"Oh, and one more thing," Alex added. "We have the mortgage for you to go with it. We knew you wouldn't want us to pay for this!" he laughed. "We all know you're loaded!"

"Well, that's a relief," Aunt Mildred played along. "I was worried that you wouldn't tell me what I owed you! I just want to know how you managed to do all of this."

"I have a confession to make," Eliza said with a big grin on her face. "You see, Alex and Lauren had been in touch with me from time to time over the past year. They had a genuine concern about you traveling alone. They knew that losing Bill was more difficult for you than you wanted them to think. One day I caught wind that this house was going to be put on the market and I knew the family history. It seemed to be the answer to our prayers. I called them, and we got things started. We have been working on this for nearly a year. Then when CJ came up with the idea of the gathering, we were going to try and contact you to come. As fate would have it, you drove up to my shop for a visit before I got that far and solved everything. All we had to do was the finishing touches, the fun stuff. Everything had been delivered from storage months before. So you see, the time you spent working on the 'Cottage' for me, well, that was sort of a little white lie. I'm ashamed of myself because I had Uncle Oliver working on that since last spring, just when he had time. I wanted to make it into a guest house someday. We weren't really planning to finish it in time for the gathering. It was just what we needed to keep you occupied and out of town while they came out early. We knew you would give it your undivided attention if you were doing something for me and we could pull this off. Sneaky, weren't we!"

"Mom, you don't know how many times we saw you drive by, and how hard it was not to run out and stop you!" Lauren said. "Alex and I drove out together to work on it, then flew back to join the families for the road trip home for Christmas. We were here for three days, and stayed with Eliza while you were working at Slipknot!"

"Sneaky is an understatement! I'm downright proud of you. Even I wouldn't have thought of something like this. And now I have a place for my family to come and visit me and spend a week when they do. No more feeling like they are intruding. Slipknot is so close, everyone can spread out and enjoy themselves. Like a vacation in a visit! Am I right?" Aunt Mildred looked at Alex, then at Lauren. "Well, am I?"

"Yes Mom," they said in unison like they did when they were kids, then began to laugh. They both went and hugged her.

"We've all been doing some soul-searching lately, and realized how important family and extended family is. We want our kids to know that and feel the same way. This is our gift to everyone, not just you," Lauren said, her voice cracking and eyes welling up.

"You couldn't have made me any happier, Christmas

or not," she said as she held on to them. "But you know, you spent a chunk of your inheritance!"

"Great investment," Alex added.

Once again the mood was lightened, and they all started to laugh.

"I want to start my memories right here for the next season of my life. Now, I need to do something, I'll be right back," Aunt Mildred said, walking toward the front door.

She quickly returned with the Christmas crock she had placed in the trunk. "Bill, look at what the kids did for us. Welcome home, honey. I'm sorry to say you won't be going to the ocean until I'm going to the ocean with you. They can take us there when our story ends. Until then, you'll stay right here with me, where you belong. That way, when they visit, they can visit both of us."

Everyone stood there, smiling, without saying a word, tears streaming down their cheeks. Even Jon was touched, knowing how he felt the loss of Annie's mom this time of year more than ever.

"Now, what do you say we lock things up and get back out to Slipknot before everyone comes looking for us?" Aunt Mildred suggested. "Oh, and one more thing, are there linens on the beds?"

"Yes, we freshened up all the beds as we put the house together, why?" Celia asked.

"Because, we will be spending the night here tonight,

instead of Eliza's apartment, so bring your suitcases," Aunt Mildred ordered.

"Great idea," Alex agreed. "Why not make the first memory tonight. We even bought coffee! That's how well we know you, Mom!"

When they got back to Slipknot, the house was buzzing with the news Aunt Mildred brought back. Not everyone knew what was going on, and they all had a good laugh learning how they pulled it off. Aunt Mildred made several trips back and forth to town to show off her new home. Everyone was so excited for her. She had a permanent address again.

They had gathered on the front porch before the daylight was gone. Family photos were now the priority. There were groups of brothers and sisters from past generations, present generations, families, and families to be. Jon and Annie had a photo taken with Pete near the barn, and the second one with CJ and JoJo in the corral standing in the background. Aunt Mildred's family gathered around her sitting in a chair with Bill, of course, setting on the table by her side, as usual.

The sun began to set, stomachs began to growl, and another Christmas Day was nearing an end.

CJ and Annie prepared supper together. He made his favorite, Hamburger Soup, and Annie made her next of many batches of Butterhorns. A great combination any way you look at it.

They all came together for a simple meal. Uncle

Oliver stood at the head of the table to give thanks. Everyone around the old farm table joined hands to complete the circle. Even Jaxon was a vital link. Amen, the room sounded.

CJ's Christmas gathering at Slipknot was an important part of their family history. Looking around the room, he recognized the common thread that held this family together. Faith. Nothing created a stronger bond.

Christmas was complete. Eliza had brought to life her dream of future generations at Slipknot. Aunt Mildred had Bill with her and a wonderful new place to call home for her children and grandchildren to visit. Annie had Pete, CJ had Annie, and Jon had peace of mind knowing his daughter was happy. Uncle Oliver had Jaxon to fill a void. Jaxon had the promise of growing up with his heritage at Slipknot, complete with a family photo of his very first visit, and everyone knew where they would be spending their Christmases to come.

(Knot) The End

About the Author

❦

My husband and I live on a farm in Southern Illinois that has been in his family for over a hundred years. We have an amazing blended family. I've been the middle generation of a five generation family for over twenty years now. Prior to this, when my daughter was born we had five generations for nine years until I lost my great-grandma.

Living in our century old twelve room farmhouse filled with antiques and unique treasures is a blessing beyond words. It is my inspiration. When I'm creating my characters and their adventures many times something in my surroundings will spark an idea. The recipes mentioned throughout my writing are actual recipes that I have found and tweaked to make my own or favorites of generations handed down through the years. It is my pleasure to share these with my readers.

For years my favorite pass-time has been going to local estate sales and flea markets. Each find has a story behind it of either the previous owner or the bargain price I snatched it up for. My dream of having an Inn gets less with each passing year, as do my collections as well as the number of flower beds I started in the early years. Although many still grace the farm, it is now in more manageable numbers. It has not been difficult passing on the treasures that I acquired through the years, sharing their story, watching the new owner leave with a smile and a story of their own to tell. Simplifying on the inside and no longer spending days with my nose to the ground planting and pulling weeds outside allows time to travel and visit my kids and grandkids or a girl's day out now and then.

Now, with a new season of my life quickly approaching I welcome these changes, ready to follow my heart and make my dream my goal. I want to write. With that said, I look forward to pouring out as many books, articles and any other bits of information God guides my nimble fingers to produce. As for now, I will continue to take care of my wonderful home, work my day job and care for our extended family. In my spare time, I will write.

Someday I imagine my time spent in a comfy chair with just enough sun to warm me, but not so much glare that I cannot see. This will allow me to continue to write about the dreams I had through the years but no longer have the energy or desire to carry out, creating characters that are as charming to my readers as they are company to me while I live a simple, but very blessed life.

Coming Soon

ॐ

Yes, *A Simple Stitch, A Time to Mend* is well in the works.

Our favorite characters return for a new season in Spring Forrest. **A Simple Stitch** is open for business. The school is out for the summer. The Café is as busy as usual. Aunt Mildred has settled and made Spring Forrest her home.

Although it has only been six short months since the gathering, the impact it left is visible. Relationships were started and strengthened during this festive time. Now that the excitement has faded and life is back to usual Eliza is feeling an unfamiliar emptiness.

With the start of summer, a chain of events bring questions as well as answers from all directions. In their usual style, adventures are taking relationships to new heights, changes are in the works, and while some have tough decisions to make, others can easily see the answers.

An accident causes everyone to step back and look at life a bit differently. During this much needed **Time to Mend** everyone pulls together. Changes are necessary. Decisions are quickly made.

You are invited back to A Simple Stitch to watch this quaint shop evolve. Slipknot in the summer is certainly the place to be for working in the garden, cooking and finding rest while sitting on the swing and watching the sun set. So while with every season there comes change, although not always easy, it can be a true blessing in disguise.

Please visit my website, **http://www. debobooks. com** and follow the progress of my new works. You will want to frequent Eliza's Recipe Box for new recipes that have been included in both ***A Simple Stitch, A Common Thread*** and in the upcoming sequel, ***A Simple Stitch, A Time to Mend.*** Follow my blog for ideas and interesting tidbits and on any given day, ask yourself, "What would Aunt Mildred be doing today?" I hope to keep your curiosity peaked and see you there from time to time. Don't forget to leave comments and suggestions. I look forward to our journey. Kindly, Deb

Eliza's Recipe Box

৩৯৫

This recipe is handed down from my Great-Grandma Bennett. I never had the pleasure of her making it for me. I was staying with my grandma after she had surgery and in passing time, she was telling me of family history. The Potato Soup recipe came up. I wrote it out as she told me, went directly to the kitchen and made a pot. She is in assisted living now, an amazing 96 years old and still keeping house. I make this soup for her from time to time. As it satisfies her appetite, it warms my heart twice. Once while making it and once while seeing her enjoy it so.

Great-Grandma's Potato Soup

6-8 potatoes of choice, scrubbed, peeled and cubed. Clean and slice 3 stalks of celery and add to potatoes. Add 1 tsp salt & 1 tsp pepper and ½ tsp celery seed.

Cover with 5 cups of good chicken stock or water

and 3 chicken bouillon cubes, simmer until potatoes are tender.

Meanwhile, fry 4-6 slices of bacon until crisp. Drain on paper towel, set aside. In same pan, drain all but about 3 Tbsp. fat, slice large sweet onion very thin and sauté in drippings until slightly browned. Remove the onions and set aside.

Melt 3 Tbsp. butter in pan with same drippings, add 1/3 cup flour, stirring and scraping until the flour begins to brown. Remove from heat and stir into pot with potatoes and broth. Return to heat and bring to a low boil, adding onions. Reduce to simmer until mixture begins to thicken. Stir in about 1 cup half and half or cream, heat just through. (If desired, add a couple slices of American cheese and stir in when melted.

Crumble crisp bacon and stir into the soup. Serve with favorite bread or biscuits. **